His fingers were stroking the skin at the nape of her neck.

His mouth was curved into a smile that was blatantly sensual. It was there again in his eyes, that heat, and she was pretty certain it was there in hers too.

'Iain, we are just pretending to be engaged.'

'Aye, but there are other things we've no need to pretend about. You know I still want you, Cordelia.'

'Did you have this in mind when you suggested our engagement?'

'No, and I won't change my mind if you're not interested. I think you are, though.' Iain laughed softly. 'Knowing that you want me as much as I want you—have you any idea what that does to me?' His expression darkened momentarily. 'I don't want you subservient to my desires, Cordelia, I want my desires to be yours. Yours to be mine.'

His words were a low, stomach-clenching growl. 'My desires to be yours?' she repeated, mesmerised.

'And yours to be mine. Admit it, we have unfinished business.'

Born and educated in Scotland, **Marguerite Kaye** originally qualified as a lawyer but chose not to practise. Instead, she carved out a career in IT and studied history part-time, gaining first-class honours and a master's degree. A few decades after winning a children's national poetry competition she decided to pursue her lifelong ambition to write, and submitted her first historical romance to Mills & Boon®. They accepted it, and she's been writing ever since.

You can contact Marguerite through her website at:
www.margueritekaye.com

Previous novels by the same author:

THE WICKED LORD RASENBY
THE RAKE AND THE HEIRESS
INNOCENT IN THE SHEIKH'S HAREM†
  (part of *Summer Sheikhs* anthology)
THE GOVERNESS AND THE SHEIKH†
THE HIGHLANDER'S REDEMPTION*
THE HIGHLANDER'S RETURN*
RAKE WITH A FROZEN HEART
OUTRAGEOUS CONFESSIONS OF LADY DEBORAH
DUCHESS BY CHRISTMAS
  (part of *Gift-Wrapped Governesses* anthology)
THE BEAUTY WITHIN
RUMOURS THAT RUINED A LADY

and in Mills & Boon® Historical *Undone!* eBooks:

THE CAPTAIN'S WICKED WAGER
THE HIGHLANDER AND THE SEA SIREN
BITTEN BY DESIRE
TEMPTATION IS THE NIGHT
CLAIMED BY THE WOLF PRINCE**
BOUND TO THE WOLF PRINCE**
THE HIGHLANDER AND THE WOLF PRINCESS**
THE SHEIKH'S IMPETUOUS LOVE-SLAVE†
SPELLBOUND & SEDUCED
BEHIND THE COURTESAN'S MASK
FLIRTING WITH RUIN
AN INVITATION TO PLEASURE
LOST IN PLEASURE
HOW TO SEDUCE A SHEIKH

In the Mills & Boon *Castonbury Park* Regency mini-series:

THE LADY WHO BROKE THE RULES

and in M&B eBooks:

TITANIC: A DATE WITH DESTINY

†linked by character
Highland Brides
**Legend of the Faol*

**Did you know that some of these novels are also available as eBooks?
Visit www.millsandboon.co.uk**

UNWED AND UNREPENTANT

Marguerite Kaye

First published in Great Britain 2014
by Mills & Boon, an imprint of Harlequin (UK) Limited,
Large Print edition 2014
Harlequin (UK) Limited, Eton House, 18-24 Paradise Road,
Richmond, Surrey TW9 1SR

© 2014 Marguerite Kaye

ISBN: 978-0-263-23984-3

Harlequin (UK) Limited's policy is to use papers that are natural,
renewable and recyclable products and made from wood grown in
sustainable forests. The logging and manufacturing processes conform
to the legal environmental regulations of the country of origin.

Printed and bound in Great Britain
by CPI Antony Rowe, Chippenham, Wiltshire

AUTHOR NOTE

I live on the west coast of Scotland and work in a room that faces right out onto the River Clyde. While I write I see the ferries traipsing back and forth across the river, I see warships and nuclear submarines making their way to and from the naval base at Faslane, and I see huge cruise ships, tankers, trawlers and tiny creelers. In the summer months I also see the *Waverley,* the only surviving sea-going paddle steamer in the world, and it was the *Waverley* which provided me with the inspiration for my ship-building hero, Iain.

Mind you, I suppose you could say that ship-building is in my blood. My paternal grandfather worked in some of the biggest yards on the Clyde during the Second World War, and in the 1960s was part of the team that built the *Queen Elizabeth II.* My maternal grandfather was a captain in the Merchant navy, and twice sunk during the same war (he survived both). When I first started to write I remember reading the mantra 'write what you know' over and over in various 'how to write' books. Since I've never found my previous life in IT particularly romantic, I guess this story is as good as 'writing what you know' as I'm going to get!

As ever with my books, the plot has gone through a whole series of changes as the characters developed. My dogged perusal of a learned tome called *Money, Mania and Markets* by R. C. Michie resulted in one fleeting reference to Cordelia's investment portfolio. The majority of the scenes that I had planned to set in Glasgow ended up on my virtual cutting-room floor, though I've used some of their ambience in the scene where Cordelia and Iain visit the Isle of Dogs. While I'd set Cordelia up with some passing references in both THE BEAUTY WITHIN and RUMOURS THAT RUINED A LADY, to be honest, I had no more idea than her sisters of why she ran away and what her fate was. I started out putting her in a convent in Italy, then I set her up in business in Glasgow building hotels for young ladies, and at one point I gave her a child, which I killed off and then abandoned altogether.

What I *did* realise very early on was that she needed a very strong hero—a self-made man to match her self-made woman. Setting the story in the year of Queen Victoria's ascendancy followed—not only because I needed Cordelia to have packed a bit of experience under her belt, but because it was with Victoria that the meritocracy started to nudge the aristocracy out of power, and I was very keen that her blackguard of a father, Lord Armstrong, was dealt if not a mortal blow then a fairly serious wound to his power base.

This is the last of the Armstrong sisters' stories—a series which didn't start out as a series at all, but as a one-off Regency sheikh story. I didn't plan to come full circle back to where it started, but as I wrote Iain and Cordelia's story, it felt right to do so.

Thanks to my Facebook friends for all their help and support, assistance with points of detail and ideas— you are stars. And once again thank you to Flo, who deserves some sort of medal for being so patient with me on this one, which had more false starts than the Grand National!

For J.

When you read this, you'll know why.

First, last and always love.

Prologue

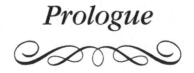

Cavendish Square, London—spring 1828

Clutching a portmanteau in one hand, a band-box tied with string in the other, Lady Cordelia Armstrong crept down the main staircase of her father's town house. It was late afternoon, and her Aunt Sophia was taking a nap. Cordelia had been pledged to attend an expedition to Richmond Park. She had been at pains, when the invitation was first issued, to inform her aunt that the company would include at least one rake, one notorious fortune-hunter and the young lady who was competing with Cordelia in a wager—registered by one obliging gentleman in White's betting book—to amass the most offers for her hand in one Season.

Lady Sophia had, as Cordelia anticipated, forbidden her to go. 'If you are seen in an open carriage in such company,' she had said, her face turning the most alarming shade of puce, 'I have no doubt whatsoever that your vouchers for Almack's will be withdrawn.'

'And all poor Papa's plans to marry me off to one of his minions will be in tatters,' Cordelia had been unable to resist retorting.

'I do not understand you. Don't you want to make a good match?'

'One that is good for me, yes, indeed. Sadly, that rather precludes it being a man whom Papa has selected.'

Her aunt had looked genuinely shocked, a reaction which had quite taken Cordelia aback. Having seen for herself how miserable trying to please their father had made Cressie, and how very changed poor Caro had become since marrying the man chosen for her, Cordelia had a very low opinion indeed of Lord Armstrong's ability to pick a husband for her, but it seemed Lady Sophia did not agree. It was true, Cordelia had originally *pretended* to go along with her father's plans for her, but she had assumed that her aunt, who was no fool, understood this was simply a ruse to ensure she was not, like Cressie, confined to the country until she agreed to do his bidding. Papa did not like open defiance. *Keep your enemies close,* was one of his maxims, and Cordelia had paid it great heed.

The moment was now ripe to strike, for her father was en route to Russia with Wellington. Sadly, it seemed the wool must also be pulled over Aunt Sophia's eyes too, for the time being. So Cordelia had said defiantly that she would go to Richmond Park no matter how low the company, ensuring that no other invitation could be accepted on that fateful date, and that her sadly abused relative would be too relieved to question her, when informed upon the day that her niece, having thought the matter over, was of the opinion that the expedition would be a mistake. Which was exactly what had happened this morning, as a result of which Aunt Sophia was sleeping soundly in her bedchamber, under the illusion that her apparently contrite charge, with an engagement-free afternoon, was resting in hers.

The house was silent, with not even a footman attendant in the marbled hallway to impede
Cordelia's departure. Placing the brief missive
on the polished half-table beside the silver salver
upon which callers to Lord Armstrong's abode
left their visiting cards, she felt a twinge of guilt.
Though her ambitious and scheming Papa deserved not a whit of loyalty or consideration in
her opinion, she did not feel comfortable deceiving Aunt Sophia, who might look like a camel,
might even upon occasion bray like one, but
had in her own way always done her best by her
nieces.

Biting her lip, Cordelia stared at her reflection in the mirror. Nature had given her the dark
golden curls, the cupid's-bow mouth and soft
curves which were deemed by society to be beautiful—this Season, at least. At one-and-twenty,
combined with an adequate dowry, her lineage
and her connections, she was under no illusions
about her value on the marriage mart—indeed,
she had already amassed enough proposals to
prove it.

'And not a single one of them could care less

what goes on behind this pretty facade,' she said aloud, her lip curling with contempt. 'Within five years, perhaps less, when I've done my duty and produced the requisite heir or two, I'll be retired to the country to grow fat and miserable like poor Bella. Or worse, if I fail, forced into hiding in the shadows like Caro.'

Turning away from the mirror, she picked up her luggage with renewed resolve. Soon, she would be married to a man of her own choosing. A man who derided politics and her papa equally. A man who paid her no pretty, facile compliments but talked to her as if she had a mind of her own, and made it very clear that he desired her not as a matrimonial conquest but as a woman. A man whose kisses made her pulses race. A man who could heat her blood by his very presence in the room. A man whose body and bed she longed to share.

'Gideon,' she whispered. Heart thumping, Cordelia slid open the heavy front door of her father's house, closing it carefully behind her. The next time she returned, she would be a married woman. 'And for once, Papa shall dance to my

tune, for the one thing he abhors more than disobedience is scandal,' she murmured to herself
as she tripped down the stone stairs into Cavendish Square and hailed a hackney cab which was
most fortuitously passing. Taking it as a good
omen, she clambered in with her luggage and
gave her direction.

The carriage rumbled off and Cordelia settled
herself for the journey to the posting house where
they were to meet before setting out on their journey. Of course, the Honourable Gideon d'Amery
had not specifically mentioned marriage, but that
was a mere detail. Papa and Aunt Sophia would
tell her that no gentleman would propose an
elopement to a lady, but Papa and Aunt Sophia
had not a romantic bone in their bodies. Cordelia
was of age, and Gideon was a man of the world
who would see to whatever details were required
to formalise their union. Not that she had any
idea what such details comprised, though she was
hazily aware they required some sort of special
licence unless they were headed to Gretna Green.

She didn't care and it mattered not a whit.
Gideon would see to it. Cordelia would concen-

trate on the important things, such as his smile and his kisses and the heated look in his dark-brown eyes when he gazed at her, and the delicious *frisson* that ran through her when he ran his fingers over her breasts in that shocking manner through her gown, and the even more shocking and even more delicious *frisson* when he pressed the evidence of his desire against her as they danced.

She touched her gloved hands to her heated cheeks. How perfectly lovely it was to be in love and to know that she was loved in return. When she came back to London on the arm of her husband, glowing with happiness, Papa would have no option but to acknowledge that Cordelia, and not her father, knew what was best for her. A month, perhaps three, if they made their marriage trip to the Continent. Rome. Venice. And Paris of course, for she would need new gowns, having been forced to leave most of her coming-out wardrobe at home.

'Six months at most,' she said dreamily, 'and then I shall return, the Prodigal Daughter, and Papa shall be forced to kill the fatted calf.' On that most satisfying image, Cordelia closed her mind to the troubles she was leaving behind her, and turned instead to the night of passion which lay ahead.

Chapter One

Cavendish Square, London—spring 1837

Though he wore the familiar livery, the footman who opened the door was a stranger to her. The name inscribed on her visiting card would mean nothing to him, so she did not place it on the silver salver he held out— The same one as had always been used, she noted. 'Please inform Lord Armstrong that Lady Cordelia is here,' she said. 'He is expecting me.'

The startled look the servant gave her informed her that he knew her by reputation if nothing else, but he had been trained well, and quickly assumed an indifferent mask. Cordelia had no doubt, however, that she would be the topic of the day in the servants' hall, and that every inch of her appearance would be recounted within minutes of her arrival.

The marbled hallway had changed surprisingly little in the nine years since she had last been here, but instead of ascending the grand central staircase that led to the formal drawing room where visitors were received, Cordelia was ushered through a door directly off the reception area. The book room. A choice of venue which spoke volumes.

'I shall inform his lordship of your arrival.'

The door closed behind the footman with a soft click, leaving Cordelia alone, suddenly and quite unexpectedly shaking with nerves. The walnut desk before her was as imposing as ever. Behind it, the leatherbound chair held the indent of her father's body. In front of it, as ever, two wooden chairs whose seats, she knew from old, placed the person who took them at a lower level than the man behind the desk. The scent of beeswax polish mingled in the air with the slightly musty smell from the books and ledgers which lined the cases on the walls. From the empty grate came the faint trace of ash. No fire burned, though there was a nip in the spring air. Another trick of her father's. Lord Armstrong never felt the cold—or at least, that was the impression he liked to give.

Nine years. She would be thirty next birthday, and yet this room made her feel like a child waiting to be scolded. There was a similar room at Killellan Manor, where she and her sisters had been reprimanded and instructed in their duties as motherless daughters of an ambitious diplomat and peer of the realm.

Memories assailed her, things she had not thought of in years, of the pranks they had played, and the games. In the days before Celia married, they had been a tight-knit group. She had forgotten how close, or perhaps she had not allowed herself to remember, in the Bella years. She smiled to herself, remembering now. Unlike Cressie, who had always been too confrontational, or Caro, who had always been the dutiful sister, Cordelia's strategy had been to give the appearance of compliance while going her own way. It had worked more often than it had failed. Rarely had her father perceived her to be the ringleader—that honour fell to poor Cressie. Cordelia had thought herself a master manipulator by the time she arrived in London for the Season. She had been so naive, thinking that her father was the only man in her orbit with a game to play.

The clock ticking relentlessly on the mantel showed her that she had been standing before the desk for almost fifteen minutes. Another of her father's favourite ruses, to keep his minions waiting, ensuring that they understood their relative unimportance. She felt quite sick. Her stomach wasn't full of butterflies but something far more malicious. Hornets? Too stingy. Toads? Snakes? Too slimy. Cicadas? She shuddered. Revolting things.

She checked the time on the little gold watch which was pinned to the belt of her carriage dress. By her reckoning, her dear father would keep her at least another ten minutes. Not quite the full half-hour. She would be better occupied preparing herself for the ordeal that lay ahead than making herself ill.

For a start, she should not be caught standing here like a penitent schoolgirl. Cordelia peeled off her gloves and laid them on the polished surface of the desk. Her fringed paisley shawl she folded neatly over the back of one of the wooden chairs. The high-crowned bonnet she had purchased, as she did most of her clothes, in Paris, was next. The wide brim was trimmed with knife-pleated silk the same royal blue as her carriage gown, a colour she favoured, for not only did it suit her, it gave her a deceptive air of severity which she liked to cultivate simply because contradictions had always amused her. The expensive bonnet joined her shawl on the chair. Pulling out a hand mirror from her beaded reticule, Cordelia shook out the curls which had taken the maid she had hired an age to achieve with the hot tongs. Far more elaborate than the style she normally favoured, her coiffure, with its centre parting and top knot, was the height of fashion and, in her opinion, the height of discomfort, but it added to her confidence, and that was, she admitted unwillingly to herself, in need of as much boosting as she could manage.

A quick mental check of the latest statement from her bank and an inventory of her stocks helped. The knowledge that her father could have no inkling of either made her smile and calmed the roiling in her stomach a little. She had no need to read the missive which had been his reply to her own request for an interview, but she did anyway, for those curt lines were a salient reminder that despite all her sisters' assertions, her father had not changed. She would need every ounce of her resolution and backbone if she was to have any chance of succeeding.

I have granted this interview in the hope that sufficient time has passed for you to have regretted your gross misdemeanour, and for mature reflection to have inculcated in you the sense of duty which was previously sadly lacking. While the pain of your wilful disobedience must always pierce my heart, I have concluded that my own paternal duty requires me to permit you a hearing.

Your self-enforced exile has wounded others than myself. Your brothers scarce recall you. Your youngest sister has never met you. You should be aware too, that my own sister, your aunt Sophia, has been made decrepit by the passing years and has likely very few left to her on this earth.

Sincere contrition and unquestioning obedience in the future will restore you to the bosom of your injured family. If you come to Cavendish Square in any other frame of mind, your journey will have been pointless. On this understanding, you may arrange a time convenient to me with my secretary. Yours etc.

Cordelia curled her lip at the reference to his heart, which she was fairly certain her father did not possess. Not that it precluded him tugging on the heartstrings of others. He knew her rather too well. The stories Caro shared with her, of their half-brothers and half-sister, were bittersweet. She had missed so much of their youth already that she would be a stranger to them. She even harboured a desire to become reacquainted with Bella, whose many foibles and viciousness of temperament she thought she understood rather more— For who would not be twisted by the simple fact of being married to one such as the great Lord Armstrong? Her feelings for Lady Sophia were both simpler and more complex, for while she had wronged her aunt, she could not help feeling that her aunt had wronged her too. And as to her father...

Cordelia folding the letter into a very small square and stuffed it back into her reticule. Neither salutation nor signature. He thought he was summoning an impoverished and contrite dependant. She wondered what penance he had in mind for her, and wondered, with some trepidation, how he would react when he discovered her neither contrite nor in need of financial support, but set upon reparation. In her father's eyes, she had committed a heinous crime. His punishment had been extreme and it had taken Cordelia, her own fiercest critic, a very long time to realise that it was unmerited. Longer still to face up to the consequences of this, for of all things, she abhorred confrontation. Focusing her decided will on achieving independence and defying convention had alleviated the pain of her exile, but success, she discovered, instead of putting an end to her grievance, allowed it to grow. Becoming reacquainted with Cressie and Caro forced her to acknowledge the huge chasm which the rift with her family had created, though it was not until that strangest of days, last year, that she faced up to the fact that in order to heal it she would have to confront the cause of it.

Her father. Were she a man, he would be impressed by her business acumen. Though were she a man, she would not be in this position in the first place. Which made her wonder what on earth she was doing here anyway, because she didn't need his permission to contact her own family. They were *her* family just as much as his.

Cordelia sighed heavily. Truth. How she hated the truth. Despite everything, despite the fact that he was far more in the wrong than she, what she wanted was his forgiveness just as much his acceptance of who she was, and the fact that she would never be the daughter he expected her to be. It was ridiculous and irrational and most likely unattainable, but there it was, that was what she really wanted from today.

The hand she held was slim. She would have

to play it with skill. Lord Armstrong must be made aware from the outset of this interview that his daughter was no mat for him to wipe his feet upon. She considered seating herself behind the desk, but her father's imprint on the leather chair made her feel squeamish. Instead, she spread the silk skirts of her carriage dress out and endeavoured to look as relaxed and comfortable as she could on the hated wooden chair. Her gown, with its wide leg-of-mutton sleeves and tight cuffs, was deceptively simple. The scalloping on the bodice and collar was subtle but intricately worked, continuing down the front panel to the the hem. The belt of the same royal blue which cinched her waist was held with a gold buckle. Her outfit was elegant and so à la mode that it screamed Paris to anyone who cared to notice. Her father, however, had little time for women and things feminine. It gave her a little kick of satisfaction, knowing that the evidence of her success, displayed in full view, would be quite lost on him.

The sound of a footfall outside the door alerted her to his arrival. Cordelia put a hand over the heart which threatened to jump out of her chest, and sternly quelled the instinct to rise from her seat.

She had thought herself prepared, but as the door opened and Lord Armstrong made his entrance, a lump formed in Cordelia's throat. There were, it seemed, some things which neither logic nor experience could tame. Here was her father, and she could not control the rush of affection which brought tears to her eyes, stemmed only by a supreme effort of will from falling. Foolish of her, but she had not expected him to look so much older. His grey hair was sparser, revealing tender patches of pink pate. Pouches had formed under his eyes, though the blue-grey colour of his irises was still disconcertingly the exact shade of her own. His face was thinner too, giving a beakiness to his nose and a translucence to his skin, though he was still a handsome man.

He still had presence too. Barely a falter in his step there was, as he nodded curtly, as if it had been a few days since last they had met. The atmosphere in the book room changed too, when he took his seat behind the desk. She had forgotten that about him. He was like a necromancer, conjuring moods at will. She was already tense, her toes curled inside her kid boots, her shoulders straight like a soldier on parade, and it was too late to relax, because his eyes were upon her and he was drumming his fingers, his chin resting on one hand. But she was no longer a child, and had, for nine years, perforce, to consider herself no longer his daughter. He had not the right to judge her, and she was not inclined to permit him to do so.

Silence stretched. Another of his tricks, but it was one which Cordelia had also acquired. By the time he raised his brows after what seemed like an eternity, she had herself under control.

'You are looking surprisingly well.'

'Yes,' she replied with a cool smile. She waited, listening to the clock on the mantel ticking. It always seemed to *tock* much louder than it *ticked,* counting out the seconds like a measured, doom-laden tread towards eternity. She wondered, as she had so many times before, if he had had it adjusted to do so.

Finally, her father spoke. 'Almost a decade ago you absconded from these premises, leaving devastation in your wake. I shall never understand what I did to deserve such ingratitude, nor such a flagrant flouting of my will.'

'Your will!' The words were out before she could stop them. 'What about my will, Father? Did you ever stop to consider...'

'Unlike yourself, I never act without a great deal of consideration.'

Lord Armstrong steepled his fingers and eyed her across the expanse of polished walnut. Furious with herself, Cordelia bit her lip, grateful that the layers of corsets and stiffened petticoats which her robe required, concealed her heaving chest. 'I did not request this interview to discuss the past, but the future,' she said.

'Indeed? You do not think the past pertinent, then? You do not feel it incumbent to explain how you have spent your years...'

'In exile? In the wilderness?'

'Outwith the shelter of your family,' Lord Armstrong concluded smoothly.

'No,' Cordelia said baldly. 'Caro and Cressie

informed you that I was well,' she continued, unable to tolerate another lengthy silence. 'They also informed you that should you wish to contact me, you could do so through either of them. You did not, I must assume because you were not interested or did not care. Both most likely. So no, I don't think it either pertinent or—or incumbent upon me to explain myself,' she concluded hurriedly, realising that she was on the brink of doing just that.

She glared at him, defying the stupid, stupid tears to fall. He didn't care. It made it so much more humiliating to discover that she, after all, cared a great deal.

'You are thirty years of age,' Lord Armstrong said.

'Next month,' Cordelia replied cautiously, wondering where this new tack would lead.

'And still, I assume, unmarried?'

'May I ask why you make such an assumption?'

Her father smiled thinly. 'Though I am sure we would both rather the case were otherwise, you are my daughter, and I do understand you. You would not be here playing the supplicant had you any other means.'

'You don't think my sisters would support me?'

'I don't think you would accept their support,' Lord Armstrong retorted.

The truth of this made her determined to destroy that smug certainty of his. 'The possibility of my having a dependant of my own has not occurred to you, I suppose,' Cordelia said.

Her father looked fleetingly appalled, but his expression was quickly veiled. 'Even you, Cordelia, would not have the temerity to foist a bastard upon the family.'

Even she! Thinking of her sisters' various exploits, Cordelia was forced to repress a smile. Marriage, no matter how belated, had obviously mitigated their actions in her father's eyes, despite the fact that not a single one of those marriages had been of his making. How pleasant it must be, to bend the facts to one's perception, as he did. She doubted he ever had trouble sleeping at night, and wished fleetingly that she too, had the knack of looking at the world through a window of her own making.

But she had not, and she did not really wish to be cast in her father's mould. What she wanted, more than anything, was to be out of this room and this house as quickly as possible. There would be no conciliation, no regrets or apologies nor even a passive acceptance. 'I didn't come here to beg your forgiveness, Father,' Cordelia said. 'I'm sorry to disappoint you, but nor am I in need of support, monetary or moral.'

To anyone who did not know him, his face remained impassive, but Cordelia did know him. Lord Armstrong sat a little straighter. His eyes lost that deceptively faraway look. 'You will explain yourself.'

'Contrary to your expectations, these last nine years have been most productive and extremely enjoyable. I do not regret an action or a moment.' Which was mostly true. 'However, I am tired of my itinerant life, and I wish to settle back home, here in England. I do not need your help with this as I have more than adequate means for the purchase of an estate.'

She waited, but Lord Armstrong seemed rather stunned. Cordelia hugged her satisfaction to herself. 'My sisters were of the opinion that you had changed, that you would regret the enmity between us. I hoped rather than believed they were right, just as I hoped rather than believed that you would apologise for the wrongs you have done me. Sadly, you have lived down to my expectations, Father. It behoves me only to inform you that I intend to re-establish contact with my family, regardless of your wishes.'

She was rather pleased with this little speech, and her own unwavering delivery. If she was expecting it to have any impact on her father, Cordelia was, however, destined to be disappointed. 'I wonder why, since you are so unrepentant and so confident in achieving your aims, you have not returned before now,' Lord Armstrong said. 'To be plain, if you truly cared so little for my opinion, Daughter, I wonder that you did not simply disregard it.' His lordship once more steepled his fingers. 'Your silence, as they say, speaks volumes, Cordelia.'

'My silence,' she retorted through gritted teeth, 'is testament to the effort I am making not to tell you what I think of you, Father. I came here to draw a veil over the past, but you will not allow it. I have done as you bid me for almost ten years, making no attempt to contact my family...'

'You do not, then, count your sisters?'

'Caro and Cressie had nothing to lose. I have not written to Celia or Cassie. I have not written to Aunt Sophia. Or...'

'Spare me the litany,' Lord Armstrong said, rising from his seat and leaning over the desk. 'Rather let me set the record straight, Cordelia. My wife will ensure that any attempt to contact your half-brothers or Isabella will be unavailing. I myself will speak to Sophia. *Her* sense of what is owed to a brother will dictate her actions, as it always has.'

Cordelia also got to her feet. Though she had quelled the urge to shrink back in her chair, she was nevertheless horrified. She was also deeply hurt, humiliated and absolutely furious with herself for having given him the chance to hurt and belittle her again. 'I don't believe you. I shall not listen to you. I don't need your permission or your forgiveness. I will allow no one—*no one!*—to dictate my actions other than myself. I thwarted you—there, I have said it—by refusing to marry a man of your choice, and you have held a grudge against me for ten years. Unbelievable! You are utterly unbelievable, Father.'

She began to gather up her things, her hands shaking with anger. Jamming on her bonnet anyhow, she bit the inside of her cheek very, very hard. So intent was she on getting out of the house before she broke down, that she did not notice the door to the book room opening until the same impassive servant, who had no doubt heard the muffled altercation, was standing in front of her father holding out the silver salver. 'Your twelve-thirty appointment has arrived a little early,' he said.

'It's fine. I'm leaving,' Cordelia said. Snatching her shawl from the chair, she caught a glimpse of the card on the tray before her father picked it up, and her heart, already beating like a wild thing, skipped a beat. It could not be. Looking up, she found her father's gaze on her. 'You know, it may very well be in your interests to remain for this meeting,' he said.

He had that faraway look. Considering. Scheming. She began to feel sick again. 'No,' she said, though her voice seemed to come from a long way away, because he had put the card back down on the desk, and she could read it.

'Politics,' he continued smoothly, as if she had not spoken, another of his tactics, 'is all about compromise. I will concede that I cannot stop you from attempting to do as you say. You will fail, but your attempt, I will also concede—you see what I mean about compromise—will be unpleasant. For all of us.'

She stared at him. Her body was screaming at her to run. Her mind was struggling to deal with her father's admission that he was— What, fallible? No. But he seemed to be offering her a deal. What deal? She looked at the card on the desk, but it made no sense, and the instinct to run got the upper hand. 'No,' she said, turning towards the door just as it opened, crashing full tilt into the man entering the room.

'Ah, Mr Hunter,' her father said, urbane as ever, 'let me introduce you to my daughter Lady Cordelia.'

Chapter Two

Broomilaw, Glasgow—1836

Cordelia stood on the aft deck of the *PS Argyle* as the paddle steamer chugged down the River Clyde on the last stage of her journey. After several weeks travelling in the Highlands, the change to this vast city was almost overwhelming. The air was thick with smoke, tasting distinctly of coal, the clouds in the tarnished sky above were a strange metallic yellow colour.

Argyle sounded her horn, a loud, low, mournful cry that made the deck vibrate, and sent a noxious plume of black smoke into the air from the high stack of funnel as she began to slow, narrowly avoiding a large three-masted clipper anchored in the centre of the channel. The sound of the water being churned up by the two huge wooden paddles changed from a torrent to a slow slap as they drew alongside their berth, scraping between a host of other craft—so many, it seemed to Cordelia, that every ship in Scotland must be vying for space here in Glasgow.

The docks were crowded as she picked her way carefully over the narrow wooden gangway from the *Argyle,* across the deck of another steamer and up on to the pier, clutching her portmanteau. Beautiful as the Highlands had been, she had felt more alien there than at any time since leaving London eight years before. The Gaelic language, with its soft, lilting tones, was lovely to listen to, impossible to decipher. She had not been prepared for her own English accent to mark her out as foreign. At times, she had encountered downright hostility. They had long memories, those whose families had paid the price for fighting for the Jacobite Prince Charlie. More recently, enclosure and the introduction of sheep to the lands had brought a new grudge against the Sassenach landowners. Cordelia, raised in a household which lived and breathed the politics of

Britain's growing Empire, had been appalled by her own ignorance of what was, in theory, part of her own country.

On a very small scale, politics had torn her own family apart. Listening to the tales of what politics had done to the Highlanders gave her rather a different perspective on her own life. In those remote, tiny, hard-working communities, family was all. Cordelia could no longer ignore how much she missed her own. She was lonely. There were times when the cost of this independent path she had chosen felt like too high a price to pay. Times, such as now, standing on the quay with the crowd pressing round her, when she would have given anything for a familiar face.

But she had never been one to mope, had always loathed regrets, and there was no point in wishing things could be different. Cordelia turned her mind to the problem of her baggage, and where, and how she was supposed to collect it. Jostled, her skirts and toes well and truly trodden on, she looked for a porter. There were many, but all were occupied, and all seemed to be deaf too. She had thought that being back in a city would restore a little of her equilibrium, but the harsh language here sounded almost as foreign as Gaelic.

'And to make matters worse, I seem to have become invisible,' she muttered to herself, resorting to using her elbows to push past a large man holding a very loud conversation with a very small man on one of the steamers.

It was then she saw him, standing quite alone a few yards down, at the end of the quay. She could not have said what drew her attention, only that it was drawn, almost as if she were compelled to look at him. He was dressed sombrely, in a black coat and trousers, black shoes. His hair was cut short. Deep auburn, it was burnished by the silver-yellow rays of the setting sun filtered through the darkening clouds, giving him the look of a fallen angel. He had been staring off into the distance, but as she watched him he turned, their eyes met, and Cordelia felt a jolt of recognition, though she was sure she had never seen him before. Perhaps it was from having listened to too many ghost stories while she was in the Highlands, but she had the strangest feeling, like seeing another form of herself. *You,* her bones and her skin and her blood called, *it's you.*

She couldn't look away. It was with a feeling of déjà vu, or fate, inevitability, that she watched him approach her. His face was not gaunt, but it had little spare flesh. The lines which ran from his nose to his chin spoke of a tough life rather than either age or decadence. A hard face with a strong chin and nose, his mouth was his only soft feature, with a full bottom lip forming into a querying smile. The quiver inside her turned from recognition to attraction. *This one,* her body was saying now, *this man.*

'Is there something I can do for you?' he asked. *Is there something ah can do furr you?* His accent was strange, a soft burr with a rougher edge lurking in the background, the sweetness of chocolate mixed with the grittiness of salt. 'My luggage,' Cordelia said, 'I don't suppose you know where I can collect it?'

'You're English.' She must have instinctively braced herself for he smiled. 'Don't worry, I'm not going to hold it against you.'

Ah'm no gonnae haud it against you. Cordelia smiled. 'I can't tell you how grateful I am to hear that. I had thought the French held my country in low esteem, until I travelled north. I am just come from Oban, but I have been travelling in the Highlands for several weeks and I—'

'I thought I knew you,' he interrupted her. 'When I saw you staring at me, I thought we must have met, but I don't think we have.'

He had caught her arm as she made to turn away. She had taken a step towards him in response. He was not wearing gloves. His skin was pale. His nose looked as if it had been broken. His eyes were deep-set and deep blue. His lashes were the same dark auburn as his hair. He was frowning at her, studying her closely, a puzzled look on his face that echoed just what she had felt when first setting eyes on him.

'I thought it too,' Cordelia said. 'That I knew you, I mean. It's why I was staring. I'm sorry, it was rude of me. I did not mean to disturb you.'

She made no move to go, however, for her body was rooted to the spot. She was acutely aware of him, of his hand on her arm, of the concentration of his gaze. He had very broad shoulders. Under that dark suit, there was a hard body. The thought made her blood heat. She could feel a flush creeping up her neck.

'You didn't,' he said. 'Disturb me, I mean.' He looked down at his hand, but instead of releasing her, pulled her towards him, linking them together, arm in arm. 'Oban, you said you sailed from?'

She nodded.

'You'll have come on the *Argyle* then. She's sound enough, though that beam engine of hers is well past its prime. Napier's steeple will become the standard, you mark my words, though if you ask me—' He broke off, smiling at the confusion which must be writ large on her face. 'I'm havering. Your luggage will be this way,' he said. 'I'm Iain Hunter.'

'Cordelia. That is, Cordelia Williamson. Mrs.'

'You're married.'

'Widowed,' she said hastily, not pausing to think why it mattered to reassure him.

'I'm glad,' he said. Then, 'I shouldn't have said that.'

He didn't look in the least bit contrite. In fact, there was a gleam in his eyes that gave Cordelia a fizzy feeling in her stomach and made her decidedly light-headed. A more prosaic woman would have said she needed food, but though she had many faults, she had not once in her twenty-eight years been accused of being matter of fact. Impetuous, yes, and heedless too. Both of those traits she had worked very hard to curb in the past few years. Now, as she tripped along beside Iain Hunter, shielded from the bustle not just by his body but by the way the crowd seemed to part for him, she felt a terrible, wicked, irresistible impulse to be both.

'What about you, Mr Hunter,' she asked, 'are you married?'

'No,' he replied.

'I am glad,' Cordelia said.

He stopped in his tracks. 'What am I to take from that?'

It was a fair question. 'I don't know,' she replied, deflated. 'I'm in a strange mood. The travel, most likely. I thought— When I saw you, I thought— But it was silly of me.'

He touched her cheek, where the pulse beat at her temple. His fingers were cold. It was the lightest of touches. She felt as if he were trying to read her mind. 'You could have asked me the same thing,' he said, 'when I told you I was glad you were widowed.'

'What would you have said?'

'Something along the same lines,' he answered. 'I was thinking— I was feeling—strange. I saw you, and I thought, oh, there she is.' He smiled faintly. 'I'm not usually the fanciful sort.'

'I am not usually the sort who talks to strangers at dockyards,' Cordelia said, smiling again.

'I thought we had established I'm not a stranger.'

'It is certainly a strange sort of day. I am beginning to wonder if any of this is real.'

'That's most likely because you haven't eaten. I'll wager the *Argyle* did not give you the smoothest of journeys.'

Cordelia chuckled. 'Poor *Argyle.* You should not be so unkind to her, for she brought me here.'

'And here you are.' He ran his fingers down her arm, from shoulder to wrist, as if to reassure himself of the fact of her presence. The gesture was intimate, not that of a stranger at all. It made her feel—not alone. 'And I'm glad for it,' he said.

The warehouse he led her to was huge, the double doors open on to the quayside, in which were literally hundreds of trunks, bandboxes, portmanteaux, boxes, parcels, crates. Though Cordelia could see no sign of demarcation, Iain Hunter made his way confidently to one of the distinct heaps. 'Which is yours?'

She pointed out her trunk, and a porter appeared at her side, looking at her enquiringly. 'Could you recommend an hotel, Mr Hunter?'

'I'll take you,' he said, and though this was exactly the sort of situation which she cautioned the readers of every single one of her guidebooks to avoid at all costs, Cordelia followed him out of the docks into the cobbled street beyond the wharf buildings, watching meekly as her chest was strapped on to a carriage which, like the porter, appeared magically, and then equally meekly followed Mr Hunter inside.

The Queen's Hotel was a converted town house in the heart of the city. Cordelia took a set of rooms looking out on to the newly built George Square. She had asked Iain Hunter to dine with her, not because she was hungry but because she didn't want him to go. He would have gone. She had only to say the word, and he would go. That was implicit between them, just as it was implicit that neither wanted him to leave. Now, he sat opposite her toying with a glass of wine, his food almost untouched, as was hers.

Not even with Gideon had she felt like this. This was not flirting. It was not the dance of will-we-won't-we? It was—communing. Ridiculous. The Highlanders must have infected her with their taste for whimsy.

'What are you smiling at?' Iain leaned forward, resting his chin on his hand.

'I've never done this before.'

'Nor have I.'

He leaned across the table and took her hand. She still wore her travelling gown, but had loosened the buttons around her wrist. He stroked the skin there with his thumb, little circles that soothed and roused, drawing all her body's focus to that point, where they touched. He didn't ask her, what, what is it you haven't done before? She liked that he didn't pretend. She had always hated that part of the dance—the pretending, the false misunderstandings, the advance and retreat.

'What were you doing on the docks today?' Cordelia asked.

'Thinking,' Iain answered, not at all perturbed by her turning the conversation. 'Planning. I'm at a—a what is the word—*hiatus?* A turning point. I need a change.'

'What do you do?'

He grinned. 'Didn't you guess? I build ships. Paddle steamers.'

'With spire engines, I assume?'

'Steeple. Aye. Though I have in mind some modifications.'

'Is that what you were thinking about, then?'

Iain shook his head. 'That's just business as usual. I need— Ach, I don't know. I need a bigger change.'

He was still stroking her wrist. Shivers of sensation were running up her arm, heating her skin, setting it tingling. She seemed to be doing the same to him, though she had no recollection of leaning across the table and touching him. It was as if her body and her mind were disconnected. 'Tell me,' she said, 'what bigger change were you thinking of?'

'New markets. New seas. New something. I don't know. What were you doing there?'

'I'm going to Edinburgh.'

'That's no answer.'

He lifted her hand to his mouth and began to kiss her fingers. The tip of each one. Then the pad of her thumb. His eyes never left hers. They were darker in the lamplight, gleaming with a combination of desire and challenge. *Did she want this?* He took her index finger in his mouth, and sucked. She released his other hand, slumping down in her chair. Her foot, clad in stockings but not her boots, found its way to his leg. She ran it up his calf over his trousers, and saw the surprise register.

He sucked on her middle finger, his tongue tracing the length of it. 'Cordelia?'

Corr-deel-ia. 'Guidebooks,' she said, sliding her foot higher, over his knee, to the inside of his thigh. He clamped his legs together, holding her there. 'I write guide books. *The Single Lady Traveller's Guide To*—Paris, Brussels, Rome, Dresden. Others. I can't remember. And now the Highlands.'

'Impressive. Surprising. You've not done any destinations closer to home?'

'I don't have a home.'

'I know how that feels,' he said.

Sadness chased across his face, but was quickly banished. *No questions.* 'No, let's not talk about it,' Cordelia said, as if he had spoken aloud. 'I am tired of thinking about it. My own turning point. There is nothing—I'm tired of it.'

'Then we won't talk of it. Should I go, Cordelia?'

'Do you want to?'

'You know I don't, but you also know that I will.'

'No.' She shook her head. 'No, I don't want you to go.'

He let go her hand. He let her foot slide back on to the floor. He got to his feet and came round to the other side of the little table and pulled her upright, sliding his arms around her waist. 'I am glad,' he said, 'because I have never in my life wanted any woman the way I want you. Now.' And then he kissed her.

He kissed her, and the connection was elemental. She understood it, when he kissed her, this feeling of knowing, of being known. *You. You. You.* She recognised him with such a strong physical pull that she staggered. As if she had been waiting all her life for him. As if none had gone before him. As if none but him would ever matter. She could analyse and question and dissect, but she had no interest in doing any of that, no interest in establishing a conflict between her mind and her body. Her body had already won. 'Yes,' she said, though he had not asked, 'the answer is yes.'

She led him into the bedchamber. No words were necessary after that, though they spoke with their lips, hands, eyes. Kissing. His mouth felt as if it were made to kiss hers, hers to fit his. His kisses were like questions. *This? And this? And this?*

And this, she replied, touching her tongue to

his, relishing the sharp intake of his breath in response. *And this.* She opened her mouth. His kisses deepened, his fingers tangling in her hair, his breath warm on her face.

Her hairpins scattered. She pulled at his coat. He threw it on to the floor, then kissed her again. She reached behind her to unfasten her gown. He turned her around, wrestling with the buttons and fasteners, kissing her neck, her shoulders, his breathing ragged. The gown took some time to wriggle out of, hindered and impeded by kisses. He pulled her against him when it finally fell to the floor, her bottom against his thighs. She was frustrated by the layers of her undergarments. He curved his arms around her to cup her breasts. She shuddered, wanting his skin on hers, her nipples hard, aching for his touch. He began to untie the strings of her corsets.

He cursed under his breath. She could not understand the language, which might have been Gaelic, but might have been something more colloquial. When her stays dropped to the floor, releasing her breasts with only her chemise to cover them, he turned her around. Slashes of colour on his cheeks. His eyes glittering with desire. Her own breath quickened, the knot in her belly tightened, the low throb lower down began. 'Take them off,' she said, pulling at his waistcoat.

He discarded his own clothes quickly, efficiently, without any modesty. He was as lean and hard as she had imagined, his shoulders broader, his skin paler, the muscles beneath tensed. And he was more than ready, his erection jutting up against his stomach. Cordelia shuddered. She had never wanted anything so much as this man inside her.

He had been watching her studying him. She smiled at him then, quite deliberately, and felt an answering heat as he smiled the same smile in response. This was going to be—everything. Anything. All. Did she say it aloud? She thought it as he pulled her to him once more, and she felt the thickness of him against the apex of her thighs. His kiss was desperate now. Her own too, her mouth ravaging his, her hands clawing at his back, at his buttocks, at his flanks.

He pulled her chemise over her head. She untied the drawstrings of her pantalettes. She wore only her stockings and her garters. He swore again, this time a word she recognised, a harsh, guttural word that should have shocked her, but expressed exactly what she was feeling. Then he cupped one of her breasts in his hand, covered the nipple of the other with his mouth.

Heat, shivering, *frissons* of pleasure, tugging, connecting up. Delightful. Delicious. But almost too late. There was no time for this, not now. She pulled his face back up to hers and kissed him frantically, pressing herself against him with abandon. *Now, now, now.* 'Now!'

'Aye. I hear you. Dear God, I hear you. Cordelia, I am so—I don't think I can wait.'

'Iain, I know I cannot.'

He laughed. A deep, masculine laugh that vibrated against her breasts, her stomach. Then he kissed her, pulling her on to the floor because even the small distance to the bed was too much. Her arms were wrapped around his neck, her legs around his waist, as he thrust into her.

She cried out.

'*Wheesht* yourself, these walls are thin,' he said, but he was smiling wickedly, and he thrust, and she covered her mouth to muffle her cries, and dug her heels into his buttocks and clenched around him, holding him deep inside her, and he stopped smiling and swore again, that shocking word that said exactly what it was she wanted from him, and inside her, she felt him thicken.

He thrust again. She felt her climax building. She never climaxed as easily as this, not this way, but it hadn't even occurred to her that she would not. He was sweating. His face was strained, his eyes were dark, but focused on her with an intensity that made her feel as if they were connected. Not just joined, but connected. He was inside her. She was inside him. When he kissed her, she responded with every part of her body.

'Come with me,' he said. She had heard that before. Had pretended before. This time, there was no need to pretend. She nodded. He thrust. She held him. He pulsed high inside her. She could feel it, the spiralling, but she could still hold on to it. He thrust again. She arched up under him, tilting her body to hold him higher, and it happened, the loss of control, the fall, the clutching, pulsing, ecstasy, and she cried out, and he thrust one more time, and cried out too, pulling himself free of her at the very last moment, and she had the urge to hold him, to keep him there inside her, regardless of the consequences. Or courting them, even.

When it was over they lay panting, sweating, tangled on the floorboards, like victims of a tempest. In the aftermath, as the urgency abated, and the bliss cocooned her, Cordelia forgot about the ending. One of Iain's legs covered hers. His hand lay possessively on her stomach. He was staring up at the ceiling, his face a blank. Empty. Sadness washed over her. Something else that was different. It had never been anything other than a pleasure before. Some more pleasurable than others, but always fun, usually satisfying, in the way that a glass of wine fresh from the cellar was satisfying, or a bowl of fresh pasta eaten in the sunshine, or a walk on hot sand in bare feet.

Not like this. This was something much more elemental. Before, during, she would have given him anything not to stop. He had invaded her, seen things she did not want anyone to see on her face. *Come with me,* he had said, and she could not have done anything but what he asked. He hadn't taken her, she had given herself to him. All of herself, in a way she never had, nor ever thought she would want to. That he had, despite the power he had over her, been so careful of her too, made it somehow much worse. That she had not wanted him to be careful, that she had for one wild, fierce moment, wanted to court the consequences, frightened her.

It was as if the whole day had been a peeling back of all her layers culminating in this revelation, the core of her, the lonely inner self. Cordelia jumped to her feet, suddenly appalled at what she had done. Her dressing gown was at the top of her trunk. Pale-yellow silk embroidered with flowers, it was masculine in cut, with straight sleeves and a collar. It was one of her favourite pieces of clothing. She tightened the belt, turning to find Iain on his feet, his expression troubled.

'I'm sorry that was so— We got carried away. I am not usually so...' He shrugged hopelessly. 'I'm sorry, I thought it was what you wanted.'

'I did,' she said shortly, unwilling, unable to lie.

She had never been the type of woman to take pleasure in making a man feel guilty.

'Then what's wrong?'

'I'm tired. I have to leave early.'

'Don't lie to me, Cordelia, and don't think you have to pander to my ego either. If it didn't work for you—though if it did not, you're a bloody good actress.'

'It did.' *Now* she was embarrassed. After all that. She would not think of all that. Cordelia began to pick up her clothes.

Iain was already wearing his trousers, pulling on his shirt. 'Then what is it? And don't give me the line about being tired.'

Don't give me the line. His accent was rougher, the Lowland gruffness taking front stage. She couldn't think what to say. *I can't believe I did that,* would give him the wrong impression, though it would certainly help get him out the door, and getting him out the door was what she needed more than anything.

Whatever he read in her face, it made him look grim. Iain picked up his coat and pulled it on, stuffing his stock into the pocket. 'So you've had your bit of rough, and now you want to be alone, is that it?'

'No! What an appalling thing to say.'

He ignored her, pulling on his shoes.

'Iain, that's not it.'

'Then what?'

Fully dressed, he looked intimidating. There was a wild look in his eye that made her think of some of the Highlanders she had seen. Cordelia ran her hand through her tangled hair, coming up with a ball of fluff and a splinter of floorboard. 'It was too much,' she admitted.

'Are you sorry?'

'No.'

The answer was out without needing to think. Iain sighed heavily, but he managed a lopsided smile. 'I'm not sorry either, but my head's reeling, if you must know. You're not the only one to find it all a bit much.'

His honesty disarmed her. 'It has been a very strange day,' she said with a faint smile. 'Extraordinary.'

'Cordelia.'

He touched her temple, just as he had on the

docks. This time, she had to fight the impulse to pull away, for she was fairly certain he *could* read her thoughts.

'I hope whichever direction you take, it makes you happier,' he said.

'Oh, I'm not unhappy.'

'I told you not to lie,' he said gently. 'I know you don't want to hear from me again, but if there should be anything you need me for, here's where you can find me. You understand, I would not expect you to deal with any consequences alone.'

He handed her a card.

'Thank you,' Cordelia said, 'but I am sure...'

'I mean it.'

'I know.'

'That's something,' he said. 'Goodbye, Cordelia.'

He did not touch her. She felt an absurd, contrary desire that he would kiss her. 'Goodbye.' She touched his temple, echoing his own gesture. 'I hope whichever direction you take, it makes you happier too.'

He acknowledged this admission of her own state of mind with a nod. Then he turned and walked through the door. She stood where she was. The outer door opened softly, then closed. She went to the window, pulling the curtains to hide her, and looked out. The lamps were lit around the square. He emerged a few minutes later, through the main hotel entrance. She could not imagine what the night porter must have thought, and did not care. She thought he would stop, look up, even though she was careful not to let him see her, but he did not. He pulled his coat around him, and headed across the square, in the direction of the river, without looking back.

Chapter Three

Cavendish Square, London—spring 1837

Iain's hands automatically went round the woman to stop the pair of them falling. His body recognised her before his mind caught up, before even he had a glimpse of her face, which was burrowed into his chest. 'Cordelia.'

Blue-grey eyes, wide with the shock, met his. Her hand went to her mouth, as if to push back the words, and he remembered that same gesture, self-silencing, only the last time it had been a cry of ecstasy she had stifled after he'd warned her about the walls of the hotel being thin. Her legs had been wrapped around his waist. The hair that was now so demurely curled and primped under her bonnet had been streaming in wild disarray over her shoulders on to the floorboards. Now, she was struggling to free herself. He let her go, but blocked the doorway, a firm shake of his head telling her he'd read her thoughts. *Not a chance,* he told her. She glared at him, but retreated into the room.

'Mr Hunter. You are a tad early.'

Lord Henry Armstrong held out his hand. Iain took it automatically, his mind racing. 'Five minutes at most,' he replied. 'Am I interrupting?'

It was a rhetorical question, for the atmosphere in the room was tense. The muffled sound of heated words had been audible in the hallway as he handed over his hat and gloves. And now he looked at her properly, Cordelia's bonnet was askew, her shawl dangling from one arm. Not, it seemed, escaping his arrival, but running from the man who claimed to be her father.

The man who was now bestowing upon him a smile which Iain found peculiarly irritating. Condescending. Patronising. Mendacious. One or all, it aroused all his base instincts, and made him want to punch something.

'Cordelia,' said his lordship, 'this is Mr Iain Hunter.'

It was the mute appeal in her eyes that kept him silent. Lady Cordelia, whom he knew as the widow, Mrs Cordelia Williamson, was obviously eager that her father should remain in ignorance of their previous acquaintance. Her father! Iain bent over the hand she extended and just touched her fingertips. The eyes were indeed the same colour as Lord Armstrong's, but he could discern no other resemblance.

'Do sit down, Mr Hunter. And you, Cordelia.'

When he spoke to his daughter, there was a steeliness that made Iain's hackles rise. 'I came here to discuss business,' he said. 'I don't see that is any concern of your—your—Lady Cordelia's.'

Lord Armstrong laughed, a dry little sound like paper rustling. 'Take a seat, Mr Hunter, and I'll explain,' he said, taking his own seat behind the desk.

Iain paid him no heed. Cordelia stood poised for flight, but he was damned if he'd let her go without an explanation. 'You'll take the weight off your feet, Mrs—Lady Cordelia,' he said, pressing her down firmly into one of the uncom-fortable-looking chairs, pulling the other closer to her, stretching out a leg casually in front of hers, just to make his message clear. She threw him a look, but he was pretty certain it was be-cause she resented his managing her, rather than any desire to flee.

'Mr Hunter,' Lord Armstrong said, addressing his daughter, 'is hoping to win a contract to build steam ships for Sheikh al-Muhanna.'

'Celia's husband!' From the tone of her voice, this was news to Cordelia. 'You mean the prince has entrusted you to award a contract to build ships on his behalf?' she demanded of her father.

'As you would know, if you were *au fait* with family matters,' Lord Armstrong replied point-edly, 'my son-in-law is very ambitious for his principality. It is not simply a matter of building ships, he wishes the skills to be passed on to his own people. Since it is a well-known fact that England is at the forefront of the industry...'

'I think you'll find that it's Scotland, actually. The Clyde to be more specific,' Iain interjected.

'Yes, yes, we are all one country,' Lord Armstrong said with a condescending smile.

'Aye, when it suits you.'

'As you say.'

His lordship took a visible breath. His daughter—hell and damnation, that woman was Lord Armstrong's daughter!—sat quite still, ramrod straight, only the nervous tapping of her little boot at the hem of her gown giving her away.

'The long and the short of it is,' Iain said, addressing Cordelia directly, 'I've the best people for the job, and I build the best ships, so his lordship here is going to grease the diplomatic wheels and jump through all the hoops of permissions and licences on my behalf. Not to put too fine a point on it, unless I have him on my side to tell me which pockets should be lined and which pieces of paper must be signed, it doesn't matter how good my ships are, they will never be built. In return for these valuable services, your father will get a hefty fee. Isn't that right, Lord Armstrong?'

Cordelia's response to this straightforward speech was, to Iain's relief, one of glee. Lord

Armstrong, who should have been put firmly in his place, had the look of a cat about to pounce.

'Not quite right, Mr Hunter,' he said. 'My terms have changed.'

'I'm not giving you any more money.'

His lordship smiled. 'I don't want *any* of your money.'

The hairs on Iain's neck stood on end, for that smile was the very opposite of benign, whatever that was. Malign? 'You were keen enough to take it when we first talked.'

'Since we first talked, Mr Hunter, my circumstances have changed.'

'Be that as it may, your circumstances have nothing to do with me.'

'On the contrary,' Lord Armstrong said. 'In fact, I hope that in the future our circumstances will be very much—entwined.'

Iain was now thoroughly rattled. 'I'm a plain-talking man, and I'm a plain-dealing one too. I'm not interested in playing games, your lordship, just name your price.'

'My daughter, Mr Hunter, is my price. I wish you to ally yourself with my daughter.'

* * *

Cordelia's jaw actually dropped. It was no consolation at all to see that Iain's did the same.

Her father took advantage of their stunned silence to inform Iain of the excellent bargain he would be making. 'Now, I accept that Cordelia here may not be as young as you would wish,' he said, 'but she comes from excellent breeding stock and her lineage, Mr Hunter, unlike yours, is impeccable.'

As if she were a prize ewe past her prime! Cordelia felt her mouth drop further. Just when she thought she had his measure, her father surprised her. Really, he quite took her breath away. A bubble of hysterical laughter threatened to escape. She made a choking sound, quickly muffling it with her hand.

'Our alliance will bring you benefits far beyond the contract with my son-in-law,' Lord Armstrong continued, getting into his stride. 'Marrying into one of the oldest families in the land will give you access to my considerable experience and influence. If I say so myself...'

'You've said more than enough. I don't want to hear any more!'

Iain's accent thickened considerably as his temper rose. It broadened even more in the heat of passion, Cordelia recalled, then wished fervently that she had not. This situation was beyond belief. Iain was on his feet, leaning over the desk. She too got up from her chair. The three of them faced each other, an oddly assorted triangle which under any other circumstances would have made her laugh.

'Mr Hunter…'

'Lord Armstrong, sit down and shut your mouth.'

The menace in his voice had finally registered with her father. Cordelia watched, fascinated, for she could almost see his diplomatic mind flicking through and discarding a myriad of responses. He seemed to be, for one of the very few times in his life, at a loss for words.

'I came here to discuss contracts for steamships,' Iain continued. 'I'm not on the hunt for a wife, and if I was, I wouldn't need you or anyone else to pick one for me.'

Iain was refusing her, which was absolutely what she wanted, so it was really rather silly of her to feel rejected, though it did give her the advantage of being able to claim that she would have complied, Cordelia thought, frowning. Not that she intended entering into a bargaining war with her father. And actually, it was insulting to be rejected so firmly and with so little consideration, especially by a man who had— With whom she had— And what's more it had been— Well, it had been memorable. Very memorable. So memorable that she had only to close her eyes to conjure up...

'...think it for the best if we discuss it alone.'

Cordelia's eyes snapped open. Was this her cue to leave? But to her surprise, Iain was ushering her father out of his own book room, and her father was making not one sound of protest. The door closed once again, and Iain leaned his really very broad shoulders against it, smiling at her in a way that made her want to run as fast as she could in the other direction—which would be out the window on to the Cavendish Square, so that was out of the question—and at the same time rooted her to the spot.

'What are you doing?' she demanded. 'What did you say to my father?'

'Weren't you listening, Mrs Williamson—or should I say Lady Cordelia?'

Corr-dee-lia. 'Mr Hunter...'

'Iain. It was Iain the last time we met, and given what went on between us, I'm not particularly inclined to go back to more formal terms now.'

He eased himself away from the doorway. She found herself trapped in his gaze. 'I see no reason why we should be on any terms at all,' Cordelia said. 'You made it very clear that you were not interested in my father's proposal.'

'I wanted to get you alone.'

'Oh.' Cordelia tried to back away, and her bottom encountered the desk. She folded her arms, unfolded them again and pulled off her bonnet. It was giving her a headache. She was deflated and depressed by the encounter with her father.

'So you've a title,' Iain said. 'Not plain missus after all, but a lady.'

He was standing right beside her now. It irked

her that she was so aware of him. Not that he was in any way bulky, Iain Hunter was tall and lean. It was not his dress either. Not for this dour Scotsman the wasp-waisted coats and padded shoulders of fashion, his brown wool suit was plain, austere even, but he had no need of artificial aids to emphasise the breadth of those shoulders, and the modest cut of his trousers only drew attention to the length of his legs. She was tall, but she still had to tilt her head to meet his eyes.

She hated being put on the back foot, especially when she was not in the wrong. 'I find that a *plain missus* attracts rather less notice than a title.' Claiming to be another man's relic also legitimised her lack of innocence, but Cordelia saw no need to point that out.

'Your father had no idea we'd met before. I'm wondering why you were so hell-bent on not telling him.'

'My father trades in information. I find a policy of withholding as much as I can works best.'

Iain laughed. 'In other words, it's better to lie. It's not a policy I'd normally advocate, but in this case—I doubt the man's ever been honest with anyone in his life. Not even himself.'

'Especially not himself. It is how he manages to be so very convincing in his mendacity,' Cordelia said with feeling.

Her cheeks were hot. There was barely a few inches between them. Beneath the tension it was still there, that—that thing between them. *Remember me. Remember me. Remember me.* She didn't want to remember. She didn't want to notice that in the year since that night, the grooves that separated his brows had deepened. She didn't want to notice that his hair was still the same shade of auburn, that he still kept it so close-cropped. She was having great difficulty regulating her breathing. She yearned for him to touch her. She would die rather than admit that. She needed to get away. Regroup. Retrench. Re-something. But first she wanted to get into bed in a dark room and pull the covers over her head and hide.

It occurred to her that he was probably just as keen to escape. Then it occurred to her that he had come to Cavendish Square expecting to conclude a very lucrative business deal and that she, inadvertently, had put a spoke in the wheel. They were both suffering at her father's hands, but Iain was utterly innocent.

'Forget about what passed between you and me,' Cordelia said, 'it's quite irrelevant. If I had not happened to be here when you called, this would not have happened. I am very, very sorry that I was. I am sure that when my father comes to his senses and realises that you will walk away from this contract rather than marry me...'

'I've no intentions of walking away from this contract.'

'Yes, I know. I mean I assumed— You told me, remember? You said that you needed new markets. I know how important this must be to you, but I merely meant you would call his bluff.'

'Oh, I'll do that all right.'

'Good. Excellent.' Cordelia picked up her bonnet again.

Iain took it from her and set it back down. 'You remembered, didn't you? The minute you crashed into me, you remembered that day. That night.'

'I said we should forget it.'

'I haven't been able to forget. Have you?'

'Oh, for heaven's sake. No! Are you happy now?'

'Do you remember, I had to tell you to *wheesht?*' Iain closed the tiny space between them. His voice was soft, a whispering burr without any trace of the Lowland growl. If it were not for that look in his eyes, she would have said it was seductive. He took one of her artful curls and began to twist it round his finger. He had an artist's hands, the fingers long and delicate, though the skin was rough.

The muscles in her belly clenched. 'You were every bit as— You enjoyed it every bit as much, as I recall.'

'I did.' He let her curl slip from her finger, only to cup her jaw in his hand, his thumb running along the length of her bottom lip. 'Too right I did,' he said, and covered her mouth with his.

She almost surrendered. His mouth fit so perfectly with hers, as no other ever had or would. Her lips clung to his, her mouth opening, her hands reaching automatically to twine around his neck, her body arching into the hard length of his. Cordelia yanked herself free and delivered a very hard slap.

* * *

Iain staggered back, his hand cupped to his throbbing cheek. Cordelia had not been messing about, and to judge by the way she was glaring at him, she would have hit him a deal harder if she'd had a chance. Or more precisely, she'd hit him again if he took another chance. He was forced to laugh. 'I suppose you'll tell me I deserved that.'

She folded her arms across her chest and stuck her nose in the air. 'You know perfectly well that you did.'

'And I suppose that you'll also tell me you didn't want me to kiss you?'

She raised her brows and pursed her lips, giving him one of those looks that managed to be both sceptical and challenging. 'I don't think I've ever met anyone whose ego is in less need of pandering than yours, Mr Hunter.'

This time his laugh was spontaneous. 'Come now, hasn't the very man just left the room! But since we're talking extremes, let me tell you that I don't think I've ever met a woman quite like you, Mrs—Lady Cordelia.'

'Is that a compliment?'

Iain shrugged. 'It's the truth. I take it you had no more idea than I of what your father was going to suggest today?'

'I am pretty certain my father had no idea either, until your card was sent in. It was a surprise attack. He was ever fond of Wellington you know, even though the duke has fallen from favour. And with him my dear father,' Cordelia said sardonically.

'They say that the king is in poor health. When he dies, there will be another General Election, though I doubt the Tories will win, even with Peel in charge.'

'No, my father's star is finally on the wane. We will have a woman on the throne too. The influential Lord Armstrong is now past his prime and stripped of influence.' Cordelia's smile was twisted. 'Not that I believe *that* for a second. My father will bend with the wind, even if he can no longer direct it.'

'What's more, he's sharp enough to see it's men like myself who'll be doing the directing in the future.' Iain grinned. 'I have to admire the devious old bugger, even if he is deluded. I've no interest in earning a fancy title, and I've certainly no desire to rub shoulders with those who've nothing better to do than spend their ill-gotten gains on clothes and parties and horses.'

'Good heavens, are you a revolutionary? Perhaps you have ambitions to put my father's neck on a guillotine?'

'No, but I suspect you would. You'll forgive me being blunt,' Iain said, 'but you don't hold the old man in much esteem, do you?'

'I doubt you are ever anything else but blunt.' Cordelia turned towards the desk and began to footer with the blotter, aligning the pen holder and inkstand up. 'No, I don't have much respect for him. About as much as he does for me.'

He could not see her expression, but something in the hunch of her shoulders made him guess at the hurt she was attempting to disguise. 'If he means so little to you, why do you let him upset you?'

She turned at that, and he saw he was right. Pain shadowed her eyes, though she was fighting it. 'My sister Cressie said something similar to me recently. She seems to have found a way of overcoming nature which I have as yet to discover, despite my attempts to do so.'

'I must consider myself fortunate not to be encumbered by parents then,' Iain said gruffly.

'You are an orphan?'

It was his turn to shrug. He had no desire to add a discussion of his pathetic history into the conversation that was already convoluted enough. 'He may be your father, but you're a grown woman, Cordelia, he can't make you do anything you don't want to do.'

'All very well for you to say that. You are a man.'

'Aye, and when you look at me like that, I'm very glad I am,' Iain replied, because the mocking look was back in her eyes, and there was something irresistible about the challenge of it, and in the sensual downward curl of that mouth of hers.

He caught her arm and turned her towards him, losing his train of thought in the scent of her, and the rustle of her gown against his legs, and in the way she reacted to the heat of his gaze, neither shrinking from it nor denying her own reaction.

'I'm not going to kiss you,' she said.

She spoke coolly, though her words were belied by the tempting tilt of her mouth. He slid his hand up her back, finding the delightful patch of naked skin at her nape, under her hair. 'You'd better not hit me again.'

'What, will you hit me back? I should warn you, Iain, I am not the sort of woman to take *that* sort of pleasure.'

'Firstly, I never hit any woman, no matter what kind.' Iain put his other arm around her waist, pulling her close. The perfume she wore was exotic, though the scent eluded him. The way she spoke his name made him shiver, made the muscles in his belly tighten, sent the blood coursing to his groin. 'And secondly, you seem to have forgotten that I know very well what particular kind of pleasure you like.'

She did not move. He knew, despite her denial, that she would kiss him back this time. It shocked him, the fierce possessiveness he felt just touching her, so much so that he let her go. 'I want that business, Cordelia. What has he got on you? I'm not daft, you wouldn't still be here talking to me if he didn't have some sort of hold over you. What is it?'

She hesitated, returning to her compulsive straightening of the desk furniture, aligning the already aligned pen holder and inkpot. Then she turned, her mouth tight with anger. 'My family. My aunt. My half-brothers I have not seen since I left nearly ten years ago, the half-sister I have never met. And most of all Celia and Cassie. They were his trump cards.' The pen in her hand snapped. 'My two elder sisters,' she explained with a curl of her lip. 'Both are married to Arabian princes. I knew Caro and Cressie—they are my other sisters—would pay no heed to my father's decree. Indeed, I was fairly certain his disowning me was sufficient for them to make a point of keeping in touch, but as to Celia and Cassie—'

She broke off, obviously near to tears. Iain wrestled with this completely unexpected revelation. 'Your father disowned you? What on earth for?'

'I refused to marry a man of his choosing.'

Iain shook his head in bemusement. 'You

wouldn't marry the man he picked for you and he took the hump?'

'I wouldn't marry *any* man he picked for me. And if by taking the hump you mean he was offended—he was furious.' Cordelia cast the broken pen on to the desk. 'I know it sounds mediaeval, but he really could have ensured that all doors were closed to me if I'd given him the pleasure of trying to open them.'

Iain stared at her in horror. 'Your own flesh and blood! Who does he think he is—some sort of god?'

'One of my other sisters calls him a puppet master,' Cordelia said wryly.

'So they don't condone what he did? But you said the eldest two…'

'Celia and Cassie. It's not that they condone it exactly, but to respond to any overture of mine would require them to keep it secret from their husbands. I have never met Cassie's husband, and Celia's but once, but the code of honour with desert princes is strong. No matter what they may think of the circumstances, my father's will must be respected. *That* is the ace he was going to play, I suspect,' Cordelia finished contemptuously.

Iain shook his head in disgust. 'I can't believe he would stoop so low. To keep your own sisters from you, and him your father.'

'Which is exactly why he does not see it as anything other than his natural right, to order my life,' she replied bitterly. 'Cressie—my middle sister—used to say that we were his pawns in the game of matrimonial chess. She was right, Iain, believe me.'

'And unless you do as he says, you won't get to see your sisters in Arabia?'

'I don't know. I had hoped today that I could persuade him to—but that was before he came up with this ridiculous idea. Now—I simply don't know.'

She shook her head, biting her lip and screwing shut her eyes, and Iain cursed himself for being so blunt. 'I'm sorry.'

'You've nothing to apologise for.'

'He's a right wee shite, your father.'

She laughed tearfully. 'I have no idea what that means, but I suspect you're right.'

'Aye, sorry about the language. You can take a man from the docks, but you can't take the docks from the man.'

She smiled at this quip, but seemed suddenly at a loss. 'I'd better be off.'

'You're not staying here?'

She shuddered theatrically. 'Good heavens, no. I have rooms at Milvert's on Brook Street. I suppose this is goodbye. I wish you luck with your contract.'

'We've both got too much to lose to turn our backs on this. I'll walk with you.'

He was not fooling himself. That day over a year ago had been in every way extraordinary. He had never, before or since, experienced that instant of certainty, that deep connection that had led them both to believe they'd met before, that had transformed into the most intense attraction he'd ever known. Circumstances had colluded to put them together on the docks at the Broomilaw at the same time in the same frame of mind. Since then, he had thought of it as a day—and night—out of time. It had not occurred to him that they would ever meet again, but now they had done so, under the strangest of circumstances, Iain couldn't help thinking that fate must have taken a hand. Not that he believed in fate, though his mother had been a great one for it.

'I beg your pardon?'

He realised, as he took his hat and gloves from the footman, that he'd spoken his mother's words aloud. 'What's for you won't go by you,' he repeated tersely, as they ascended the steps into Cavendish Square.

'You think that fate has brought us together?' Cordelia asked.

She had a smile that did things to his insides. Provocative, that was the word for it. Iain never spoke of his mother. His memories of his family were so painfully tarnished that he rarely allowed himself to remember the few happier times when Jeannie was still alive. His heart felt as if it were being squeezed, and he automatically closed his mind to that memory. He had always been driven, but this last year, he had immersed himself in his work to the exclusion of all else. He hadn't realised he'd missed Cordelia until he saw her today. It didn't matter that their entire acquaintance spanned less than twenty-four hours either. At some elemental level, he and she were the same.

Iain took her hand and tucked it into his arm. 'You want to know what I really think?' he said, smiling down at her. 'I think we should tell your father we're getting married.'

Cordelia's rooms at Milvert's exclusive hotel were on the corner of the second floor. Pushing open the window of her sitting-room, she gazed out on to the busy street, her head whirling. With the Season starting to get into full swing, there was a steady flow of carriages and horses making their way past Grosvenor Square to Hyde Park.

'You haven't said what you thought of my suggestion,' Iain said, throwing his hat and gloves on to the table.

She pulled the casement closed and began to wander disconsolately about the room, tidying her notebooks, folding her cuffs, wiping her pen, absent-mindedly straightening the various objects which sat on the tables, the mantelpiece, the hearth, before finally taking a seat opposite him. 'I don't know what to think.'

'Do you have an alternative plan?'

She shook her head, pursing her lips. 'Though I am more determined than ever to act, despite the fact that my father could make things very difficult. What's more, now that he has set his heart on this ridiculous idea of us marrying, he will not listen to any alternatives.'

'Which is all the more reason to pretend to give him what he wants.'

'Pretend we are engaged, you mean?' Cordelia asked, for she was still unsure about how serious Iain had been. 'Lie to him, make him think we are doing exactly what he wants, so that we get exactly what we want, and then, when we have succeeded, tell him it was all a ruse?'

'Strictly speaking, it would not be a lie. "Ally yourself with my daughter" is what he said, not "marry her".'

'Semantics.'

Iain shrugged. 'He's a diplomat—or he was. Don't they trade in semantics?'

'When you put it that way...' He really was serious, Cordelia mused. It really was a scandal-ously attractive idea. She really could not believe he meant it. 'But I thought—you said it yourself, Iain, you are a plain-talking man, an honest man. I can't believe you are contemplating this. You are so—so straight.'

'Unlike your father, who is as crooked as a bent pin,' Iain said with a grin.

She spluttered. 'No, no. Devious, scheming, but never criminal.'

'He deserves to be locked up for the way he treated you.'

'Yes, I quite agree, but I rather think this would be better punishment.' Her laughter faded. 'You really want this business badly enough to achieve it by deceit? I confess, you surprise me.'

'I'll take that as a compliment. The man I'll be dealing with will be Sheikh al-Muhanna, and I've no intention of deceiving him.' Iain stretched his long legs out in front of him, tugging at his neckcloth as if it was too tight. 'I'll be straight with you, Cordelia. This deal means a lot to me. It's not just the money—in fact, it's not about the money at all. It's what we talked about that day in Glasgow, you remember?'

'Your turning point.'

'Aye.' He smiled at her. 'The engineering challenges alone would have tempted me to go in at a loss. I don't just want the deal, I need it.'

'And you could have it, can have it, if I tell my father I won't marry you. I'm sure he wants it as much as you.'

'I'm sure he does, but after today, I'll be damned if I'll let him have anything the way he wants. I won't be manipulated, and I won't have you pay the price of my victory. You're a feisty wee thing, and you've been hard done to.'

She threw back her head and glared at him, immediately on the defensive. 'I don't need your pity, Iain.'

'I don't feel sorry for you. I admire you, and I don't see why you should sacrifice yourself so that I can have what I want, when we can both win. He's no right to keep you from your own flesh and blood. Your own sisters. If I wasn't the best person for the job, it would be different,' Iain said earnestly, 'but I am, and I'm not about to lose it because the likes of your father wants to stick his oar into my business. *Chan eil tuil air nach tig traoghadh.*'

'Is that Gaelic?'

He seemed somewhat disconcerted, as if he had not intended her to hear the words. 'It means every flood will have an ebb. Your father's day is coming to an end. It's not blood that will count in the new age, it's science, and industry, and people like me who aren't scared to get their hands dirty.'

Cordelia shivered. 'Remind me never to get on the wrong side of you.'

'We are both on the same side. Don't you want revenge?'

She stared at him, sifting her responses, measuring them carefully. 'If you had asked me a few hours ago, I would have said revenge was the last thing on my mind,' she said finally. 'I went to Cavendish Square today thinking to achieve reconciliation. Foolish of me, but I had to try. One last time. I shouldn't have bothered, but at least I can be in no doubt of his feelings. Not even I could persuade myself he cared after that.'

Fury, red-hot and vicious, caught her suddenly in its grip. The muscles in the backs of her legs actually trembled from it. Her hands were clenched into painful fists. What had she been thinking of! He would never, ever agree to what she wanted from him because he simply didn't care. 'He doesn't love me.'

There, she had said it out loud. Cordelia looked out of the window. The sky had not fallen down. 'My father doesn't love me. My *father* doesn't give a damn about me!' It felt good. It felt very good. There could be no excuses, no mitigating factors. He had been cruel, deliberately so, and malicious too. She forced herself to recall in great detail, every word he had said, determined this time to etch it on to her mind, a sort of memory-prompt should she retract, as she had so often in the past. He didn't love her, but he thought, he still thought, he owned her, and it was *that* fact she had until now never truly questioned. Every act of hers had been in defiance. She had never felt entitled to her own life even when she had acted as if she did.

'My God, what a fool I have been.' It really

was as if she had lifted the shutters on a darkened room, allowing the light to filter in, displaying the murky contents for what they were. She owed him nothing. What she had taken for love had been a sense of duty, a habit, nothing more. She didn't love her father. Right now, thinking of how he had so nearly managed to manipulate her, she almost hated him.

'So you'll do it?'

She had almost forgotten Iain in the heat of her anger. It faded now, replaced by something else. She came back across the room towards him, smiling. Power, that's what she felt, and it was intoxicating. 'A double coup,' she said. It was a very satisfying notion. 'You know, it is really very liberating, being freed from guilt.' She stretched her arms wide, laughing as she twirled round, the skirts of her gown whirling around her. 'I feel quite giddy with it.'

'I can see that.' Iain got to his feet, catching her as she stumbled. 'Mind you don't fall.'

'I can mind myself perfectly well. Just because we have an—an alliance doesn't mean that I can't fight my own battles.'

She spoke more aggressively than she intended, but Iain merely smiled. 'I know that fine, and it's one of the things I like about you.'

'You mean there's more than one?'

She meant it simply to deflect the compliment, to distract her from the realisation that it would be very nice indeed to have someone fight her battles for her, just once. But it was a mistake.

'You know perfectly well there's more than one,' Iain said.

He was doing it again. Looking at her with intent. And it was having the same effect as it had before, heating her blood, making her heart beat too fast. 'Stop that.'

'It's your own fault. If you had not reminded me of all the things I like about you—and don't tell me you're not thinking of the things you like about me too, for I can see it in your face.'

Cordelia tilted her chin, defying the flush to creep on to her cheeks. 'One of the things I don't like about you is the way you make assumptions about what I'm thinking.'

'You've a very speaking face, which is why I'm

going to suggest something else you won't like. Let me handle telling your father our news.'

Instinctively, she wanted to refuse him, but for once Cordelia paused to think. 'You mean I might give the game away?'

'He knows you too well.'

Much as she wished to deny it, she could not. 'Very well, though I should warn you that—'

'You prefer to make your own decisions. As do I.' Iain grinned. 'We're like to have some interesting clashes, my wee love.'

'I am not your *wee love.*'

He slipped his arm around her waist, pulling her up against him. 'For the time being, that's exactly what you are.'

Her heart began to beat erratically. She had that feeling, that her corsets were too tightly laced. She wished he would not smile at her like that, because it was nigh on impossible not to smile back at him. 'What does that make you for the time being,' she asked, determined not to let him see the effect he was having on her, 'my great big darling?'

She felt his laugh rumble in his chest. He pulled

her tighter against him, sliding his free hand into her hair. 'Flattering as that is, I think it would be best if you didn't go bragging to the world about it.'

She felt herself go scarlet. 'I did not mean great big—I did not mean that!'

'There now, that's put me in my place. And yet I seem to remember there were no complaints from you at the time.'

His fingers were stroking the skin at the nape of her neck. His mouth was curved into a smile that was blatantly sensual. It was there again in his eyes, that heat, and she was pretty certain it was there in hers too. 'Iain, we are just pretending to be engaged.'

'Aye, but there are other things we've no need to pretend about. You know I still want you, Cordelia.'

Corr-dee-lia. 'Did you have this in mind when you suggested our engagement?'

'No, and I won't change my mind if you're not interested. I think you are though.'

'I think I've already mentioned that you've a very high opinion of yourself, Mr Hunter.'

Iain laughed softly. 'I don't want to play games, Cordelia. Knowing that you want me as much as I want you—have you any idea what that does to me?'

His voice was low, making the hairs on her skin stand on end. No man had ever been so— so blatant before. 'You do not subscribe to the belief that men shall hunt and women shall be hunted?' she asked.

His expression darkened momentarily. 'I told you, I'm not interested in playing games. I don't want you subservient to my desires, Cordelia, I want my desires to be yours. Yours to be mine.'

His words were a low stomach-clenching growl. 'My desires to be yours,' she repeated, mesmerised.

'And yours to be mine. Admit it, we have unfinished business.'

'You think to finish it while we pretend to be engaged?'

'Yes.'

'You think proximity will engender indifference?'

'It always has before.'

This, in Cordelia's experience was very true. Iain did not ask her about her experience. Thinking back over their earlier conversation, she realised there was a distinct possibility he thought it acquired when she was married to the mythical Mr Williamson. Disabusing him now would raise all sorts of awkward questions that were none of his business, any more than his experience was hers, she told herself firmly. If he asked her directly of course, she would not lie, but he had not asked, nor was he likely to.

'The point of a betrothal is usually to nurture love rather than breed contempt,' Cordelia said.

'Faux betrothal. And our aim is indifference,' Iain said. 'I can't imagine ever holding you in contempt. To be honest, though I'm certain of the outcome, I'm a bit more interested in the journey, aren't you?'

'Even though it's likely to be anything but smooth. I am after all a—what did you call me—a feisty wee thing?'

'It's because you're a feisty wee thing that I think we'll both enjoy the journey. You don't strike me as a woman with much interest in a smooth path, Cordelia.'

She had only to make the tiniest movement and he would let her go, but she didn't want to. She wanted him every bit as much as he said, and she wanted not to want him every bit as much. 'You're right, I'm not in the least bit interested in a smooth path.' Cordelia smiled, deliberately provocative. And then she kissed him.

Chapter Four

Her lips were warm, soft. She wobbled, put her arms around his neck, pulling herself against him, and kissed him again. Iain sank down on to the sofa, taking her with him. She was splayed across him, her breasts brushing his chest. He slid his arms around her waist and pulled her upright so that she sat astride him, his hands curving over her bottom. Her eyes widened with surprise and she smiled that smouldering smile of hers, and dipped her head, her lips already parted as he kissed her back.

His heart skittered to a frenzy as he was enveloped in her scent, her skin, the rustling silk of her gown, as he slid his tongue into the warmth of her mouth, and she shuddered against him with a little moan of pleasure. The kiss deepened.

Her hands slid under his jacket to his back. He could feel her fluttering fingers through the silk of his waistcoat and the linen of his shirt. She squirmed, her knees on either side of his thighs to hold her balance. He knew from experience that her underwear made her top half impregnable, and instead pulled at her skirts, his hand fighting with layers of petticoats until he found the softness of her flank, separated from her skin by just one layer of cotton.

She arched her back, rubbing her breasts against his chest. Her tongue touched his, retreated, touched his again in the most tantalising of dances. He was already hard. His hand cupped the delightful curve of her buttock. She lifted herself from him to allow him to slip his hand beneath her, but her voluminous petticoats were getting in the way. He wanted to roll her on to the floor and push up her skirts and bury himself in her. His shaft throbbed in anticipation. He hadn't allowed himself to remember how she felt around him, hot and wet and tight, gripping him, urging him deeper. Now he could think of nothing else. Though actually, there was plenty he should be thinking about.

'Cordelia.' He tried to lift her from him, but she protested, kissing him deeper, her fingers plucking at his hair, at his back, tugging at his shirt.

'Cordelia, wait.'

She stilled and lifted her head, blinking at him, her skin flushed, her eyelids heavy, her eyes glittering. 'Too much already, Iain? Or are you having second thoughts?'

'No! God, no. I'm not having any thoughts, though I should be,' he said distractedly. 'There are a million things I should be doing, thinking of, preparing for.'

'And this is rather far down the list,' Cordelia said, attempting to clamber from his lap.

He stayed her, putting his hands firmly round her waist. 'The problem is that this is at the top of my list. In fact, right now, it's the only thing on my list, and we haven't even formalised our betrothal.'

'Faux betrothal. Are you suggesting we wait until there's a formal announcement?'

He ignored the mocking note in her voice. 'No,

but I am suggesting we wait. I—Cordelia, we've waited a year already. It was—the last time, it was...'

'Extraordinary.'

This, she said without any trace of irony. 'Yes,' Iain agreed, relieved. 'And also—well, frankly rather hurried. I do possess some finesse, you know.'

'I don't, but I'd like to.'

That smile again, curling like smoke. His shaft throbbed in response. It took a supreme effort not to kiss her. 'You shall find out, I promise you.' He eased her to her feet, getting up from the chair and putting some very necessary distance between them. 'After...'

'We are formally betrothed,' she finished for him.

He had meant to say after he had spoken to her father, but perhaps she was right. There would be so many arrangements to make, and all the blasted formalities that Armstrong was facilitating to be gone through. The promise of Cordelia at the end of it would certainly be an incentive.

'I don't mean it that way,' she said, interrupting his thoughts. 'As an incentive,' she explained when he looked at her blankly. 'That was what you were thinking.'

'I was, but not in the way *you* were thinking. You're not the type to hold a man to ransom.'

He had meant to say it lightly, but the words came out sounding like a threat. Her lips tightened. 'No, I'm not,' she said. 'Perhaps if I had been—but I never have, so what is the point in discussing it?'

Which meant, quite clearly, that she would not discuss whatever *it* was, Iain realised, at the same time as he also realised that he wanted to know, and that he had no right to ask. How could he have thought her easy to read! Right now, her face was as inscrutable as a cat's. Odd, this feeling of knowing her so intimately and yet not knowing her at all. He wondered if she felt the same. At the back of his mind, he registered that he was spending rather too much time wondering about Cordelia, when he should be thinking about the problems of building ships in Arabia. Frustration, that's what it was. That's all it was.

Best cured by action, though sadly not of the sort his body clamoured for.

'I had best be off.' He picked up his hat and gloves. 'I'll call on your father first thing.'

'You are sure...'

'I won't change my mind.'

'I was going to ask if you were sure you would not rather I accompanied you?'

'I'm sure of that too.' He risked a very brief kiss, the most fleeting touch of his lips to her cheek.

She caught his arm as he turned to go. 'I am sure too,' she said, with a deliberate hint of that smile of hers, 'on both counts.'

'Feisty.' He pulled her back into his arms. 'Most definitely feisty. I never thought I'd say this, but I'm looking forward to being shackled.'

'Faux shackled.' She ran her hand possessively down his back to rest on his behind.

'Nothing faux about this,' Iain said, and kissed her once more.

Cordelia had spent a restless night torn between regretting that she had agreed to allow Iain to see her father alone, and thinking of the thousand-and-one questions she should have asked him to cover on her behalf. At one point, she had almost written everything down and sent Iain a note, for he would assuredly not think to discuss the half of them with her father. In fact, she wouldn't be surprised if he spent the entire time discussing contracts and permissions and all those things which would facilitate his blasted steamship building and not think about any of the things Cordelia needed to know. The knowledge that he was right, that she was likely to betray herself, kept her back, though it was devilish difficult, to let another manage her fate. Devilish!

It was therefore an enormous relief when the maid informed her, not long after eleven, that a Mr Hunter awaited her convenience downstairs. She selected a walking dress of her favourite powder-blue merino wool with navy frogging which fastened over a white-silk underdress. Twisting her hair into a simple knot, brushing away the maid's offer of hot irons, she donned a poke-bonnet whose only ornament was an ostrich feather the exact shade of blue as her gown.

Despite the throng of people in the reception area, she spotted Iain immediately. It wasn't that he looked out of place, rather that something emanated from him which drew the eye. He was plainly dressed as he had been yesterday, in a black coat and trousers, but as yesterday, the austerity of his attire drew attention to the man himself as he stood by the doorway, looking out on to the street.

He turned as she began to make her way towards him, and any illusion a person might have had, that the plainness of his dress betokened a man of the cloth must have been banished, for surely no man of ecclesiastical pursuit would look at a woman in such a way. Blatant desire, washed with—what? Cynicism, scepticism, worldweariness or simple wariness? Whatever the combination, Cordelia wished he would not look at her in that way, and at the same time felt her skin heating as he did.

His greeting, however, was brief and to the point. 'I've seen your father. As you'd expect, he has his terms. I've business to attend to in the Isle of Dogs. You can come with me, and I'll bring you up to date.'

Which was exactly what she wished, but his high-handed manner put her hackles up. 'And what if I have another engagement?'

He drew her a level look. 'I thought we agreed we wouldn't play games?'

'Actually, you said you didn't want to play games. I cannot recall that I made any commitment either way—where are you going?' Cordelia said sharply, as Iain turned away.

'I told you, I have urgent business. There's a lot to be done if we're to make Plymouth in time.'

Her irritation fled. 'Plymouth?' Another of those looks, but this time she could see the gleam in his eye. So much for his avowal not to play games. She caught at his sleeve. 'Iain, why are we going to Plymouth?'

His mouth quivered on the verge of a smile. 'Actually, we are merely passing through Plymouth. We're going to…'

'Arabia?' She was shaking. Her knees really were turning to jelly. 'Do you mean it, Iain? I'm going to see Celia?'

He nodded. 'I do. All being well, you'll be with your sisters in a matter of weeks.'

Forgetting all about her surroundings, Cordelia threw her arms around his neck and burst into tears.

'*Wheesht,* now.' Totally taken aback by the strength of her reaction, Iain pulled her into the relative privacy of an alcove and put a sheltering arm around her. 'I thought it would be a nice surprise, not a shock.'

She sniffed, smiled, and dabbed frantically at her face with the handkerchief he handed her. 'It is. A nice surprise I mean, not a shock. I'm fine now, I'm sorry to have made such a fuss.'

She held out his damp kerchief. He took it, folding it into his pocket. 'I shouldn't have sprung it on you like that. I didn't realise it meant so much to you.'

'I don't think I did either. At least, I think I didn't allow myself to admit how much it meant. Are we really going to Arabia? I'm going to see Celia, and Cassie too?'

'That's the plan.' She was looking at him as if he'd just handed her the crown jewels, smiling at him mistily, her cheeks still damp with tears he suspected she rarely shed. He wanted to pull her into his arms, and at the same time, he wanted to punch that smug, manipulative bastard who called himself her father.

'Thank you, Iain.'

She stood on her tiptoes, and to his surprise, kissed his cheek.

'Don't be daft. Come on, let's get out of here, and I'll fill you in on the details.'

Outside, he tossed the urchin a shilling and helped Cordelia up into the gig before taking the reins. The streets were crowded, a nightmare bustle of carriages, coaches, carts, horses and pedestrians that made Glasgow seem like a village. He had always preferred walking—a legacy of his youth, no doubt, when the only roads were the drovers' tracks. The bucks and dandies who took such pride in driving to an inch, which in Iain's book meant driving to within an inch of killing someone, made him want to laugh, but as he gritted his teeth, prayed and manoeuvred the gig out into the stream of traffic, for the first time he wished he had a little of their skill.

* * *

It was with relief that he reached the relative quiet of Holborn. Cordelia, either realising his need to concentrate or caught up in her own thoughts, had been silent by his side, but perhaps now she sensed him relax, and turned towards him. 'I really am grateful, you know. I am sorry I behaved so childishly this morning. I thought I was beyond playing such stupid games. It is rather mortifying to discover that I'm not.'

'I suspect it's even more mortifying to have someone else act for you,' Iain replied, smiling at her.

'And even more to be so transparent,' she said with a wry smile.

'No, it's only that I'm the same myself, I like to be in control. There's no need to be grateful you know. We're both gaining from this, and we're both paying a price too.'

'What do you mean?'

'Despite the fact that I know we're in the right of it, it doesn't sit well with me to deceive, any more than it does you. Come on, Cordelia, there's a hundred things we'll have to do that you won't like. You're going to have to lie to that aunt of yours, for a start—for the while, at least. And what about your stepmother, never mind your sisters? I know you've a conscience—you wouldn't be in this tangle if you didn't have—and despite what you might try to tell yourself, it extends to your dealings with that man who calls himself your sire.'

She gave a spurt of laughter at this. "'Calls himself!" Believe me, if I thought for a moment he was not… When we were younger, Cressie and Caro and I, we used to pretend that Mama had had an *affaire*—or *affaires,* who knows?—and that we were all of us cuckoos in the nest. Sadly, we are all rather too alike, and even Cressie, who considers herself the plain one, though I cannot see why, has Papa—our father's eyes. Iain? What's wrong?'

'Nothing.' She looked entirely unconvinced, and he realised his face must have betrayed him. 'Your father has many faults, but at least—' *You can be sure of who he is.* Iain broke off. 'I'm sorry, I shouldn't have made a joke of it. I didn't mean to suggest—*that.*'

'I wasn't taking you seriously.' Cordelia waited, but he remained silent, taken aback at how near he had come to betraying the doubts which he'd thought long dismissed. 'Well,' she said, when he kept his mouth resolutely shut, 'what I was trying to say in a roundabout way was that I owe you an apology. I didn't think any of those things— my concerns, that is—would occur to you. I did you a disfavour.'

'What, did you think I'd spend my time talking to your father about paddle steamers and permits?'

She flushed. 'Yes.'

'Well, that's told me.' He was hurt, but he was dammed if he'd let her see it. 'In fact, we spent the better part of the time talking about *your* business, not mine, though to be fair, that's partly because Armstrong considers the nuts and bolts of industry beneath him, and passed me on to his own man of business to discuss the detail. He's efficient, I'll give him that—or perhaps he knew that he'd need to give me some proof of good faith,' he added wryly. 'I've already had the first of the appointments he made for me at that ramshackle house in Downing Street they call the Foreign Office.'

'Which is all very well, but doesn't change the fact that I underestimated you, and I'm very sorry for that,' Cordelia said contritely.

'Well, it's good of you to admit it.'

'Yes, it is.' Cordelia grinned. 'I wouldn't have, you know, when I was younger. I hate to be in the wrong, and I hate even more having to admit it.'

Her smile was infectious. He was quite disarmed. 'Were you often in the wrong, when you were younger?'

'Oh, yes, lots, but I am afraid I was one of those children who took delight in pulling the wool over everyone's eyes. I turned into a young, heedless woman who did the same,' she said, 'and look where that got me. But never mind that, you have not yet told me the detail of what passed between you and my father this morning. You mentioned that he had his terms.'

'Aye.' They were heading east, roughly following the path of the river, the area known as the Pool of London. He bought himself some time by pointing it out, and the diggings which marked the excavation of the new Thames Tunnel.

Cordelia looked where he indicated, then looked back at him, raising her brows questioningly. 'I'd rather you just came out with it, whether you think I'll like it or not.'

'For a start, he wants the announcement formalised. I tried to put him off.' Iain grinned. 'I developed a patriarchal concern for the state of the king's health, but your father's determined to puff off his new acquisition to all and sundry, though I've no idea what good he thinks it will do him.'

'I suspect he has an eye to his sons' future,' Cordelia said disdainfully. 'He can see that self-made men such as yourself will hold increasing sway in the corridors of power.'

'So it's not just his daughters whose futures he maps out, then?'

'I suppose not. I had not thought of that. What else?'

'He wants to make the announcement himself, before it's in the press. At a family gathering, is what he said.'

Cordelia frowned. 'My father has never been keen on socialising unless he has something to gain. He has never seen the point of family gatherings. I remember the last Christmas I was at Killellan, he arrived in time for dinner and left almost immediately after. Bella—that's my stepmother—was furious.'

'Well, he was quite adamant on the subject. A family gathering at which the announcement will be made,' Iain said. 'It's to be in ten days' time.'

'He's already set the date?'

'A couple of days before our ship is set to sail from Plymouth.'

'Did he arrange that too?'

Iain nodded. 'A frigate. He pulled yet more strings. It will take us to Lisbon, and from there we'll meet up with—I can't remember the name, but that will take us to Greece, and from there on to Egypt.'

'Surely you will need more time to sort out your business?'

'Until I speak with Sheikh al-Muhanna, I don't know exactly what my business will be—how many ships, what specification. I need to understand what use they will be put to before I can decide—it doesn't matter, but there are a host of technical issues I need to resolve face to face with the man. In the meantime, I have, believe it or not, a more than adequate deputy running my yard on the Clyde.'

'Delegation, Mr Hunter?'

'Aye, it pains me to admit it, but Jamie is more than capable. That's because I trained him myself, mind.'

Cordelia smiled abstractedly. 'I wonder that my father agreed to my accompanying you merely as your affianced bride and not your actual bride. I wonder if the truth is that he wants rid of me.'

'I'm afraid you might be right.'

'What do you mean?'

Her eyes were narrowed. Iain took a deep breath. 'Cordelia, he doesn't want you to see any of your family until the party. I'm really sorry, but he was adamant, and there was nothing I could do to change his mind.'

Cordelia stared at Iain uncomprehendingly. 'Not see them?'

'I'm sorry.'

'Did he give a reason? Is he afraid I shall contaminate them—corrupt them—did you even ask him?'

'Of course I asked him,' Iain snapped.

He pulled the gig over to the side of the road. The banks of the river were lined with wharves on both sides. Through the gaps could be seen the waterfront, bustling with ships of all sizes. Two- and three-masters were moored two and three deep. The steamships, with their tall narrow funnels, were smaller and wider. The thick, grey smoke from the tugs billowed up into the air, the powdery tang mingling with the overriding smell of new coals—according to Iain, the main cargo. She noticed it all, but did not take any of it in. 'What did he say?'

'That they were in the country and there was no point in you going there when he was holding the party in London. That Lady Armstrong would wish to prepare the children because they'd not seen you in nearly ten years. That if we were to leave for Arabia in less than two weeks you'd have more than enough to occupy yourself with. That he wanted to give us both time to reflect on our commitment before he made it public.' Iain transferred the reins into one hand, reaching for her with the other. 'You know what he's like, Cordelia, the way he can make anything sound reasonable.'

She snatched her hand away and glowered at him, knowing perfectly well that it wasn't Iain's fault, but needing to blame him anyway. 'But he wasn't being reasonable. It's outrageous. He is just doing it to spite me.'

'Aye, of course he is.'

'He had not even the courage to tell me to my face, but must use you as a messenger.'

Iain grabbed her wrist and held it firmly, giving her arm a little shake. 'It's as well he did. Would you really want him to see you like this? He's nothing to you, remember?'

'Don't shout at me. I am not the one who's being unreasonable.'

'I'm not angry with you.' Iain dropped the reins and covered her hands with his. 'You're right, it's outrageous, but it only matters if you let it. No, *wheesht* and let me talk. Aye, he's trying to pull your strings, have things his own way, but he's doing it because we've outmanoeuvred him.'

'How?'

Iain looked sheepish. 'You'll think me daft, but it stuck in my craw to tell him that we were getting married...'

'Betrothed.'

'Betrothed, just to please him. So I—well, I told him that after he left us alone together yesterday we both realised that we were—that there was—that we—I told him we had fallen in love.'

For the second time in two days, Cordelia's jaw dropped. 'In the space of twenty-four hours?'

'In the space of a few minutes. I said it was love at first sight.'

Colour tinged Iain's cheeks. A bubble of hysterical laughter caught in Cordelia's throat as she tried to imagine the scene. 'You actually used those words?'

Iain nodded.

'You said—you actually said...'

'That I had taken one look at you, and fallen head over ears,' Iain said soulfully.

She stared at him, utterly lost for words for a

few seconds, then the gleam in his eye was too much to resist. She let out a peal of laughter. 'Oh, dear God, did he believe you?'

'My ain wee love,' Iain said, looking quite wounded, 'how could he doubt it?'

Cordelia's jaw dropped further. 'My ain big liar, I did not think that you had it in you. You should be on stage, Iain Hunter.'

He laughed. 'To be honest, I didn't plan it that way, but when I told him that we'd agreed to a betrothal he looked that smug I wanted to belt him one, and it was the only thing I could think of to bring him down to size. You should have seen his face, Cordelia, it was a picture, and I couldn't help rubbing it in just a wee bit when I realised he was actually embarrassed.'

Her hands were still enveloped in his. He had turned towards her on the narrow bench of the gig, so that one of his knees brushed against the outside of her leg. Not that she could possibly feel it through her voluminous skirts, but it felt as if she could. His face was quite transformed when he smiled, it was utterly beguiling. It was making it very difficult to concentrate. She struggled to recover the thread of their conversation. 'Yes, but—but the outcome of your deluding him is that I am not to see my family until this blasted party.'

'I suspect he'd already decided that.' Iain pressed her hand. 'He is an old man who can see his powers slipping from his fingers, and must resort to increasingly petty revenge to assert himself. You're above all that, Cordelia. Remember, though he doesn't know it, it is you and I who are pulling the strings. More importantly, you're getting what you want. Much as I know you wish to be reconciled with your half-siblings and your aunt, it is Celia and Cassie who matter most to you, isn't it?'

She sighed, but smiled too. 'Are you always right?'

'I'm rarely wrong.'

'You will be hoist by your own petard you know, when we make an appearance at this party, for you must now play the besotted swain.'

The gleam in his eyes was back, though it was a very different kind of gleam. 'A man who cannot wait for the pleasures of his wedding night, you mean? A man who cannot look at his bride-to-be without picturing her naked? Without imagining the softness of her flesh quivering to his touch?'

Iain ran his hand up her arm to touch the nape of her neck. 'A man who dreams of her mouth on his,' he said, leaning closer, his voice a whisper. 'Of the sweetness of her curves.'

He traced the outline of her breasts with the flat of his palm, resting his hand on her waist. 'A man who wants to taste every inch of her.'

His lips touched the corner of hers, his tongue the briefest of caresses. 'And you,' he said, his accent noticeably thicker, 'you will have to play a woman equally in thrall. A woman who wants to touch, and to taste every inch of her man.'

He took her hand and placed it on his thigh. 'A woman so sure of her power that she only has to look at him in a certain way to send the blood rushing.'

Of its own volition, her hand crept up his thigh, and found that the blood had already rushed. Iain's eyes flickered closed, then open. His pupils were dark. Her heart was pounding. A pulse beat in her neck, and at the top of her thighs.

'When you look at me, they will see it in your eyes,' Iain said. 'Power. Passion. It's a heady mix. Do you think you can do it, Cordelia?'

His breath was coming fast and shallow on her cheeks. His fingers were curled into her waist. She opened her mouth to speak, and his lips descended on hers. A strange little moan escaped her as she wrapped her arms around him and bowed her body towards him, instantly afire with desire. He kissed her hard, and she kissed him back with equal passion. He moaned, the same sound, lower, as her own.

A catcall made them jump apart. Looking around her in bewilderment, Cordelia remembered they were in an open carriage. Blushing furiously, she tried to right her bonnet. Iain swore, bending to unravel the reins, which seemed to have become wrapped around his ankle. The urchin who had interrupted them shouted something vulgar, and Iain grinned, said something incomprehensible but without doubt equally vulgar back, and tossed him a penny.

'I think we might have to tone our performance down a wee bit,' he said to her.

'I have no intentions of *performing* in such a way in front of my family,' Cordelia snapped. 'That was not love, it was simply lust.'

'We know that,' Iain replied, 'but I doubt your family will know the difference.'

Which was very true, but she was tired of Iain being right. 'All the same, if you think that I am going to kiss you just to prove a point…'

'No, no, my wee love. I think you're going to kiss me because you want to. All you have to do in front of your family is look at me as if you want me to kiss you, and I'll look at you as if I want to kiss you, which won't be difficult, because I'm always wanting to kiss you.'

'One of the things I dislike about you, Iain Hunter, is the way you make it very difficult to be angry with you. Stop being so charming.'

He put his hand on his heart. 'I can't help it, for I am charmed by you.'

Cordelia turned away to hide her smile. 'Shouldn't we be on our way? I thought you had urgent business.'

'Indeed I do, though you should know that there can never be anything more urgent than kissing you.' He picked up the reins and set the reluctant horse back into motion.

'Iain.'

'Yes?' He gave her an innocent look.

'I am not your wee love.'

The visit to the docks, contrary to Cordelia's expectations, was fascinating. Being at the centre of so much industry, the ships with coal and sugar and tea and silks and tobacco converging on one bit of river made her feel as if she were at the very hub of London.

'Not a place many ladies would care to be,' Iain said when she told him so. 'They'd think it vulgar.'

But it struck Cordelia that without all this noise and bustle and dirt and smoke, ladies would have no gowns to parade in Hyde Park, no sugar confections to decorate their dinner tables or coal to burn at their parties.

The Millwall Iron Works, where Iain had business, were on the southernmost tip of the Isle of

Dogs, which was not an island at all, but a bulge of land encircled on three of its four sides by the River Thames.

'It's not that long been taken over by Sir William Fairbairn and David Napier,' he said, helping Cordelia down from the gig, which he had pulled up in front of the main building. 'Both fellow Scots of course,' he added with a grin, 'and fellow engineers too. Napier built the boiler for the *Comet*—the first steam-paddle ship—and he built the *Aglaia* too. She was one of the first paddle steamers to have an iron hull, though she still had a wooden keel. My own *Eilidh* has an iron keel. Here he is now.'

Mr Napier had a head of unruly white hair which looked rather like an unspun fleece. His beard, equally white and unruly, descended seamlessly into his white stock. Craggy eyebrows gave his face a forbidding look, but he cracked a genial smile at Cordelia, and shook Iain heartily by the hand, muttering something that sounded defamatory, though it made Iain laugh.

The Iron Works built small ships, mostly for the Admiralty. Napier escorted them around the site, discoursing at length on the advantages of his patented steeple engine over the side lever, arguing vehemently with Iain over a plethora of technical detail that left Cordelia quite bemused. Iain more than held his own in the discussion. It became obvious to her that when he said he built ships he had at some point literally built the things, and probably could still, for it was not just Napier he talked with so knowledgeably, it was his workers too.

Watching Iain peering into a section of paddle, his hands smoothing over the casing in a way that was almost sensual, his face creased into a smile as the shipwright cracked a joke, Cordelia began to understand a little of his love for engineering and a lot more about the man. He was not just a businessman content to make a profit from a blossoming industry, but a man who built ships. It wasn't the money he wanted from the contract with Celia's husband, it was the opportunity and the challenge.

She almost wished she had not come. In some ways, seeing him in his own milieu was even more intimate than sharing his body. It made her uneasy, having this private window into his life, she wasn't at all sure she wanted it. For one thing, it reminded her of her own solitude. She tried to remember a time when she had been different, and struggled. When Celia left? When her father married Bella? She had been eleven or twelve then, not much older when Cassie left too, so there were just the three of them at Killellan.

'They've some problem with the boiler. Napier has gone to look at the plans. Are you all right?'

'Fine.' Cordelia smiled at Iain, thrusting the past away. 'What is the problem?'

'You really want to know?'

When she nodded, Iain explained patiently in a way even she could follow, and in response to her questioning, led her back round some of the yards, explaining what the new developments Napier had been holding forth on meant in practical terms to the ships and their function. The Works were noisy, dirty and very smelly, but with Iain pulling the whole picture together, piece by piece, Cordelia caught some of his enthusiasm.

'I've actually made a few modifications to Napier's engine to give us more deck room on our new steamers,' he told her conspiratorially. 'I've got the blueprints with me, I'll let you see them later, and the patents are pending. It will revolutionise the Clyde, I'm sure of it.'

'It will?'

He laughed at her bewilderment. 'Trust me, it will. With the expansion of the railways, we'll be able to take people from Glasgow to Greenock and Gourock at the tail of the Clyde in a snap of your fingers. And from there, they'll board my paddle steamers to take the sea air. Holidays, Cordelia, not just for the well heeled, but for the working man and his family, and it will be my steamers that take them.'

'You know, I believe everyone should take a tour of the Isle of Dogs. All this noise and dirt are part of progress. These ships of yours won't just make it cheaper and quicker to import and export goods, they'll make the goods themselves cheaper. And all these ships must mean more work, more money to spend, more leisure in which to spend it.'

'You have been listening.'

Cordelia smiled, despite herself, proud of the

little glow his admiring look gave her. 'You made it easy. You tell a very fascinating story. It's one I think other people should hear.'

He laughed. 'In one of your guidebooks? I doubt very much you'd find an audience.'

'I hope you might be surprised.'

Several days later, Cordelia dined in her rooms on some rather stringy goose, thinking not for the first time since returning to England how much she missed the freshness and simplicity of Italian cooking, the complexity of French. She had forgotten how cold it was here too, despite the fact that summer was just around the corner. And she had forgotten how much more *propriety* there was here. Walking alone in the Regent's Park, she had been accosted twice and ogled several times. It was why she was dining here alone, rather than venturing out.

She gazed disconsolately out of the window at the carriages that were, tonight, arriving at a different house in Grosvenor Square. Was it a mistake, coming here? She had set her heart on moving back to England, but it no longer felt like home. Her younger self was too present here, and she suspected it would be worse in the country. Already she knew that she could not purchase any house in the vicinity of her old home, even with Caro as a neighbour. Besides, Caro spent several months of the year with her family in Italy, where Cressie was settled too. When she met Iain in Glasgow, Cordelia had been tired of her nomadic life. Perhaps it was rather the idea of a home than the bricks and mortar she wanted?

She had no idea, and she couldn't think about it while so much remained unresolved. Returning to her dinner, she began to spoon the minted peas around the serving dish. She had seen nothing of Iain, save for the notes he sent her, updates on his progress, other tasks for her to execute. She could not possibly miss a man she barely knew, ridiculous to think so. It was because she was here in London that she felt more alone, though truth be told, the approaching reunion with her family filled her with as much trepidation as anticipation.

And then there was tomorrow. Cordelia ate a mouthful of cold peas. She had not been surprised to receive Aunt Sophia's summons, for despite what her father thought, his sister liked to make her own mind up. It was a good thing, Cordelia told herself staunchly, a chance to apologise. Cressie had been of the opinion that Aunt Sophia would understand and would not bear a grudge, but Cressie had not been in her aunt's care when she ran off with Giovanni, nor had she led everyone, her sisters included, on a merry dance. What's more, Cressie's elopement had been with the man to whom she was now married, while Cordelia's elopement...

What a little fool she had been back then. She could hardly bear to recall that naive, vain young woman gleefully anticipating how shocked everyone would be by her elopement, so smugly proud of herself for pulling the wool over their eyes, so stupidly, foolishly sure she was shaping her own glorious future. She had shaped her own future, that was for sure, but in a very different mould from what she'd anticipated. She would not allow herself to regret it. It had shaped her, and she liked the shape it had made of her— eventually—so she would not regret the deed, though she deeply regretted how she had gone about it.

Iain wanted to accompany her tomorrow, but she had refused, telling him that she wished to see her aunt in private, though merely thinking about the meeting made her feel sick with nerves, and the idea of him beside her, an ally, a solid, reassuring presence, was shamefully attractive. Her independence, it seemed, was not sacrosanct.

Her conscience nagged at her. 'Admit it,' she said, glowering down at her reflection in the serving spoon, 'the real reason you don't want him to come with you is because you don't want him to know the truth.'

Her distorted face gazed back at her, looking troubled. Cordelia threw down the spoon, scattering peas across the table. What had the past nine years been for, if not to ensure that she was answerable to no one but herself? '*That* is something very few women can claim,' she declared, 'and it is something I have no intentions of ever surrendering.'

Still, her conscience would not quiet. 'He will judge me,' she told it, realising as she did that here was the nub of the matter. If she was not ashamed, she would not be ashamed to confess. If his opinion did not matter, she would not care whether Iain knew the truth or not. And that, she thought wearily, heading for her bedchamber and her nightly tussle with her corsets, was something she really didn't want to think about right now.

Chapter Five

Iain was waiting for her outside her aunt's house. 'Don't be angry,' he said, as she descended from the hackney carriage.

Cordelia was horrified. 'What the *devil* are you doing here? I *told* you—I made it very clear I wanted to do this on my own.'

He took her arm and pulled her to one side of the steps. 'I'm not presuming to know your own mind better than you do, if that's what you're thinking.'

'Then what were you presuming?' She glared at him.

'That you could do with some moral support. No, don't bite my head off,' he added hurriedly, 'I know you can manage this on your own but—

Cordelia, why make it harder for yourself when you don't have to?'

Conscious of the fact that her fingers were digging into his arm, she tried to disengage herself, but he wouldn't let her go. Did he think that her legs wouldn't support her? Did he think she needed him here to protect her? Or was he simply playing the attentive bridegroom? Attentive faux bridegroom. 'What do you mean?'

'Are you going to lie to your aunt?'

'I don't know.' After a sleepless night, Cordelia was beginning to wonder if she knew anything.

'You need to remember why we're doing this,' Iain said, with that uncanny knack he had of reading her thoughts. 'Tell me, has your aunt made any attempt to contact you these last nine years?'

Cordelia frowned. 'No, but—but nor have I, and she is not the one who...' She stared at him helplessly. 'Iain, there's something...'

'Let me put it another way. She's going to assume that our betrothal is real, isn't she?'

'Yes, but...'

'So, unless she asks you outright, you're not going to have to lie to her, are you?'

'No, but, Iain…'

'And if I'm with you, right by your side, playing the devoted fiancé, then she's even less likely to doubt you, isn't she?'

'Yes, but…'

'So,' he said, tucking her hand more firmly into his arm, 'it makes perfect sense that I come with you.'

There was something in his voice, in the way he looked at her, that told her he was determined. She could fight him, but he had logic on his side, besides which the sense of release at having the decision taken from her was difficult to resist. He was steering her towards the house. She felt as if she were on a frozen mountaintop. One step and she would slither out of control. The door was opened by Aunt Sophia's very decrepit but still recognisable butler, and the familiar slightly mouldy, dusty smell of the panelled hallway hit her.

Cordelia handed over her gloves. 'There's one thing you need to know,' she said.

Her voice sounded strange to her own ears. It

must have sounded even stranger to Iain's, for he spoke sharply. 'What?'

'My aunt—the reason I am so—or at least one of the reasons.' She drew a ragged breath. 'I eloped when I was in my aunt's care. Nine years ago. I—that's when it all started.'

Iain had no time to react to this revelation, for the butler was already leading them up the stairs. Lady Sophia was ensconced in a large leather-covered chair, her heavily bandaged foot resting on a stool in front of her. 'You'll forgive me for not getting up,' she said. 'Come in, come in, don't just stand there gawping.'

Cordelia had turned quite pale. She was not quite gawping, but her countenance showed clearly how shocked she was at her relative's appearance, though she tried to mask it as she let go of his arm and covered the short distance to Lady Sophia's side, where she dropped into a deep curtsy.

'You never used to be so formal, come here.' Lady Sophia held out an imperious and very gnarled hand. 'Let me look at you.'

His mind reeling, Iain studied the aunt as the aunt studied her niece. Her face was gaunt and lined with both pain and age, little trace of the camel, which is how Cordelia had jokingly described her. The iron-grey hair was set into regimented curls around the papery-white skin of her forehead. Iain decided it must be a wig, though it looked as if it were provided by a wiry and ancient poodle. Her cheeks were sunken, the lack of flesh on her face drawing emphasis to a very strong jaw which, along with the blue-grey eyes reminded him of Lord Armstrong. Frail though she appeared, a bag of bones under her grey silk gown, there was life and a great deal of intelligence in the look she was concentrating on her niece. A force to be reckoned with, Iain thought, and readied himself to do battle, at the same time telling himself that there was no need, and that it was not his fight.

'You look well,' Lady Sophia said, breaking the uncomfortable silence, 'which is more than you will think of me, I expect. I am getting old. No, don't deny it, for you were never a good liar. A prevaricator, yes, but not a liar.'

'Aunt Sophia, I am so very, very sorry. I did not mean to deceive you— At least, I did, but I meant it to be— I thought it would be only for a few months. I did not mean— I am so very, very sorry.'

Silence fell once more. Cordelia stood in front of her aunt, hands clasped in front of her, looking like a penitent. Lady Sophia was staring off into space, her jaw working. Fearing that she was about to terminate the interview before it had even begun, Iain stepped forward, though he had no idea what he was going to say, but the movement broke the older woman's reverie.

'So this is Henry's latest protégé, is it?'

He narrowed his eyes, but though she stared him down, and though her words sounded as if they were designed to make his hackles rise, he had the distinct impression that she was testing him. 'I'm not anyone's anything,' Iain said.

Lady Sophia raised a pair of sparse but none the less forbidding eyebrows. 'A Scot, and a ferocious one at that. My brother gave me the impression that he was taking you under his wing, Mr Hunter.'

He was right, she was definitely testing him. 'I'm sure he did,' Iain replied, ignoring Cordelia's anguished look. 'Your brother likes to think the world can't turn without his say-so, but it's not true.'

Lady Sophia gave a crack of laughter. 'I see you have Henry's measure.'

'Right now, Lady Sophia, I'm a mite more interested in taking yours, if you don't mind my saying so.'

'I do not, Mr Hunter, for I intend to do the very same thing, and you have now spared me the trouble of being polite about it,' she replied. 'How do you do?'

He took the hand she held out and bowed over it. He would do much better if he was in possession of the facts, but he was not about to reveal his ignorance to this formidable woman, any more than he was about to overset the fragile hold Cordelia had on herself, by demanding to know the truth.

'Sit down, the pair of you, or I'll get a crick in my neck, and I've more than enough ailments to bother me already.' Lady Sophia waved them at the sofa facing her. 'Help yourself to refreshments. I will take a Madeira, if you please. It is a little early, but I feel the need of it. I don't have any whisky, Mr Hunter, but...'

'I'm fine,' he said, handing her a glass, and pouring a second for Cordelia which she took, but made no attempt to drink. Her smile was faint, apologetic and at the same time defiant. Sorry and not sorry. Looking up, he was disconcerted to find Lady Sophia's eagle eye on him and decided that his best course of action would be silence.

'Aunt Sophia.' Cordelia was pale, but her voice did not tremble. 'I need to explain to you about my elopement. I need you to know that I—'

'Henry knew, didn't he?' Lady Sophia interrupted. 'He knew where you were, long before your sisters did. Well,' she said, her voice sharp, 'am I right?'

'Yes.'

'How much did he know?'

'He had—he had all the salient facts.'

The look Cordelia slanted him as she said this made Iain wary. He wondered what salient facts she hadn't told him. He wondered what other salient facts she was keeping back from that aunt of hers, and saw the aunt wondering the same thing. Lady Sophia was drumming her bony fingers on the arm of her chair. Her brother did that too, Iain had noticed, when he was scheming. It was like watching a game of chess. No, if he was honest, he was beginning to feel like a pawn in Cordelia's game of chess, and he didn't like it. Not one bit.

One thing life had taught him however, was not to show his feelings. Cordelia might be playing games, but he wasn't about to let her see that he knew it. Not yet.

'My brother did not see fit to inform me that you were safe,' Lady Sophia said.

'Nor did I, Aunt.'

Cordelia's face had gone from pale to pink. He wondered that she made no attempt to defend herself when she could have so easily, by explaining that she had been forbidden contact. She was protecting her aunt. No, not just her aunt. She was protecting her perfidious father. If it had been up to Iain—but he caught himself just in time. It was Cordelia's choice. He couldn't help but admire her loyalty, even if he didn't agree with it.

Lady Sophia, however, seemed to have a pretty good grasp of her brother's Machiavellian mind. 'My brother made his wishes clear in the matter of communication when Cressie finally told me of your whereabouts. I expect he made them equally clear to you.' She took a deep draught from her Madeira, and waved the glass at Iain for a refill. 'Very well,' she said heavily, 'I can see you do not wish to speak against your father, and I must condone you for that, though you are misguided if you think he needs your protection.'

Cordelia snorted. 'I assure you Aunt Sophia, I am not so misguided.'

Her aunt smiled thinly. 'No, you always did seem to me to have his measure.'

'I thought so too, but it turns out in this instance I was mistaken,' Cordelia said. 'Be that as it may, what I did was inexcusable. I caused you a great deal of worry.'

'You did, that I will not deny. When the weeks passed without any word after that first letter, I thought the worst, despite Cressie's assurances. I blamed myself, for you were in my charge.'

'Oh, Aunt, it was not your fault. I was irresponsible, and headstrong, and...'

'And a lot more,' Lady Sophia said with another of her grim smiles, 'but you were in my care all the same. No, please don't get emotional, Cordelia, for I am not—this gout, my age, I am not as strong as I once was, and I find tears—so please do not.'

Cordelia blinked furiously. Lady Sophia took another large swallow of her sherry. 'So, now you are to be married,' she said.

'We are betrothed,' Iain replied quickly, sparing Cordelia the need to lie.

'Though I understand your acquaintance has been extremely brief.'

'We'll have plenty of time to get to know one another in the next few months.'

'Ah, yes, you are going to Arabia. To Celia. Fortuitous, is it not, that Mr Hunter has business in exactly the place you wish to be, Niece?'

Cordelia looked flustered. 'Yes. That is, Aunt Sophia, you should know that...'

'I shall thank Lady Celia's husband myself,' Iain interrupted. 'Though he doesn't know it, he brought us together, and I'll be forever grateful.'

'Ah, yes, the ships. My brother was most enthusiastic about this deal he brokered, Mr Hunter. Really, very enthusiastic. He seems to think that you will be of great use to him—more specifically his sons—in the future.'

Iain snorted. 'I know he does.'

Lady Sophia cackled. 'Playing him at his own game, eh?'

'I made no promises on that score,' Iain said, thinking that in her own way, her ladyship was as devious and as knowing as her brother.

It seemed he was right. 'Take care that you do not get burned, Mr Hunter, my brother always has a few tricks up his sleeve,' she said, ringing the handbell which sat at her side. 'I am tired. No doubt I will see you again at this party your father has arranged. You know that Bella will be there?'

Cordelia nodded, getting to her feet.

'You want to know if you are forgiven?' Lady Sophia pursed her lips. 'I could castigate you for not confiding in me, but that would be hypocritical since everything in your upbringing and that of your sisters has encouraged you to distrust and secrecy. We are a family with far too many skeletons in our cupboards, Mr Hunter, and it is contagious I fear. Those who marry into the Armstrongs—but there, that is only the women.'

'What on earth do you mean, Aunt? The only women who have—do you mean *Bella* has a secret?'

'We all have secrets, Cordelia. I find that it is better not to ask, unless one's own cupboard is empty of bones.'

Lady Sophia's smile was enigmatic, catlike, and very disturbingly like one of Cordelia's. Looking from one woman to the other, Iain had the distinct impression that there was a quite different conversation going on that he knew nothing of. He saw the precise moment, however, when Cordelia decided not to pursue the matter, which reminded him once more that they had their own conversation to be had on the subject of skeletons and closets, so he made his bow. 'Until Saturday,' he said.

A regal nod, he received in return, but her niece was given a hand to kiss, he was relieved to see.

'I will forgive you,' her ladyship said gruffly, 'because you are my niece and because I understand you. But be aware, Cordelia, that I can never condone your actions, no matter what the circumstances. You acted very wrongly. No matter how much you may rail at it, this is a man's world. You cannot change that, and you will always be judged accordingly.'

It was a beautiful sunny day outside, but Cordelia could not stop shivering. Her aunt's parting words had wounded her deeply, but they had also, paradoxically, salved her conscience. Despite her claims to understand her, Lady Sophia was far too much the product of society to do so. No matter how right Cordelia believed herself, in her aunt's eyes, she would always be in the wrong. It infuriated her and saddened her, but more than anything, it made her absolutely determined to stick to her own course.

'I owe you an explanation,' she said to Iain, sounding far more aggressive than she intended.

'You do,' he said. 'I think we'll walk back to Milvert's. You need to calm down first.'

It was on the tip of her tongue to tell him that she was perfectly calm, but one of his level looks made her think again. Had he made any attempt to take her arm, she would have taken great pleasure in pushing him away, but to her annoyance he didn't, matching his step to hers, his face irritatingly inscrutable while she was sure hers was showing every single one of the storm of emotions she was feeling. Her fists clenched and unclenched. Head down, she quickened her steps, colliding with a baker's boy, who cursed, and only just held on to the tray of currant buns he was carrying on his head.

Cordelia glowered at the boy, aware that she was being ridiculous, yet unable to stop herself. Iain tossed him a coin and took one of the buns. 'It's not funny,' she said.

He gave her a bland look. 'I'm not laughing.'

Perfectly well aware that he had the right to be furious with her, she rubbed her eyes, and forced a smile. 'Is it a good bun?'

'Nothing like as good as the ones my mother used to buy.'

'Your mother?' Cordelia frowned, trying to remember what little Iain had told her of his family, happy to be distracted from her own. 'I thought you said you were an orphan.'

'I think it was you who assumed so.'

'So you're not?'

Iain threw the rest of the bun into the gutter. His face was quite closed, and there was a bleak look in his eye that gave her shivers on the back of her legs. 'I think one cupboard full of skeletons is enough for today.'

It was none of her business, he meant, and meant it very clearly, which made her all the more intrigued, but with her own confession pending, now was hardly the time. Tempted as Cordelia was to pursue the matter, it was not merely Iain's intimidating expression which stopped her. Having slithered so far down the icy slope of revelations at Aunt Sophia's house, she was anxious to get the rest out of the way.

She should be glad that he had turned up today. She would like to think she would have plucked up the courage to come clean before their betrothal was announced, but she was not entirely convinced. She shuddered to think of how it would have been if he had walked unknowing into a room filled with her nearest and dearest, all of whom knew more than he. Telling him would be unpleasant, but at least it would allow him to walk away before it was too late.

Braced as she was however, she took the precaution of ordering a bottle of wine to be sent to her rooms when they arrived at the hotel. Excusing herself, she retired to her bedchamber to remove her hat and gloves. Dashing some cool water over her face, she stared at herself in the mirror.

'What's the worst that can happen?' It was a trick she had used many times to boost her courage. 'He can walk away, and I'll be no worse off than I was before we agreed to this charade,' she told herself. It ought to be true. That it was not, made her feel quite ill. It mattered to her what he thought. It mattered to her that he understood, which was silly, because no one else ever had.

Not that she'd ever explained herself, not even to Cressie. She was being quite irrational. Still as she straightened her shoulders and headed for the door, she could not deny the fact that it did. Too much, to tell him the whole truth. Which, she reminded herself once more, was none of his business.

Cordelia entered the room looking like a soldier facing execution. Iain had been telling himself that whatever she had to say couldn't be that bad, but now he changed his mind. He had so many questions he was having difficulty keeping track of them, trouble in stopping himself from blurting them all out, one after another. He poured himself a glass of wine and handed one to Cordelia, taking the seat at right angles to the couch on which she perched. Beneath her skirts, he could see her foot tapping. 'Go on then, out with it,' he said, putting his wine down untouched, 'I'm braced.'

'Right.' She emptied her own glass in one long gulp. 'Well, the first thing you need to know is that I've never been married.'

Of all the things he'd thought of, this had simply not occurred to him. Iain gawked. He knew he was gawking, but he couldn't help it. 'But…'

'When you met me, I was not a virgin,' she said.

What he'd been about to say was that she'd told him she was a widow. This blunt statement rendered him speechless. Cordelia, on the other hand, now she had launched into her story, seemed less ill at ease. She stood and poured herself another glass of wine, swallowed it back and then sat back down, determinedly holding his gaze, daring him to judge her. He was far too dazed to do any such thing.

'I'll stick to what my father would call the pertinent facts,' she said with an ironic smile. 'You already know that he saw us girls merely as assets he could marry off. We have none of us done as he wanted. Though he is adept at twisting the truth, neither Cassie nor Celia's marriages were of his making. Caro did marry the man he picked.' Her mouth curled with disdain. 'A man who beat my sister, and then he threw her out without a penny. Poor Caro, the only one of us who ever tried to do what our father wanted, was utterly miserable. And Cressie too, not because she was married but because she couldn't bring herself to behave in an encouraging enough manner to attract any of the suitors on my father's list.'

She was almost snarling now as she spoke. 'Oh, yes,' she said in response to his sceptical look, 'he really did have a list. When Cressie failed to pluck a candidate from it, that duty fell to me. I was one-and-twenty when I came up to London for the Season, and I was absolutely determined that I would *not* give him the satisfaction. You may say that was ungrateful of me...'

'I would say that you were damned right,' Iain said, 'you're not a bit of horseflesh.'

'Well then, at least we are agreed on that,' Cordelia said. 'Though actually, when I first came to London I really did intend to marry some man off the list just to escape, but I discovered I simply couldn't stomach it, and so I—I am ashamed to say, I decided to see how many proposals I could amass, just to prove a point. I had persuaded myself that I didn't care what my father thought of my behaviour at that point, when in fact, my behaviour was designed to bring myself to his attention. Not that I saw that at the time.'

Cordelia sighed. 'I'm sorry. It is one thing to know one's limitations and faults and to judge oneself, but quite another to spread them out for someone else to pick over.'

'I don't have the right to judge you,' Iain said.

'No, but that won't stop you doing so, even if you do keep it to yourself,' she replied frankly.

He couldn't deny it, and didn't try, merely indicated that she continue.

'There was a man. Is there not always a man, you will be thinking, when there is a tale to be told of a young flighty, pretty girl?' she said mockingly. 'For I was considered one of the pretty sisters, along with Cassie. That we had minds of our own didn't matter, needless to say. But I digress. As I was saying, there was a man, and as in all such stories, this man was suitably handsome and suitably profligate. A lady's man, is what my aunt called him. A libertine is what she meant, meaning to ensure I kept well away from him, not realising that I was bound to be attracted, because not only was he everything a young lady should flee from, he was everything my father would have hated. Not a scrap, not a single scrap of political influence did he have.'

'So you let him dangle after you,' Iain said. 'Despicable as he is, I didn't have Lord Armstrong down as an idiot. I'd have thought he'd be wise to that.'

'You forget he was otherwise occupied with Wellington. *How* my father reveres that man. Second only to himself of course.'

Cordelia began to pace the room restlessly, speaking in short bursts. 'He wanted me, you see, that man. He didn't give a damn about my father or my family, he wasn't in the least bit interested in politics.' She stopped to poke the fire, rising with her face flushed, though it might have been the heat. 'He was the only one who showed an interest in me. For myself, I mean, Cordelia, and not Lady Cordelia Armstrong. I thought he loved me. I thought I loved him. We eloped. It was his idea, but I took little persuading. I ran off with him thinking we were to be married—

though to be fair, he never actually proposed, not then. Of course I thought that since we were getting married there was no point in waiting to consummate our love, and neither of us wanted to wait in any case, and so—and so we didn't.'

She went over to the window, leaning her cheek against the pane, looking over at him with that mixture of defiance and defensiveness that reminded him so much of his younger self. Iain waited, expecting to hear the predictable sorry tale, relieved, truth be told, for that was an explanation he could understand. The twisted logic of this bothered him, for it was also a tale which left Cordelia much wronged. She began to speak again before he could pick through this paradox.

'You think I'm going to tell you that it was all a ruse, that we didn't go to Gretna, that he planned only a seduction all along,' she said, and smiled that twisted smile of hers when his face gave him away, resuming her seat opposite him, speaking with a new hardness in her voice. 'You would be right, but you would be wrong to think of me as a victim. He didn't need to seduce me. I went to him willingly and I enjoyed it.'

She glared at him, daring him to speak. He wanted to, but her words conjured up such mixed feelings. He was not a man who expected a woman to lie on her back and endure, but nor did he like to imagine the woman he ached for with another. 'There's no sin in that,' Iain managed.

Cordelia laughed. It wasn't a pleasant sound. 'Not when there's a bit of paper legitimising it, no. Otherwise, there is, in the eyes of the world, a great deal of sin—for the woman, at least. My lover duped me, but not as much as I duped myself. He was the antithesis of what my father wanted for me, and I thought that was love.'

'But—I don't understand. Your family could have hushed it up, couldn't they? Surely that sort of thing happens all the time?'

'I don't know. Probably. You cannot comprehend, Iain, how much I hate to be wrong, and how impossible it was for me to admit that I'd been wrong, especially to my father. So—so there could be no hushing it up because I didn't go back.'

There was so much of what she was telling him that troubled him. So much he admired, and so much made him angry too. As to the man—no, he could not afford to think of him. 'So it was because you wouldn't allow him to hush it up that your father disowned you?' Iain asked.

Cordelia hesitated, then nodded.

'And presumably it is this that your aunt meant she couldn't condone?'

'"This is a man's world. You cannot change that, and you will always be judged accordingly",' Cordelia quoted bitterly. 'Had I claimed to have been ravished, had I fled from my seducer, I would have been forgiven. Because I would neither pretend nor flee, because...' Cordelia's hands curled into two tight balls on her lap. 'Because I am a woman,' she said through very gritted teeth, 'my behaviour cannot be condoned.'

Her knuckles were white. Her eyes were bright, not with tears but with anger. She looked like a vengeful goddess. 'By God, remind me never to make an enemy of you,' Iain said. 'What did you do to him in the end, boil up his entrails and have them on toast for breakfast?'

'Worse than that,' she replied with a satisfied little smile, 'I refused to marry him. The cardinal sin.'

Iain couldn't help it; a guffaw of laughter escaped him. 'Sorry, it's just—you look so bloody magnificent. What really happened?'

'That's what really happened. Perhaps my charms grew on him, or perhaps he grew a conscience. Whatever the reason, he asked me to marry him, and I refused. He wanted to do right by me. I could see that tying myself to him could only be wrong. Instead, I became a widow and a writer, and so I have been until now.'

'So you threw away your reputation by running off with a libertine to thwart your father, and when the libertine offered to make an honest woman of you, you ran away from him too because…'

'Because another lesson I learned the hard way, Iain, is that as a woman you can only live the life you want by being alone.' Cordelia poured herself another glass of wine. This time she drank only half of it in one swallow. 'Independence is what I wanted. Is that so difficult to understand? I suppose it is. As my aunt said, it is a man's world. You no doubt take such things for granted.'

'No, I don't, and I'm not sure it's true that men have it all their own way either,' Iain said darkly.

'How so?'

He tried to imagine telling her. His own family history would make hers seem like a bedtime story. 'It was a brave thing to do, not to marry that man. Do you regret it? Do you wish you had accepted him?'

'No, and definitely not.'

'If you had, we would not have met.'

'If I had, there would probably be no need for this discussion.'

'What did you do when you left him then—how did you survive?'

Cordelia smiled an oddly secretive, self-satisfied smile. 'Cressie is not the only one in the family with a head for figures. I put mine to good use in the gambling halls of Europe. It's where I made the beginnings of my fortune, before I discovered it was much more profitable and much less chancy to gamble on the Exchange.'

'I thought your money came from your writing.'

Cordelia laughed. 'Good grief, no, I doubt there is anyone who can make a living with their pen. That is what I do, not how I live.' She drained her wine. 'So there you have it. All that remains is for me to say that I will perfectly understand if you wish to change your mind about our little—arrangement. In fact, it will make it easier for me to get you off the hook, for I shall inform my father that as you are now in possession of the sad, sordid tale of my fall from grace, you quite naturally wish to be released from our engagement.'

Her face was flushed. Her voice was a tiny bit slurred. When she poured another glass of wine, she slopped some of it on to the table. 'I've not changed my mind,' Iain said.

Cordelia lifted her glass in silent salute. 'Very honourable, but I believe it is perfectly proper to cancel a contract made under false pretences. No one would blame you, and you need not worry that you wouldn't be able to build your precious ships, for my father would certainly wish to salvage that from the débâcle.'

'There isn't going to be a *débâcle,* because I'm not going to change my mind.' Iain watched as Cordelia took yet another large gulp of wine. He could take the glass from her, but he was pretty certain she would see that as a swipe at her precious independence, and he had bigger battles to fight. 'It's been nine years since it all happened. Your father can certainly bear a grudge.'

'Sticking to his principles, I think he would call it, and so too have I, in the interval,' Cordelia said. 'It is remarkably freeing, being told that one no longer exists. I promised myself I would never allow anyone to dictate my actions again, and I have stuck to that promise.'

'Why did you tell me all this? Why now, I mean—for the chances of my finding the truth out for myself must be quite low. It's hardly in Armstrong's interests to tell me.'

Cordelia felt herself flush. She had not lied, save through omission, so she had no reason to feel guilty. If Iain had asked her—but he had not. If she was a man, she wouldn't be feeling like this. She was not deceiving him. She would not think that way. 'To be honest, I had no intentions at all of telling you anything,' she admitted. 'Since we are not actually getting married, you would not be discussing settlements with my father, so the fact that I wasn't a widow—you wouldn't have found that out.'

'So why then?'

She hesitated, for she was not entirely sure of her own motives herself. 'There was the risk that someone would say something—though that's slight, for aside from my father no one really knows the full story. But that's my point, I suppose. My father knows, and he'll think that you do not, and I suspect that it gives him a sort of perverted pleasure, thinking he has duped you— or that I had duped you at his command. I won't have him laughing up his sleeve at you, and I won't have him thinking he can make me dance to his tune. You are an honest man, and a principled one. In fact, it is partly your honesty and your principles that have led us into this situation in the first place.'

Cordelia stopped abruptly, realising that she was sounding a little hysterical. She should not have drunk that last glass of wine. It had not escaped her notice that Iain had drunk nothing. Nor had she failed to notice that he'd refrained from commenting on her consumption. She sank back down on to the sofa and eyed him from under her lashes. Why did he have to be so very nice! And why did he have to be so very attractive! And how was it that she was even thinking such a thing when this was probably the last time she would see him. 'I don't know if that makes sense, but that's why I told you. And also to give you the chance to change your mind.'

'I don't want to.' He left his chair to sit beside her on the sofa, taking her hands between his. 'What you've told me makes me absolutely certain we're doing the right thing. You're a brave lass. There's not many who would have chosen such a difficult path as you.'

'You mustn't be thinking that I have been miserable, or that I was treated badly.'

'There we must beg to differ. Whether or not you went willingly, the man seduced you,' Iain said grimly.

'I don't want you to feel sorry for me, Iain. I don't need your pity either. I am not a damsel in need of rescuing.'

'And I'm hardly the knight-errant type,' he replied with a bitter smile. 'I take your point, and I have to admire you for it. You go your own way, no matter how difficult that way may be. You're a woman after my own heart.'

'Stubborn, you mean. Maybe that's what drew us together that day in Glasgow.'

'I prefer to call it our independent spirit.'

She chuckled. 'Not something that is conducive to connubial bliss. It's as well we are only pretending.' Her expression became serious again. 'Are you sure, Iain?'

'I am.'

He spoke firmly. It was like that first time, on the docks, as they gazed into each other's eyes for just a moment. That connection, a tangible thing, tightened between them, pulling them towards each other. It would be so easy to kiss him.

So easy to surrender to the passion which was there, lambent, smouldering, wanting only the smallest of contact to burst into life. Their fingers entwined, they leaned closer to each other and, at the same time, they pulled back.

Iain got to his feet. 'It's been a long day, and I've another appointment in Whitehall before I'm done yet. We've a hundred things to do before we go, so I doubt I'll see you before this party. I'll call for you, we should arrive together.'

'Yes. Iain, do you...?' She had been about to ask him if he had evening dress, but stopped just in time. She had no idea whether he would have had cause to wear such a thing, and consequently no idea whether he would find even an informal family party at Cavendish Square uncomfortable, but she was loathe to ask, and suspected that whatever was the truth, Iain would not admit to being uncomfortable about anything. 'Do you have any other errands I can add to my list?' Cordelia asked instead.

'Your list must already be as long as a wet Sunday in the Highlands. If I'm stuck, I'm quite capable of employing someone to help me out.'

He kissed her cheek and left. She watched him from the window, following his tall, lean figure as he strode off in the direction of Piccadilly.

Chapter Six

Cordelia wore an evening gown of powder-blue velvet fitted with a belt of the same fabric at the waist, and two deep flounces at the hem. Aside from the cream lace which trimmed the décolletage, it was very simple, relying on the shape of the wearer and the rich colour of the fabric for effect. She wore no jewellery, only a pair of long evening gloves which left the narrowest band of flesh on display beneath the sleeves, which were cut less full than was the fashion, for she hated to wear plumpers with evening dress.

Judging by Iain's face when he arrived to escort her, the effect was as she had hoped. She dropped him a curtsy, deliberately allowing him the most fleeting glimpse of her powdered bosom, and was rewarded with his sharp intake of breath. 'I doubt I'll have any difficulty in pretending to be besotted with you tonight,' he said.

'I doubt I'll have any difficulty returning the favour,' Cordelia replied, 'you look most distinguished.' He looked much more than distinguished. His black tailcoat fitted his lean frame perfectly, hugging the breadth of his shoulders, making the most of his narrow waist. The pristine white of his shirt drew attention to the tanned, harsh face, and the discreet silver of his waistcoat, the first such garment she had ever seen him wear, somehow drew attention to the very male body it hugged. Iain was charismatic in plain day clothes. Tonight, he was quite simply the most attractive man she had ever seen.

'Have I a button undone?' he asked.

She had been staring, probably like a child in a cake shop. Cordelia shook her head.

'You're not worried I'll eat with my spoon, or maybe end up tongue-tied in front of that stepmother of yours?'

She chuckled. 'Being stuck for words is the last thing I'd imagined you would be.'

'So you admit you were worried?'

She had the grace to blush. 'A little.'

'For all you know, I've never been to a society party before.'

'I'm sorry, it was presumptuous of me.'

'To think I couldn't handle myself in any company—aye, it was,' Iain said harshly. He cupped her chin, tilting her face so that she met his eyes, and spoke more softly. 'I'm not in the habit of going to such things, but I won't embarrass you.'

'I didn't think that for a moment. I was worried for you.'

He smiled. 'I know that. It's why I'm not angry.'

She touched his cheek. 'It's as well you're not, since you are to play my besotted swain.'

'As I've said, I've no problem in doing that the way you look tonight, my wee love. I'm just a bit concerned that every other man in the room will be the same.'

'It's a family party, the only other men will be my half-brothers and my father.'

'Gathered together to meet the prodigal daughter and to celebrate her betrothal.'

'Our betrothal.'

'Speaking of which…' Iain reached into his pocket and pulled out a slim box. 'I believe it's customary for a man to give his affianced bride a gift.'

'But we are not really getting married.'

'Open it.'

Cordelia stared at the box, filled with excitement and anticipation. Jewellery was such a very personal thing. What if she hated it? 'You open it,' she said, closing her eyes, making a silly little wish, opening them again, and letting out a gasp. 'Iain!'

'Well?'

The necklace was a simple circlet of sapphires trimmed with diamonds. The earrings were drops of bigger sapphires, the clips studded with smaller diamonds. 'It's perfect,' she said with difficulty, for there was a lump in her throat. 'My favourite colour. How did you know I'd be wearing blue?'

'Because you almost always do.'

'Will you put it on?' She turned so that he could do so, not just the necklace, but the earrings too. It was such an intimate gesture, the fastening on of jewellery, his fingers on her nape, on her lobes, herself acutely aware of him, his legs brushing her skirts, his head bent down towards hers.

'There.'

His hands on her shoulders turned her back round. There was a hint of colour on his cheeks, a hint of something darker in his eyes as he looked at her. 'What do you think?' she asked.

'I'm more concerned with what you think.'

She went through to the bedchamber to look in the mirror, taking his hand, leading him with her. In the soft light of the lamp, her skin looked pearlescent, the stones of the jewellery glinting, reflecting the colour of her gown and her eyes. 'Beautiful,' Cordelia said. 'It's exactly what I would have chosen for myself.'

Gentle hands on her shoulders turned her round again. 'I didn't mean to make you cry.'

'I'm not. It's only that no one ever buys me presents. Thank you, Iain.'

She stood on her tiptoes to kiss him, steadying herself with one hand on his shoulder, the other behind his head, pulling him towards her. His lips were cool. She meant it as a simple thank-you. He would have taken no more, except that her lips clung to his and her body nestled closer, and his hand crept around her waist, and her mouth opened to him, and the kiss was not so simple after all. Heat, and wanting, and longing. It was the longing that made them cling, and the longing that ended the kiss too, for it was unexpected, new, dangerous. They stared at each other, confused. Then Iain let her go.

'We'll be late,' he said, holding out the dark blue evening cloak which lay ready over the bed.

He said nothing else as they completed the short journey in the town coach he had hired. Beside him, Cordelia too was silent. Every now and then, her fingers strayed to the necklace at her throat, to the earrings, as if she needed reassurance. No one ever gave her presents. He'd been so caught up in the upheaval of the past two weeks, feeling as if he was being tossed, emotionally and physically, from pillar to post, that he hadn't considered what Cordelia's life must have been like. She was so confident, so—so vivid a woman, so assured, that he hadn't thought about her being alone, or lonely.

Hardly surprising, since he hadn't considered himself either, until he met her again. The strength of his resistance to ending their agreement made him realise how much he counted on her company for the next few months. He was accustomed to being alone, but he wasn't used to being lonely. Cordelia made him see that he was, because when he was with Cordelia he wasn't. Cordelia, who never received presents. Cordelia, who had been almost as much an orphan as he for the past nine years.

Who'd have thought two people born on two such very different sides of the fence could have so much in common? No one ever bought her presents, and he'd had no one to buy presents for, until now. Funny, but that hadn't occurred to him before either, because her family were just as out of reach as what was left of his.

He was so accustomed to thinking them all dead, it took him aback that his mind made the comparison before he could stop it. It wasn't the same at all. There was no comparing the two, none, and no point in thinking about it either. What he needed to be concentrating on was

Cordelia. Her mind must be in flitters, yet here she was, sitting calm—except of course she wasn't calm! He could be a right eejit sometimes.

Iain reached for her hand, enfolding it in his. 'I'll be right here,' he said. 'There won't be a single moment in the whole of tonight when there isn't at least one person completely on your side.'

'I wish you would stop reading my mind.'

Her fingers trembled, and so did her voice. 'Remind me now, what are all these half-brothers of yours called,' Iain said.

As he had hoped, she was distracted from her inner reverie. 'James is the eldest. He will be seventeen now. Then there's Harry, who is two years younger, and the twins, George and Freddie, who must be nearly fourteen. They were only little, the last time I saw them. And Isabella, who is six, I think, I have never seen. I doubt she will be at dinner tonight, though I hope that Bella will allow me to visit the nursery. I was thinking that... Oh, dear heavens.'

'What is it?'

Cordelia pointed wordlessly out of the carriage window. They had turned into Cavendish Square, but the carriage had slowed to a crawl, caught up in a jam of other carriages. 'Someone is having a fairly grand affair, looks like,' Iain said, peering out.

'Not someone.'

Her voice was tight. She was angry. He was about to ask her why, to reassure her that they would be delayed only five or ten minutes, when he noticed the flambeaux on the railings, and the red carpet that was laid on the steps, and the door it led up to, and he cursed, long and hard, in the language of the docks. 'What the *hell* does he mean by this! He said a small family gathering.'

'Bastard!'

The word, spoken in a low, vicious tone, shocked him to the core. 'Cordelia!'

'Don't *Cordelia* me. My father is a conniving, scurrilous, scheming, scabrous, contumelious, duplicitous, selfish, arrogant, lying *bastard!*'

The coach had come to a halt. Lord Armstrong's liveried footman was opening the door of the carriage two ahead of them. 'Cordelia,' Iain said urgently, 'your father has every one of the traits you so eloquently ascribe to him, I couldn't have put it better myself, but in a couple of minutes we're going to have to greet him, and the two hundred or two thousand other guests he's invited, and you can't let him see you like this.'

'He's doing this because of you,' she said, ignoring him. 'He's showing you off, Iain. *I might be out of the government, but look what I've got.* This isn't about me being welcomed back into the bosom of my family. It's not about me at all. I can't believe this. No, actually I can. Did I not say to you that he never gives a party unless he can get something out of it? Well, prepare yourself to be hounded and courted and touted about like a—a prize bull. Were it not for the fact that I'm fairly certain he wants you to do something for my brothers, I doubt I'd even get to meet them. *Bastard!* He's a complete—'

Iain put his hand over her mouth. 'Aye, he is, and when we've time, I've a few more choice words to add myself, but you need to get control of yourself, Cordelia. You can't let him see you like this. Are you listening to me?'

It took her until their carriage crept forward again to do as he bid. 'I'm listening,' she said, pulling his hand away from her mouth but cling-ing on to it. Her eyes were wide, her colour, from what he could see in the dim light, high.

'Good. First, you can take a horse to water and all that. He can tout me about and flatter me as much as he likes, but I assure you, I don't feel under any obligation at all to do any more than listen politely, and if he tries to push me, then I won't be so polite. Understand?'

Cordelia nodded.

'Secondly, I'll be having a word with him on the finer points of our agreement. You'll get your time with your brothers and sister, if not tonight, then as much as you want over the next few days. I know we're leaving for Plymouth soon, but we can put that back a bit and still make our ship, if need be.'

'But how will you make him if he won't agree?'

'He's in too deep to pull out now, but I'm not—or at least, that's what I'll tell him.' Iain smiled in what he hoped was a reassuring manner. 'It won't come to that, don't fret.'

'Thank you.'

'There's no need. We're in this together, re-member? I'll be right by you.'

'You don't mind all this—this show?'

He laughed. 'Honestly, that's exactly how I think of it, a show. I'm annoyed to be done out of my dinner though.'

'There will be at least two suppers, if Bella has anything to do with it. My father's wife is very fond of her food, as you will be see from her girth. Thank you, Iain—again. I am, as you would say, braced,' Cordelia said as the carriage began to inch towards the foot of the steps and the waiting footman.

'Aye, but you've forgotten something.' He pulled her towards him. 'It's not braced, you've to be, it's in thrall,' he said, and kissed her hard, swiftly and passionately.

As the carriage slowed to a stop, and the door was flung open, Lord Armstrong's footman was treated to the spectacle of Lord Armstrong's daughter in exactly the kind of compromising position he'd expect of such a scandalous female.

The town house had been transformed. Every window blazed. The huge hallway was awash with people glittering in jewels, powdered, primped and pomaded to within an inch of their lives. It reminded Cordelia of her coming-out ball. This was the milieu in which she had been raised, which she had been expected to inhabit and in which she now felt utterly and completely alien. She recognised several faces as she crossed the hallway, having discarded her cloak. False smiles. She returned them, equally falsely.

Iain was waiting for her, propped against the doorway of the book room, looking perfectly at ease, a smile, half amused half contemptuous, on his face. 'The fallen daughter returned to the fold seems to be as much of an attraction as the rich, influential shipbuilder,' Cordelia said under her breath as she took his arm.

'They must lead boring lives, if all they have to do is talk about others.'

'These people have made a career out of talking. Diplomats, politicians, half of Whitehall seem to be here. I noticed several Whigs too. There was a time my father would never have given them house room.'

'There was a time when this could have been your life,' Iain said.

'I know. You'll not be surprised to hear that I was thinking the same thing a moment ago.' Cordelia looked around her, at the procession of finely dressed men and women ascending the stairs, listening to the low, anticipatory buzz of conversation that always preceded a party, no matter how tedious it turned out to be. She smiled up at him. 'It's certainly not a life I wish to return to. Shall we get this over with?'

'Ready?'

'As I'll ever be,' she said, feeling absurdly nervous.

They ascended the staircase arm in arm. While Cordelia received knowing smiles and the occasional leer, it was Iain who attracted more attention. Her father had obviously been doing his groundwork, puffing up his prospective son-in-law's fortune and influence, for the men were clearly sizing him up. The ladies on the other hand, looked rather more predatory. She was not surprised, she had been looking at him hungrily enough herself, earlier, but she was taken aback by how proprietorial she felt. She tightened her grip on his arm.

They had reached the top of the stairs, and Cordelia caught her first glimpse of her father, resplendent in evening dress. The tall young man beside him was unmistakably James, made in his father's image, with her own blue-grey eyes. No sign of any of the other boys, but there was…

'Good grief!' She covered her mouth too late. 'Bella,' she whispered, in answer to Iain's enquiring look. 'She is quite transformed.'

Indeed, the woman standing at Lord Armstrong's side was a shadow of her former self, no longer corpulent, but slim, and really quite pretty, in the pink-and-cream style of a faded English rose. Cordelia had always thought of her as old, yet she looked to be no more than forty—and a young forty at that.

'Cordelia.' Her stepmother studied her, as a collector would study a specimen. 'You look well.'

'Bella. You look…'

'Thinner,' her ladyship finished for her.

'Younger.' From the corner of her eye, Cordelia saw Iain usher her father out of the line into an alcove on the landing.

'I find that country life agrees with me very much, now that I have my daughter,' Bella was saying. 'You must come tomorrow to meet Isabella. She is quite enchanting. So unlike any of her brothers or sisters.'

'I would love to come. And to meet the rest of my brothers too. James, it is lovely to see you again. You have grown considerably.' Her brother blushed and bestowed a very awkward kiss on Cordelia's cheek. Iain had his back to her, but she could see her father, looking rather dwarfed and not at all happy.

Bella was also eyeing the altercation in the alcove. 'Could they not have waited until later to discuss business?' she said waspishly.

'Personal business. We were under the impression, Iain and I, that this was to be a small family gathering,' Cordelia replied, and when Bella looked surprised, explained tersely, 'I would have been more than happy to have you come to Killellan, but that option was not given to me.'

Lady Armstrong cast a fulminating look at her

husband. 'I never come to town these days, your father and I lead very separate lives, but he told me that this party was what you wished, and if I did not play his hostess I would not meet you.'

The two women stared at each other, but before they could speak, the perpetrator of the deceit came back to the line, and the crush of bodies behind Cordelia began to push forward. 'Come to me tomorrow,' Bella said hurriedly, 'I shall ensure that you have time alone with your brothers and sisters.'

'What was that all about?' Iain asked, taking her hand again.

'You first.'

He grinned as they entered the drawing room. 'I think I managed to put him straight on a few things.'

'He lied to Bella too. He told her this party was my idea. He told her— Iain, she said they lead separate lives. And I have just remembered something Aunt Sophia said about skeletons. Do you think…?'

'I think it's time for us to play our parts.'

She looked up to find a sea of faces gazing

at her. Her father was pushing his way into the centre of the room, Bella following in his wake. Lady Sophia was already ensconced in state in a thronelike chair.

'Ladies and gentlemen.' Lord Armstrong raised his hands for silence. 'Tonight, we Armstrongs welcome another member into the family fold. Mr Hunter, as those of us who know about such things will be aware, is what we call an up-coming man.'

He touched his finger to his nose, smiling in that condescending way that made Cordelia's hackles rise. Looking up at Iain, she saw it had the same effect on him.

'Mr Hunter's shipbuilding company is currently the foremost in this great island of ours. With his new connections, namely myself—' Lord Armstrong anticipated the polite laughter with a modest bow '—I predict that Hunter will soon be a name recognised throughout the world. In a matter of days, thanks to my connections, he sets out to conquer Arabia. Ladies and gentlemen, please raise your glasses to Mr Iain Hunter. And of course, to my daughter.'

They were still standing in the doorway. Cordelia was trying very, very hard not to be inflamed by her father's speech in which she had not even been named and more to the point, in which Iain had been patronised to a point well beyond acceptability. She would happily have stalked out, if he had not taken her hand. And cleared his throat.

'Ladies and gentlemen,' Iain said, halting the toast in midair. 'I'm sure he didn't mean to, but his lordship has made my betrothal to his daughter sound like a business alliance. Welcome though his contacts may be, let me assure you that I've no need of his help to build my ships, unless Lord Armstrong here knows how to rivet steel.'

This time, the laughter was spontaneous. Her father's smile looked as if it were forged in the metal Iain used for his ships' hulls.

'While I'm thankful for his pulling of the various diplomatic strings which have enabled me to open up discussions with Prince al-Muhanna, as far as I'm concerned, there's one thing, and only one, that Lord Armstrong has done that matters, and that was bringing this wonderful woman into the world.'

He took her hands between his. Their eyes met, and Cordelia forgot about all the other people in the room. *This one.* She remembered in that moment how it had been that first time. How he had looked at her, and she had looked at him, in just this way. *This one.*

'I'd like you to raise your glasses to my betrothed,' Iain said. 'A woman who treads her own path. I'm very glad it led her to me. Ladies and gentlemen, I give you Cordelia.'

And then, in front of a drawing room full of the great and the good of her father's world, Iain kissed her. And the great and the good clinked their glasses and burst into spontaneous applause. And her father looked as if his champagne were vinegar. And Cordelia smiled up at Iain, quite lost for words, because he hadn't lied, and he had praised the thing she had worked so hard at, and even if they weren't really betrothed, it felt so good, so very good to be standing beside someone who really understood her. She was about to say so, when a man pushed his way through the crowd.

'No!'

That one word stilled her heart in horror. Tall, dark, handsome and utterly sure of himself. Gideon hadn't changed at all.

The silence was sudden and complete as he stood in front of her. 'No, Cordelia, I don't think so,' Gideon D'Amery said, turning to Iain. 'It should have been me seven years ago, but it's not too late. I had her first. She's mine. She always will be.'

The words were barely out of Gideon's mouth when Iain knocked him down with a vicious, extremely effective blow that sent Cordelia's former lover sprawling on to the drawing-room floor, a fist-sized bruise already blooming angry red on his jaw.

No longer the distinguished man of business, Iain looked like a great big brawny Highland warrior as he stalked menacingly towards his prey, fists clenched. For a moment, Cordelia felt a wild elation, a ridiculous feminine pride in being so defended, but the cruel glint in Iain's eye brought her rapidly back down to earth. It frightened her, as if his civilised veneer was wearing very thin.

'Iain...' She grabbed at the sleeve of his tail-coat. He swatted her away.

Gideon, the light of battle in his eye, was already on his feet. 'You will name your seconds,' he said.

This brought Iain to an abrupt halt. 'Don't be so ridiculous, man. You can't possibly be thinking of calling me out.' He sounded quite dumb-founded.

'Of course I'm calling you out. Any gentleman would, after...'

'I'm not a gentleman,' Iain said, proving his point by thwacking Gideon squarely on the nose.

He did not go down this time, but came at Iain with his fists raised, landing a blow to his shoulder that sent him staggering. With a snarl, Iain landed a third punch in Gideon's stomach, and would have followed through if Cordelia had not thrown herself between the two, taking both by surprise and narrowly escaping Gideon's counter-blow.

'Are you all right? Did he hit you? Cordelia, speak to me.' Iain's face was white with fright.

She shook herself free. 'I am perfectly well, thank you, but I prefer to fight my own battles. I did tell you that.'

He flinched. 'You did.'

'Not that I am not grateful, for he deserved to be punched,' she said, softening the blow, 'and I could not have done half so well as that,' she added, smiling maliciously at Gideon, who was mopping his nose with a handkerchief.

Gideon sneered. 'I will call you out for this, Hunter, gentleman or no gentleman.'

'Oh, for God's sake, shut up,' Cordelia snapped. 'What the devil are you doing here anyway? I cannot imagine that you were invited.'

'There, my dear, you are wrong. You forget, my mother was a Lamb. Lord Melbourne's cousin, in fact. Now that the Whigs are in power, your father is rather eager to cultivate my acquaintance.'

Cordelia felt her jaw drop. It seemed to be making a habit of it. Glancing up at Iain, she could see her own disbelief reflected on his face. Gideon laughed, a brittle sound that sent shivers down her spine, because she remembered it of old, when he walked away from the tables a loser, before she had begun to play for them both. 'Blood, it seems, is not really thicker than water, my dear Cordelia,' he said maliciously, 'at least, not in your father's case.'

She became aware of the silence. She had forgotten that they were in the drawing room, in the middle of a party. Across the room, her aunt Sophia was looking pale. Bella, on the other hand, was looking positively gleeful. And her father— her father, no longer the great orchestrator, was slumped in a chair, looking down at his shoes. She should have felt triumphant, but he was a pitiful sight.

'You're right,' Iain said, as if she had spoken. 'Lady Armstrong, will you see to Lady Sophia? I think she needs a brandy. And you—I don't even know your name?'

'Gideon D'Amery.' Gideon sketched a very brief bow.

'Aye. We've business to discuss. After you.'

The crowd parted as Iain and Gideon left the drawing room and headed down the stairs, Cordelia in their wake. As they crossed the threshold, the room burst into conversation.

'Well, what they merely speculated about us before has certainly been confirmed, my dear,' Gideon said as Iain closed the door of the book room.

'No doubt as you intended it should be when you made such a dramatic entrance tonight.' Cordelia was furious. 'How dare you! What on earth were you thinking?'

'Exactly what I said. You were mine first, and you will always be mine. Come, Cordelia, you know that perfectly well. Now why don't you step outside while I finish my business with this usurper, and we can…'

Her hands formed into fists. She was beginning to understand Iain's instinctive reaction. In fact, if he had not made such an excellent job of it, she would have thrown a punch just to make herself feel better. 'This is *my* business,' Cordelia hissed.

'She's in the right of it,' Iain said. 'You don't know her very well if you think to ride roughshod over her without consulting her.'

'But that's the point, isn't it? I rode her first, though as to roughshod—I do believe I have rather more finesse than that, do I not, my dear?'

This time, Cordelia was faster than Iain, landing a resounding slap, right on top of the purpling bruise. It might have hurt her as much as Gideon, but it was his eyes that were watering. 'How dare you! I am not some filly you broke in, and if you think to shame me into marriage, or shame Iain out of it—forget it. He knows about you.'

Gideon's eyebrows rose. 'How very—noble of him to stand by you, my dear, but there is no need. No, don't try and hit me again, save that tempestuous nature of yours for something more worthwhile.'

Cordelia lunged. Gideon took a hasty step back. Iain grabbed her by the waist. 'Stop rising to the bait,' he whispered, putting a very firm restraining hand around her waist.

He was right. Again. He was also behaving far better than she. Cordelia sent him a shaky smile before turning back to her ex-lover. 'Why are you here, Gideon?'

'The second time you've asked me that. My answer remains the same.'

'I haven't heard from you in seven years.'

'You would have done, had I known where to find you, but you seemed to disappear off the face of the earth.'

'Perhaps because I didn't want you to find me,' Cordelia said tartly. 'Please don't tell me that you've been wearing the willow for me.'

'There, you underestimate me. When I asked you to marry me, it was nothing to do with honour you know, and everything to do with sentiment.'

'A shame you were not so sentimental when we eloped.'

'I think so too. I was a fool not to make you mine when I had the chance. You loved me then, Cordelia.'

He smiled at her. Despite the bloody nose and the blossoming bruise, he was still a very handsome man. Her heart used to flutter, just imagining his kisses. When he had smiled at her across a crowded ballroom, that same complicit smile he was smiling right now, she would have gone to the ends of the earth with him. Had that been love? 'It was nine years ago, Gideon.'

'I've missed you,' he said, holding out his hand to her.

She was no longer anchored to Iain's side. She hadn't noticed him letting her go, and now he was avoiding her eyes. She looked at Gideon again. The reality of his touch had never lived up to her imagination. He was an accomplished lover, she knew that now. Skilled, considerate, almost never selfish. It had taken her a long time to realise that's all he was.

He was still holding out his hand. There was still complicity in his smile. And knowledge. It made her deeply uncomfortable, that knowledge. Nine years. Nine years! He didn't know her at all. How could he have, when she was scarcely formed? 'I expect what you've missed is my presence at the tables,' Cordelia said. 'Have the cards been going against you, Gideon?'

His smile wobbled. 'We made a good team, you and I.'

'We were never a team, Gideon.' Cordelia placed Iain's arm back around her waist and held it there. He was looking at her strangely. There was no time to worry about that now, she had to deal with Gideon first.

'If it's your father you're worried about,' he was saying, 'I'm sure that my connections would weigh heavier than any trade.'

Cordelia managed to laugh. 'I rather think you're behind the times. Besides, my father has nothing to do with my betrothal to Iain.'

'I heard he was the one who introduced you. You've known each other barely a few days.'

'You're wrong. Our—our relationship is of much longer standing.'

'Relationship? What do you mean, relationship? I had you first, Cordelia, what can be more important than that?'

Power. It was surging in her veins. And revenge. She hadn't even been aware that she had thirsted for it, but she had. 'I had no other man to compare you with, Gideon. Now I have,' she said, turning to Iain. Standing on her tiptoes, she put her arms around his neck. 'Believe me, there is simply no comparison.'

It was a kiss performed for an audience, and

Iain played his part, bending her back theatrically in his arms, his mouth clinging to hers, until they heard the muttered exclamation and the slam of the book-room door.

Cordelia refused to return to her father's party, and Iain, silently brooding, was happy to take her back to Milvert's, commandeering the town coach waiting at the steps of Cavendish Square rather than wait for the one he had hired.

'*That* certainly turned out rather differently from what any of us planned.' Cordelia threw her cloak over a chair in her sitting-room and began to wrestle with the buttons on her evening gloves. 'So much for the small family gathering. I hope my father is pleased with himself. You know, I always thought Bella hated me, but I got the distinct impression tonight that it was my father she couldn't bear. She said they lived separate lives. Not that they were ever very much together, for he rarely came to Killellan. Though they did manage to produce five children, so they must have— Actually, I don't much like to think of that.'

She was nervous, that much was certain, Iain thought. Avoiding the issue. Or waiting on him raising it. She threw her gloves down on top of her cloak, and continued with her inane chatter. 'I'm to call on her tomorrow. Bella promised me *he* wouldn't be there, that I shall see the children. James is more of a young man than a child. He looks very like my father, don't you think? I would have recognised him anywhere, though he looked rather askance at me. I should not be surprised he did not recognise me, really. He was eight years old the last time he saw me, and the only portrait of me at Killellan was done when I was about the same age. I was so nervous about meeting them all, and as it turns out that was the least of my worries.'

She was stirring ineffectively at the fire now. Iain took the poker from her. Cordelia jumped and retired several feet away. Iain added some coals. 'The main thing is, our betrothal has been announced,' he said.

'I suppose you're sorry for it.'

He studied her carefully. 'Are you?'

She paled, but stood her ground. 'I should have told you the full story.'

'You lied to me. I'm still not sure what the full story is. Why didn't you tell me?'

'I didn't lie. You assumed— I thought it was none of your business.'

'D'Amery made it my business.'

'Tonight! I had no idea he would be there tonight. If I had known, of course I would have told you.'

She was glaring at him, that mixture of defiance and shame that resonated horribly with him. 'How long were you with him as his mistress?' he asked.

She looked as if she would not answer him, but then gave a little shrug. 'About two years. I learnt very quickly that I did not love him any more than he loved me but we were—compatible.' Cordelia ran her fingers through her *coiffure*, dislodging a pin. 'We travelled. As you'll have gathered, Gideon was a gamester. It was he who taught me to gamble, and in the end it was my winnings which kept us going. So you see, I was never a kept woman. He never paid for my—I gave myself freely, not by way of recompense.'

Again that mixture of defiance laced with shame. Iain frowned, trying to recall their previous conversation, her exact words, his own questions. 'You lied to me.'

'I did not!' she said indignantly. 'I might not have told you the whole truth, but I never lied. I told you I wasn't miserable. I told you he didn't seduce me. What difference does it make, Iain, how long I stayed with him, whether it was one week, one month, one year or two? I didn't tell you because I knew you would judge me, just as Aunt Sophia does and probably Bella and certainly my father and—and Cressie and Caro would too, if they knew.'

'They don't?' He couldn't keep the surprise from his voice.

'Not all of it.' She wouldn't meet his eyes now, was concentrating on twisting her hairpin round her finger. 'I don't think they'd understand. Caro and Cressie, they have not exactly been conventionally courted, but their husbands—well, they love them. They're happy with them. Will be happy with them always, if they are to be believed. While I— It's different for me, can't you see that? I have no husband to redeem me, and nor do I want one.'

There was pain shadowing her eyes which surprised him and a shade of insecurity too, that touched him. She had told him what she had not told her sisters. But—two years? It shouldn't matter, but it did, and he disliked himself for that fact. Iain took the hairpin from her and threw it on to the hearth.

'I was right not to tell you,' Cordelia said. 'You are judging me.'

'I'm trying not to.'

'I do not object to you having had other lovers,' Cordelia said.

'I've never introduced you to any of them at a party,' Iain snapped.

'That was unfair.'

He held his hands up. 'It was, and I'm sorry. Look, I know fine that the way I'm feeling isn't right. If you knew—' He broke off, closing his eyes briefly. He would not compare Cordelia to his mother. 'It's one thing to know about him, another to meet him. If I could eradicate that man from your past, I would.'

'If I had not run off with Gideon, I would not have met you,' Cordelia said. 'He helped make me the person I am, and I like that person, Iain.'

Iain was forced to smile. 'I like her too. I doubt your father will be saying the same, mind, after the way I behaved in his drawing-room.'

Cordelia chuckled. 'I confess I was rather thrilled. It is a shocking thing to admit, but you see no one has ever fought for me before. You looked like one of those wild Highlanders in a painting.'

'You mean I looked like a savage?' Somehow, his arm seemed to have wound round her waist. She didn't try to remove it.

'I mean, it was romantic. Even though I was perfectly capable of handling the situation myself, and even though we are not really betrothed. That is, if we are still betrothed?'

'You need to learn that I don't go back on my word. We are betrothed.' He had an excellent view of her delightful cleavage. He dragged his gaze back to her face and twined one of her ringlets around his finger. The atmosphere between them had thickened. Somewhere along the way, his anger and hurt had given way to the hunger which lurked just below the surface whenever they were together.

'I haven't thanked you for rushing to my defence.'

Iain let the ringlet unravel. 'I don't need thanks, Cordelia, and as you pointed out at the time, you didn't really need defending.'

'Not thanks then, but—this should be our night, Iain. Our victory. We have what we wanted.'

He remembered what she'd said, just before he pretended to kiss her in her father's book room. *Believe me, there is no comparison.* She'd sounded as if she meant it. It would be so easy to kiss her. So easy to lose himself in her. He wanted her so much. Wanted her more than he'd ever wanted any other woman. *No comparison.* He was the one she was with now, the one she wanted, his fevered brain reminded him, and he surrendered to the inevitable.

He kissed her hungrily. Passion raged, fierce, sudden and unstoppable. Cordelia kissed him back with an equal fervour. Tongues touched, retreated, touched. His hands roamed over her back, her bottom, her flanks, everywhere frustrated by the sheer volume of her clothing.

Believe me, there is no comparison. But his mind kept returning to the first man she had given herself to. He dragged his mouth away. 'Did you love him?' he asked.

'No. Yes. I thought I did. It was nine years ago. It doesn't matter now.' She was panting. She tugged at his coat. It dropped to the ground. She began on the buttons of his waistcoat. It landed on the fender.

More kissing. She tasted lush. Her kisses were heady. He burrowed his face in the swell of her breasts, breathing in the scent of her. She reached behind her and began to perform the kind of contortionist's dance required to unbutton her gown, cursing under her breath. He turned her round to help, kissing her neck, her shoulders, easing the lacing wide enough to expose her breasts straining against her corsets, turning her back again to kiss his way over the tender flesh. Her breath was coming fast and shallow. She wriggled. He tugged. Her nipples sprang free, and he caught one between his lips, drawing a harsh cry from her.

'You don't regret it then?' he asked, his own breathing ragged.

'Regret what?'

'Refusing him tonight.'

'No.'

'You don't think you could love him again?'

'Iain! No!'

He kissed her again. She tugged his shirt free from his trousers. Her hands were warm, smoothing over his muscles, making him clench beneath her touch. He tugged at her lacings, and her gown finally fell open. She stepped out of it. He picked her up. She wrapped her legs around his waist. He carried her through to the bedchamber and laid her on the bed. He pushed her petticoats up, and helped her wriggle free of her pantaloons.

Dear God, but she was gorgeous. He kissed her mouth, her breasts. He sucked on her nipples. 'But still,' he said, unable to stop himself, 'it must have been strange, seeing him after all this time.'

Cordelia sat up, propping herself up on her elbows. 'Iain, can we please forget about Gideon?'

He wanted to. He desperately wanted to. He rolled on to the bed beside her and slid his hand between her legs. She was hot and wet. She moaned. He began to stroke her, trying to concentrate on what he was doing. He shouldn't have to concentrate.

I rode her first...

Save that tempestuous nature of yours...

I have rather more finesse than that...

It was one thing to have the tale of a lover told, another to be confronted with said lover, flesh and blood and bloody handsome into the bargain. A gentleman. But Cordelia didn't want D'Amery. Cordelia wanted him. Why else would she be lying here beside him, almost naked, wet with longing?

Except she wasn't as wet as she had been. And she could be lying here because she wanted to make sure he kept to their bargain. Iain kissed her desperately. It seemed to him that she kissed him back with equal desperation. She fumbled for his trousers, and found, at the same time as he, that there was decidedly less to fumble for than there had been a few moments before.

'Iain? What's wrong?'

It was the worst thing she could have said. 'Nothing.'

He kissed her again. He slid his fingers inside her and began to work her feverishly, but she was now almost as dry as he was limp. If only she hadn't said anything. If only she hadn't noticed. Mortified, furious at himself, but angrier at her, for it was her lover who had thrust himself between them, Iain rolled away and got up from the bed, tucking his shirt into his trousers.

'Iain?'

'You're obviously not interested.'

'I beg your pardon?'

'Don't pretend you don't know what I'm talking about. I know what I'm doing, and it was perfectly obvious you weren't enjoying it.'

With an exclamation that might have been disgust or frustration or annoyance, Cordelia jumped up and grabbed her robe from the chair, tying it tightly around her waist, her eyes flashing. 'You are not the only one who knows what they are doing. It was perfectly obvious to *me* that you were supremely uninterested.'

'Because *you* were not.'

'And is it any wonder! How could I possibly concentrate when you kept on and on and on about Gideon?'

'You should not need to *concentrate*,' he threw at her, managing to be both hypocritical and unfair, since he'd had the very same problem. He was being ridiculous. He didn't care. This didn't happen to him. This had never happened to him. 'I did not *go on and on* about that man. I asked you some perfectly reasonable questions.'

'Under perfectly unreasonable conditions.'

Also true, and it made him even more furious. 'You started it.'

It was an outrageously provocative thing to say, but he couldn't stop himself. Cordelia's breath hissed. She looked as if she would hit him, then to her credit, she turned away, opening the bedroom door and stalking ahead of him into the other room.

He followed her and began to harvest discarded garments from the hearth, the floor, beneath the sofa, the window-seat, deliberately stoking his fury with his frustration. 'I won't be used, Cordelia. I don't want you to plaster yourself all over me because you want to forget another man.'

'That's not what I was doing.'

'And I don't want to be thanked, either.'

'I was not thanking you!'

'You said it yourself, you liked it when I hit that— Him.'

'So now you're some kind of knight in shining armour and I am a grateful damsel in distress!'

Cordelia glared at him, hands on her hips. At her ears and throat, the jewellery he had given her sparkled. She looked magnificent. To his shame, Iain felt his shaft stirring. He was so confused, he had no idea what he thought, but one thing was for sure; if he remained here, whatever he said or did would be the wrong thing. He stuffed his gloves into the narrow pockets of his tailcoat.

'You're going?'

'I don't see any point in staying.'

'You don't think it would be better if we talked about this?'

'No,' Iain said, extremely decidedly, 'I do not. I think we should forget it happened.'

'Forget! But—we leave for Plymouth in three days. That is— Are you saying we should forget that too?'

She looked as confused as he felt. He hadn't a clue how they had got to this point, and he had even less of a clue on how to go back. 'If that's what you want,' Iain said, which was not at all what he meant, but now it was out, and sounding exactly like an ultimatum, he would not take it back, even though Cordelia, clutching at the ties of her robe, looked as if he'd stabbed her or slapped her. And now he came to think of it, he'd seen that robe before. It was the same one she'd put on that night in Glasgow. No doubt D'Amery had seen it too.

Iain picked up his hat. 'He was serious you know, when he asked you to marry him. He'd take you now. I doubt you've burnt your boats with him.'

'You think I'd take him after he made sure the entire drawing-room full of society knew we had been lovers? They would have speculated before, but they wouldn't have known.'

Iain shrugged callously. 'He just wanted to make it difficult for you to refuse him.'

'So you're advocating I accept, is that it?'

Cordelia was on the brink of tears, but she was determined not to cry. He could have kicked himself. He wanted to take her back into his arms, but he knew even now, through the fog of his confusion, that D'Amery would be there between them if he did. 'He says he loves you. You've a history, the pair of you.'

'They have a saying in the Highlands. I learnt it in my travels. *There's no need of history when memories are long.* An old man translated it for me, when I asked him why they hated the English so.'

It was one his mother used to cast up at him regularly. He'd only ever meant to save her the inevitable pain of rejection, but she never did abandon the hope that the next one would be *the* one. *The man who matters is the last.* No, he would not take that path. The circumstances were very different. Cordelia was not his mother. Iain caught himself, just in time, biting back the Gaelic translation of the quotation. 'We were talking about more recent history,' he said. 'D'Amery is obviously in your father's good books, with his political connections. What's more, you're from the same side of the fence, you and him. I'm sure if you jumped ship Armstrong would be happy enough.'

'There speaks the shipbuilder. You mean I should jilt you.'

'We're not really betrothed, Cordelia.'

'But we do have a deal, Iain. I thought we were on the same side of the fence, you and I?'

'All I'm saying is that you've got options you didn't know you had until this evening, and maybe you should think about them.' Though the last thing he wanted to think about was Cordelia and D'Amery. The very strength of his revulsion propelled Iain towards the door. 'Goodnight, Cordelia.'

'Do you mean goodbye?' she asked, looking quite forlorn.

'I mean you need to think about it.' He was being unfair. He didn't want her to think about it. He wanted her to tell him he'd got it all wrong. He wanted to unsay almost every single word he'd spoken in the past half-hour. He most certainly wanted to undo the fiasco in the bedroom. Most of all, what he wanted was to get away, out of here, right now. 'Goodnight, Cordelia,' Iain said again, and left.

Chapter Seven

'I shall return to Killellan tomorrow. It is a pity you cannot come with me, Isabella seemed quite taken with her new sister.'

'And I with her,' Cordelia said to Bella with a smile, accepting a cup of tea. They had spent the best part of the day together with all of the children. Isabella was a most taking little thing, not at all in awe of her, and eager for stories of her other sisters, quite unlike her brothers who were, sadly, already exhibiting that combination of extreme exuberance and shyness in the company of females which their school seemed to encourage. They were, in fact, all four of the boys, rather too much like her father for comfort. She had no doubt that she loved them, but as to liking, she was much more ambivalent—and that, she thought rather guiltily, was unlikely to improve with age. 'Isabella is very different from her brothers,' she said.

'I believe she takes after me,' Bella said with what seemed to Cordelia a very secretive smile. She was still struggling to come to terms with the changes in her stepmother. It was not simply the alteration in her form, but her manner, which verged on the warm and the confidential, neither of which traits had ever been in evidence before.

'You find me changed,' Bella said, as if she had been reading Cordelia's thoughts.

'I confess—yes, I do.'

'Having a daughter is part of it. I had so wanted a daughter, and had quite given up hope, for your father—frankly, he was never actually interested in that sort of thing, save for the procreative purpose, and he considered four boys more than sufficient. My needs—of any sort—were never a consideration for him.'

Cordelia, who considered herself a woman of the world, was both embarrassed and intrigued by this confidence, which put her father in a very different light. She couldn't help wondering what

Iain would make of it, or of Isabella, whose colouring, of dark-brown eyes and black hair, was either a throwback to some distant generation, or, as seemed increasingly likely, testimony to another parentage all together. Though Iain was not likely to make anything of either thing, because she most likely wouldn't hear from him again, and in fact, there was no reason for her not to visit Killellan as Bella suggested, except she could not face the explanation that entailed and…

'Is there something wrong, Cordelia?'

'I'm sorry. I—I have the headache.'

'You were not used to have headaches. Cressie it was, who claimed to have a headache when she wanted to be left alone. You now, you were always rather more inventive with your lies.' Lady Armstrong surveyed her complacently. 'I always did see more than you realised. I remember saying so to Cressie—oh, it must have been around about the time you were in London and she was having an *affaire* with that Italian she eventually married.'

'You knew she was having an *affaire*?' Cordelia positively goggled. 'And you did nothing to stop her?'

Bella shrugged. 'A pointless waste of energy. Nothing I said would make a difference, and frankly, it suited me to have her out from under my feet.'

'But my father—good heavens, if he had known...'

'Then no doubt he would have acted as he did with you. And with Caro, now I come to think of it. *Off with her head.* He does so like a dramatic gesture, it makes him feel as if he is in control.' Bella pursed her lips. 'I tried to stop him, you know. When he found you were Gideon D'Amery's mistress, I mean, after he returned from Russia. If you had not been so pig-headed, he would have been able to cover it all up. But there—you are all the same, Catherine's daughters, determined to have your own way, and in the end—you know, I really do think it's one thing I've learned from you. It took me a long time, but since I too decided to go my own way, as all of you have, I have been very happy.'

Cordelia put down her empty teacup and

brushed the crumbs of rather good seed-cake from her gown. She could not be mistaken. Bella was positively bursting to be asked. 'Isabella is not my father's child, is she?'

'Of course not. After the twins, save one time, he did not come near my bedchamber. He had enough sons, he told me, and he'd had enough of servicing me—not that he put it in such words, he is far too much the diplomat, your father, to be so blunt,' Bella said with a sneer.

'But—but—but he does not deny…'

'He tried to, but I pointed out to him how very bad it would look, that such a prominent figure as he could be cuckolded, and I suggested that he would not relish having the details of his short-comings revealed to the world.'

Cordelia stared at her in utter astonishment, then burst into a peal of laughter. 'Good grief. How absolutely—marvellous!' She covered her mouth, but it was too late, the words were out, and her stepmother was actually preening. It was shocking too, absolutely outrageous, but more than anything, she wanted to applaud Bella for her unique form of restitution.

'I am relieved to hear you say so,' Lady Armstrong said. 'The outcome has been most serendipitous. Had Isabella been a boy, it would have been a different matter, needless to say, but your father has a very poor opinion of what he believes to be the gentler sex. And I have to tell you, Cordelia, as one woman to another, that since I met my—Isabella's father, it has been quite a revelation. I did not realise it before, for I had none to compare your father to, but suffice it to say, I know now that such things do not have to be simply endured.'

Cordelia caught her jaw just before it dropped again. 'Now? So you still see Isabella's father?'

'Oh, yes. It is what the French call a *grand amour*. I believe I have finally shocked you.'

'I rather think you meant to.' Cordelia replied drily.

'Let us not pretend, my dear. You very much disliked my taking your mother's place, and I very much disliked having you girls foisted on me. However, that is all water under the bridge now. I think we can both appreciate that we were all miserable in our own ways. In fact, the only person who benefited from the arrangement was your father.'

'You are right, and I am sorry for it.' Impulsively, Cordelia gave her stepmother a hug, surprised and touched when Bella returned the embrace.

'Do you know, that is the first time that you have ever done such a thing of your own free will?' Bella said.

'I'm sorry,' Cordelia said, aghast, trying in vain to remember a single other occasion when she had done so. 'I really am sorry, Bella. It never occurred to me that you— I was so selfish.'

'Yes, in that sense you are very like your father.' Bella poured herself another cup of tea. 'In fairness, I never encouraged any of you to be tactile. Even with my boys— It is only since I had Isabella, who is so very fond of cuddles. But I see no point in recriminations. Your father married me to play the broodmare, not mother to you and your sisters. If he had wanted that kind of woman, he'd have married someone else.'

'I have often wondered why it took him so long to marry again, to be honest. Mama had been dead more than ten years before he married you. I used to think that he must have loved her very much, but from what you've said…'

'No, he didn't love Catherine.'

Cordelia frowned at the certainty in Bella's tone, remembering Aunt Sophia's hints about skeletons. But Aunt Sophia must have been referring to Bella, surely. 'How can you be so sure?'

Bella pursed her lips. 'You will be looking forward to seeing Celia. If anyone was a mother to you, it was she, I gather. You must ask her.'

'Yes. If I— To be honest Bella, I am not sure that I— Iain and I, we had an argument.'

'After last night's fiasco, I am not surprised. No man likes to be confronted with the evidence he has not been the first to possess his lover.'

Once again, Cordelia stared at her stepmother in astonishment. 'How on earth did you know that we have— That *is* what you meant, isn't it?'

'Come now, Cordelia, have I not just told you I'm not a fool?' Bella sighed in exasperation. 'For a start, there had to be a reason behind your sudden desire to please your father, other than your wish to have your name restored to the family bible.'

'You know perfectly well that I can't see Celia and Cassie without his consent.'

'I also know that you could have obtained his consent without agreeing to marry Iain Hunter,' Bella responded tartly. 'I know too, having seen the pair of you together, that your acquaintance is not of a mere few days' duration. And I can recognise from my own experience, that particular—familiarity—between a man and a woman which makes it very clear that they have shared more than a few chaste kisses.'

'Bella!' Cordelia's face was flaming.

'Oh, spare me your blushes.' Bella got to her feet, putting her slice of cake untouched on its plate, back on to the tea tray. 'You are nigh on thirty years of age, Cordelia, far too old to pretend to be coy, and most likely far more experienced than I, for I believe Gideon D'Amery's reputation as a libertine must mean he is rather more than competent in that area.'

Bella looked as if she were waiting on some sort of commendation. Cordelia could only nod.

'I thought so, though I have to say, I can *perfectly* understand your preference for Mr Hunter. That combination of the primitive and the powerful is very appealing. There is something about him that draws the eye, is there not?'

This whole conversation was beginning to feel quite surreal. 'Yes. Yes, there is,' Cordelia replied, dazed.

'A man who has made his fortune with his own hands. A very manly man. Your Aunt Sophia was most taken with him.'

'She was?' Cordelia asked faintly.

'Oh, very. So, as I was saying, I am not at all surprised that he became rather possessive. A man such as Mr Hunter, who fights for what he wants, that sort of man is worth having. I should know, having lived with one who would not lift a finger for me.'

'Iain said that I should consider Gideon's offer.'

Bella frowned. 'I expect what he meant is that he won't be second choice.'

'But he's not.'

'Were you clear about that?'

'He pushed me to accept. He said that Gideon came from the same side of the fence.'

'An undoubted truth. It didn't occur to you, I suppose, that Mr Hunter might be jealous?'

'Of Gideon!' Cordelia snorted. 'Why should Iain be jealous of Gideon?'

'He is rich—and not from trade either.'

Cordelia shook her head. 'I got the impression that his gambling— I rather thought he was in need of money, Bella.'

'Cash flow is not really a problem when one has an inheritance to fall back on,' her stepmother replied dismissively. 'The point is, his wealth comes from the land. He is very good-looking. He comes from your own milieu. He knows the people you know. And he knows you, Cordelia. Intimately.'

'But—but he doesn't know me.' Not the way that Iain did. And she didn't want Gideon, had never wanted Gideon, the way she wanted Iain. 'Besides, why on earth would Iain be jealous when…?' *He doesn't love me,* she had been about to say, biting back the words when she remembered what Iain had told her father.

Bella though, was not so easily taken in. 'Men are like dogs with a bone. It's not about love, it's about possession. Iain doesn't want to be reminded that you belonged to someone else, and he certainly doesn't like to be confronted with the evidence.'

'Gideon did not *possess* me. Just because I have— Just because we shared a bed does not mean he had the right to my mind—or my body, for that matter.'

'You were his mistress, Cordelia. He paid your bills.'

'At the start, that's true, but as soon as I could, I paid my own way. I'm a rich woman now, you know.'

Bella raised her brows. 'Congratulations,' she said, sounding not a whit impressed.

'I don't need a man to support me, and I certainly don't intend to allow one to claim ownership of me—ever.'

'Not even when you are married? Or perhaps you have no intentions of actually getting married?' Bella drew her a quizzical look. 'Your father was right, when he said you had unortho-

dox views. I wish you luck treading that particular path. It is a man's world, Cordelia. It would
be easier if you came to terms with that.'

'Aunt Sophia said the same thing.'

'Lady Sophia is right.' Bella looked at the clock
and sighed. 'It is Isabella's bath time. I must leave
you—unless you wish to help me?'

'No, thank you. I need to think.'

'Don't think too hard. If I were you, I would
come down from my high horse and apologise
to your Mr Hunter before it is too late.'

'I've nothing to apologise for.'

Bella sighed again. 'Cordelia, do you want to
go to Arabia?'

'You know how much it means to me.'

'Then is not a little compromise a price worth
paying? You are due to leave for Plymouth in
three days. I would prefer to return to Killellan,
but I *am* willing to compromise, and would like
you and Isabella to be better acquainted before
you go.'

'*If* I go.'

Bella ignored this. 'So we will remain here
until you leave. You understand, she may not be

your flesh and blood, but I want you to think of her as your sister.'

'Bella, since we are being frank, I suspect I will like Isabella a great deal more than my brothers, who are, as you put it, my flesh and blood. Thank you.' Cordelia embraced her stepmother again. 'I mean it. I appreciate the sacrifice you're making, I really do.'

'Until tomorrow then, by which time I trust you will have resolved this other matter. Whatever your reasons for engaging yourself to Mr Hunter, I advise you to have a care. He is not a man to play games with, but he seems to me a man who would be worth having on your side. If I were betrothed to him, I would work very hard to keep him there.'

It was after six when Cordelia left Cavendish Square, her mind awhirl with Bella's various confidences. She felt as if she barely knew the woman revealed to her today. Subversive, selfish, insightful, with her own particular brand of morality that was in its own way every bit as wayward as Cordelia's own, this Bella was, shockingly, a much more *interesting* person than the one Cordelia had known previously. Aunt Sophia would condemn Bella for not protecting Cressie, but Bella's deliberate neglect had allowed Cressie the freedom to pursue her true love. And Bella's adultery had given her the daughter she craved. A lovely child Isabella was too, her mother was quite transformed in her company. Bella had done her duty, and now she was pleasing herself.

'Good for Bella,' Cordelia said under her breath, 'though it would not be me.'

She paused on the corner of Margaret Street. The sensible thing would be to go back to Milvert's and send Iain a note asking him to call on her in the morning, by which time she would have had plenty of time to think matters over. But she didn't feel like being sensible and she had already spent one tortuous, self-castigating night with her mind going round and round in circles, so she turned her steps impulsively towards Regent Street. It was absolutely not the done thing for a lady to call at a gentleman's lodgings, or indeed for a lady to walk alone at this time of the evening down St James's, but Cordelia was not in the mood for convention. She wanted to know where she stood, and she didn't want to take a chance on due reflection imbuing sense or cowardice.

Last night— Oh, God, last night. She came to an abrupt halt at Conduit Street. *Had* she been thinking of Gideon when Iain was kissing her, touching her, taking her clothes off? Not at first, she was certain of that. But he had been there, in the back of her mind, all the same. Confronted with the flesh-and-blood man she had once desired, whose body was once as familiar to her as her own, had been such a shock. She did not recognise the woman he had tried to recall as herself—or did not want to, more likely. No, she had not been thinking of Gideon when she was with Iain, but she had been using Iain to blot Gideon out.

It had never happened to her before, that—that failure. Her body had betrayed her. And Iain—was it worse for him? She suspected so, from his reaction. That had never happened to her either. Was it her fault, or perhaps Gideon's fault—

which was the same thing, in a way? It was ironic and rather dreadful that something she wanted so much had been such a catastrophe. They could not ignore it, no matter how wretched she felt at the thought of discussing it, for it would taint everything. *Gideon* would taint everything.

Bella had said that Iain had pushed Cordelia towards Gideon as some sort of test. She had also said that men like Iain didn't play games. Cordelia had not precisely been playing games, but she had most decidedly been cautious with the truth. All very well to tell herself it didn't matter, that her past was none of Iain's business, that if she were a man it would not be an issue. The fact was, she was a woman. The fact was, it mattered to her what Iain thought, and it was making her uncomfortable because she was not being honest with the one man in the world she had ever wanted to be honest with.

Which was such a disconcerting thought that Cordelia cut it off immediately, taking off again along Regent Street apace, arriving at Jermyn Street slightly out of breath and so caught up in her inner lecture, to speak the truth and damn the devil, that she was fortunately quite oblivious to the increasing amount of attention she was attracting from the gentlemen she passed.

The lodging-house was situated next door to a tavern— At least, Cordelia hoped it was the right lodging-house, suddenly aware of the fading light and the extreme masculinity of her environment as she waited for her knock to be answered. A suggestion put to her from a very drunk man standing outside the inn made her laugh. She was about to tell him that she doubted any woman capable of such contortions, when a very severe-looking man answered the door. In reply to her query as to the whereabouts of Mr Hunter, his expression turned positively disapproving, but he allowed her to wait—in the narrow hallway—while he ascertained whether Mr Hunter would receive her.

Which meant that Mr Hunter was at home. Cordelia's heart began to bump uncomfortably. The creatures which had been resident in her stomach during that first interview with her father returned. Cicadas, she thought distractedly, that's what she had decided they were. All scales and big eyes and spindly legs and fluttering wings. Revolting things.

'Cordelia. What the hell!' Iain was in his shirt-sleeves, his waistcoat unfastened, his shirt open at the neck. 'You shouldn't be here,' he said as she moved towards the stairs.

'*You* have called on *me* several times at Milvert's. Besides, I rather think we are beyond worrying about the proprieties.' She looked up at him from the bottom step. She liked him better dishevelled. He needed to shave. His hair needed brushing. There was a spot of ink on his cheek. Shadows under his eyes. A golden fuzz of hair on his forearms. The cicadas began to disperse, their leaping and fluttering giving way to a different kind of tension.

'I would have called on you in the morning if you'd sent me a note,' Iain said.

'I did not want to wait until the morning,' Cordelia replied. 'I did not want to have to spend the night wondering if you would come.'

His smile was a little twist of his mouth, the faintest lift of his brow. 'I wouldn't have, this morning.'

'Well, I've saved you the bother this evening. Can we go up?'

He stood back to allow her to precede him. Her skirts brushed against him as she passed. His rooms were practical, simply but comfortably furnished. A fire burned in a small grate. A lamp sat on a table strewn with papers. Through a half-open door she could see a bed, a chest of drawers. She sat down on a worn leather chair by the hearth and pulled off her bonnet, stripped off her gloves. Iain took the seat opposite her, sitting up straight in the chair, his legs curled under it.

Silence. He stared not at her but into the fire. Waiting. The cicadas were back. He looked forbidding, distant. Not a man to accept second-best, Bella had said. Not a man to play games. Cordelia squared her shoulders, physically and metaphorically, and launched in.

'We made a deal, you and I. Our betrothal has nothing to do with this other thing between us. You said yourself that regardless of what happened on—on that front, you would still honour our contract.'

She spoke carefully, clearly, without a tremor.

Businesslike, was what she was aiming for. Man to man. Man to woman? Correct, but not right. Iain was looking at her and not the fire now, but still he said nothing. 'The circumstances which necessitated our contract have not changed,' Cordelia continued. 'I am most eager to meet my sisters in Arabia. I presume you are similarly eager to build your steamships?'

He nodded.

'So when you suggested—last night, when you suggested that our contract be terminated— No, that's not what you said.' Cordelia tugged at a pin which was sticking into her scalp and pulled it free. At a loss as to what to do with it, she stuck it into the arm of the chair. There was a faint tearing sound. 'What you suggested was that I might wish to end it,' she continued. 'But why would I wish to do that, Iain, when it will not get me to Arabia?'

He looked quite nonplussed by this, Cordelia was pleased to see. 'That's not what I meant,' he said.

'I know. You were confusing our—let us call it

the business side or our relationship —with the other, personal aspect of it.'

He gave a short bark of laughter. 'Aye, you're right, but I wasn't the only one.'

'No, you were not. We were both overwrought last night.'

'Overwrought,' Iain said heavily. 'That's one way of describing it.'

Cordelia frowned down at her hands, tightly laced in her lap. 'We made a deal. As far as I am concerned, it stands. We are, for the moment, betrothed, and we are going to Arabia.' She met his gaze unwaveringly. His eyes were very blue. Every time she saw him, it gave her a little shock, the blueness of them. Which was entirely beside the point. 'So unless you have changed your mind?'

Iain ran his hand through his already ruffled hair. 'But this isn't just business, is it? It's not about whether I've changed my mind or not, it's about your future.'

'Which, beyond the duration of our contract, is none of your business,' Cordelia replied tartly. 'And even while we are betrothed—faux betrothed—I do not recall that there was anything in our agreement about meddling in each other's lives. I would not dream of interfering in your matrimonial plans.'

'I don't have any. I've no intentions of getting married.'

'What, never?'

'What, no interest, Lady Cordelia?'

She bit back her angry retort with difficulty. 'Touché,' she said instead. In the silence which followed, the fire crackled. The conversation seemed to be going around in circles. Because despite her resolution, Cordelia realised, she was dancing around the issue. She gave a frustrated little sigh, which came out sounding like a strangled kitten, not that she'd ever actually heard a kitten being strangled, but...

Cordelia got to her feet and paced the short distance to the window. When she got there, when she turned around, then she would speak up. She got there. She turned around. Iain's expression was unreadable. She turned back to the window. Why didn't he say something!

She turned back to face the room and took a

deep breath. 'Two things,' she said. 'I came here to get two things cleared up. First of all, I want to go to Arabia. It is what I want more than anything. I want to be on that ship out of Plymouth in three days' time. So I need to understand once and for all whether you're prepared to go through with our betrothal—faux betrothal?'

Iain shook his head, but his expression had softened considerably. 'Of course I'm prepared to go through with it if you are, that was never in doubt—at least if it was, then I'm sorry. I would have called on you tomorrow to say as much. I was— Last night, we were both, as you said, overwrought. But it's the other matter that still bothers me, Cordelia, for if you are thinking that you and D'Amery have a future together, I don't think sailing off to Arabia with me is very wise.'

'My future plans don't involve Gideon.'

'Are you sure about that?'

'Iain, I couldn't be more sure. Actually, I thought I couldn't be more sure until last night. Now I'm very, very sure indeed.'

'Then it's a deal.'

'Good.' Cordelia took a quick turn to the window and back again. 'Which brings me to the second thing I wanted to clear up.'

'If it's about last night, I don't want to talk about it.'

'It's not exactly a subject I relish either, but—frankly, Iain, I don't want Gideon's ghost following us on to that boat.'

'You admit it was your fault then.'

She could argue with him, but where would that get her? 'I'm not trying to apportion blame, I'm trying to— Look, you were right, for what it's worth. Gideon was there with us, in the room. And I wasn't thinking about him, but I knew you were, and I— So it— I couldn't. And so— But that is not what I— Oh, why is this so confusing!'

It had all seemed so clear when she was hurrying here, but now it was all jumbled in her head. She had his agreement on the betrothal. She would sail with him to Plymouth in just a few days. She could forget about this other thing between them, pretend last night never happened, quit now while she was ahead. Then she remembered Bella, complacently telling her that she had chosen too difficult a path. Maybe so, but it was *her* path.

The cicadas in Cordelia's stomach had multiplied. Bred? She shuddered at the image she had inadvertently conjured up. She clasped her hands behind her back, very tightly. She wished fervently she had a glass of wine. She imagined taking a steadying sip and felt her resolve return.

'Iain.'

The change in her tone alerted him. She wasn't going to let this go. He couldn't help admiring her for that. As he watched her take another turn to the window and back, a total of eight steps, he was almost relieved to have the topic which had kept him awake the entire night forced on him.

'Iain.' Cordelia took another deep breath. 'Last night, I was wrong. I didn't realise it at the time, but I was using you. I was trying to—to reclaim the night, I think, to make it ours, to push Gideon away from—from centre stage. I'm sorry.'

Guilt and admiration made him feel about six inches high. 'It wasn't just you. There were two of us there in—in the bedchamber. You were right, I did *go on and on.* I just couldn't let it go.'

'And there, as the Bard would say, is the rub.' Cordelia managed a faint smile. 'I won't lie, Iain, I won't rewrite my history in order to make things easier between us. That's what I was trying to do, I think—not lying so much as failing to tell the whole truth. It's what Bella does now. Do you know, her daughter is not my father's child?'

'You seem remarkably sanguine about that fact.'

'I'm shocked, of course I am, but when she told me the circumstances...'

Cordelia related them. Iain listened with growing astonishment tinged, it had to be admitted, with a sense of satisfaction that Armstrong was getting his just desserts, though the satisfaction waned when he realised that he was applying standards that were more than double when condoning Lady Armstrong for something far worse than he was condemning her stepdaughter.

'Bella blackmailed my father into acknowledging Isabella as his own, and my father allowed himself to be blackmailed. She threatened to expose him as a cuckold, but he could just as easily have labelled her an adulteress. He chose not to, because—I think because he felt he owed it to her. She had done her duty in giving him the sons he craved. It was due payment, not bribery. That's how Bella sees it anyway. I'm pretty certain my father does too. He would not play along with it elsewise.' Cordelia was frowning. 'I'm not like that, Iain. Unorthodox, Bella called me. I suppose I am, though as you know, I prefer to call it independent. Bella thinks that she is making her own terms with her life, but she's not, she's— I don't know, playing within someone else's set of rules. Paying lip service. Lying. Whatever you want to call it, I won't do it. I won't pretend. I thought you had no right to know about Gideon, I thought it was history, but maybe the Scots have a point.'

'There's no need of history when memories are long,' Iain explained in response to her puzzled look, realising he'd spoken the Gaelic first.

'You speak like a native.'

'My mother was from the Highlands. I was born and bred in Glasgow. I only have a few words.' It was more than he ever told anyone, and he was as taken aback as Cordelia by this revelation. Iain resorted to throwing more unnecessary coals on the fire to hide his confusion. His mother again. He had to be rid of this association. 'I was jealous,' he said abruptly, 'I had no right to be and I'm not proud of the fact. As you keep reminding me, our betrothal is not real, but there it is, I was jealous.'

Now that it was out, he felt better. Iain began to straighten the papers on his table, then realised this was one of Cordelia's habits. 'It's— That— What happened— What didn't happen in the bedchamber— It's never happened to me before.' He could feel himself flushing like a wee lassie. 'I couldn't sleep for thinking about it, if you must know.'

'I can see you haven't.' She touched his face briefly, her fingertips soft on his bristles. 'I didn't sleep either.'

'You look a hell of a lot better for it than I do.'

'Perhaps I'm more practised in concealment. Bella thinks I am. She said that I was always an inventive prevaricator. I fear she was right.'

'Poor wee soul. You really have had quite a day of it.'

Cordelia grimaced. 'Home truths, the kind I hate the most. I notice you don't defend me.'

Iain caught her hand. 'I don't doubt you had just cause.' Her fingers curled into his. It was the simplest thing, the most basic of contact, and yet more intimate than anything that had happened last night. The only other hand he'd ever held had been Jeannie's. Her wee hand was so tiny, the fingers chubby, the nails grimy. Closing his eyes, he could feel it, hot and usually sticky, always trusting. He gazed down at the slenderness of Cordelia's fingers twined in his. Trust. 'I had a sister once.'

He felt the shock of his revelation in the way her fingers tightened around his. 'Jeannie,' he said, though her name came out sounding strangled. He couldn't remember the last time he'd said it aloud. It was the reason he'd been unable to name a single one of his ships after her. 'Jeannie,' he said again.

'What happened to her?'

He couldn't answer, but his face must have spoken for him. 'Oh, Iain.' Cordelia lifted his hand to her lips, pressing a kiss to his taut knuckles. 'I'm so sorry. Was she very young?'

'Seven.' He squeezed his eyes shut, shaking his head. Already he had said more than he had to anyone. Already it was too much.

'It's why you are so determined I shall see my own sisters?' Cordelia kissed his hand again, her fingers twined even tighter around his.

'Aye.' He had a grip on himself now, and forced his eyes open. Hers were wide, fixed on his, more grey than blue today, shadowed from her sleepless night. She'd not lied about that. She had not lied at all. Yes, she had omitted salient facts, but faced with his reaction, who could blame her? Didn't he have his own shameful secrets? Cordelia had at least had the courage to reveal hers, while he…

Iain reluctantly disengaged his fingers. 'It's because of Jeannie that I feel so strongly you've a right to go to Arabia, but she's not the only reason I'm here, pretending to be your future husband, Cordelia. I tried to kid myself on, told myself that I was being noble, and I tried to pretend that it was about my ships as much as your sisters, but last night proved me wrong. It's about us. This— What did you call it?'

'Personal aspect?'

'Aye, that.' Iain grinned. 'I can't believe we're having this conversation. I'm a Glasgow docker, when all's said and done.'

'I think you're underestimating yourself.'

'A wee bit, maybe.' Iain realised he'd been aligning his papers again. Cordelia's habit. 'I've said some things that I'm ashamed of—not because they were lies, but because I've felt them. It is a man's world, and I'm but a man. Humbling as it is, my reactions last night were about as clichéd and unthinking as it's possible to be. You've not once cast my experience up at me.'

'Rather because I haven't let my mind dwell on it than because it doesn't affect me,' Cordelia interrupted, looking faintly uncomfortable.

'I'm glad to hear it, but all that goes to show is that you're a lot more honest than me.' He meant it as a compliment, but she looked even more uncomfortable. 'What have I said?'

'I— It's nothing.'

'It's because I'm rambling, isn't it? I'm trying to get to the point, but it's difficult.' Iain strode over to the window and back. Six steps. Two less than Cordelia. 'Look, I'll stop beating about the bush. I want you. I've never wanted any woman the way I want you, but I don't want that—that man to come between us. I need to be sure I'm not just paying lip service.'

'Pretending to come to terms with it, then casting it up later, you mean?' she said drily.

He flinched, but did not deny it.

'At least we know where we stand now.' She moved past him to pick up her bonnet and gloves, her expression for once quite closed to him.

'No, you misunderstand me. I'm saying that I'm wrong and you're right, but I'm also saying I need time to be sure of that. And for you to be sure of that.'

'Yes. You know I can't help feeling that all this talk of something that simply happened that day in Glasgow is putting the whole thing out of proportion. When all is said and done, it is simply an act that people do every day.'

'Is this your attempt to sound like a man?'

'It's my attempt to put things in proportion.'

'And to remind me, no doubt, that you're not interested in our faux betrothal becoming real.'

Cordelia eyed him warily. 'You don't need reminding. You are not interested in marriage any more than I am. Besides, I seem to recall that we agreed familiarity would breed indifference.'

Iain swore under his breath. 'If we go on at this rate, we'll end up hating each other. I think you'd better go.'

Her expression clouded. 'I see.'

'You don't. You're not the only one who struggles with home truths, and you've dealt out a fair few this evening. It was a brave thing to do, to come here and talk to me like you did, even if it wasn't quite the done thing, and I am very glad you did, but I can't look at you without thinking—frankly, wanting to prove to you that last night was an aberration. I need a bit of thinking time and I need to be alone, that's all, and before you ask, for the last time, I'm not going to renege on our contract. As far as the world and your father are concerned, we are betrothed, and in three days' time, we'll be aboard that ship sailing from Plymouth.'

'Bella suspects it is a ruse, our engagement.'

'You know, there's a bit of me that would like to consign Bella to the devil.'

'There's a bit of Bella that would like to take my place by your side. If she were betrothed to you, she told me, she would take care to remain there.'

Iain shuddered. 'Spare me.'

He followed her from the lodging house, escorting her out into St James's, where he hailed a passing hackney. Back in his rooms, he struggled with a gust of longing for a good dram. The knowledge that the dram he'd get would be second-rate, even if they had such a thing as whisky in the London taverns, held him back, rather than the usual memory of what the stuff had done to his father.

Feisty, he'd called Cordelia and he'd not been wrong. He should be honoured that she'd confided in him and he was, as well as shaken up, turned inside out by what he'd learned about himself and—aye, still plain jealous. *There is no comparison,* she'd said last night. She had turned D'Amery down. It was Iain she wanted. He was the only man she'd ever told the truth to. The only man she'd ever been betrothed to. Faux betrothed. But all the same, it was more than she had given D'Amery.

He put a guard over the fire and returned to the table strewn with papers feeling just a bit better. He picked up his pen and dipped it in the ink-pot. As to last night—an aberration, just as he'd said. She was spot on as to the cause of it too. A perceptive wee thing, was Cordelia. A mite too perceptive for comfort. Ink dripped on to the letter he'd been writing in response to one of the many notes he'd received today from men he had failed to meet at Armstrong's excuse for a small family gathering. He blotted it hurriedly.

'Devil take it, when did I become someone who has to pick apart every idle thought!' Iain kicked back his chair and strode through to his bed-chamber, retrieving his coat from the back of the door. He would not go in search of whisky, but there was nothing wrong with a bit of food. With his stomach full and at least one of his bodily needs satisfied, maybe he'd get some perspective.

Chapter Eight

It took HMS *Pique* four long weeks to sail to Gibraltar, and a further six days to reach Zante, during which time Cordelia, the only female on board, was forced to spend most of her time alone in her cabin for lack of what their stern captain termed adequate supervision. Iain, whose enthusiasm for the power of steam over sail had offended the ancient mariner, fared little better. Arriving at the island close to Greece known locally as Zakynthos, currently a British protectorate, they were both overwhelmingly relieved to quit the claustrophobic atmosphere of the frigate, and to make the most of the brief interlude before they continued their journey.

Zante was a beautiful island. The Mediterranean sun was hot. Not the tentative warmth of an English summer, but the true dry heat of the south. The sea itself had turned from azure to turquoise as they sailed into shallower waters. The town of whitewashed stone houses, seemingly pristine in the bright sunlight, stretched out from the harbour, which nestled in the crook of a rugged range of low-lying hills, the dark green, velvetlike tree cover giving way to a burnt brown halfway up. The distinctive wooden fishing boats, their pointed prows and narrow hulls testament to the island's Venetian occupation, crowded the white sands of the beach, while a large frigate, several cargo ships and a host of other brightly painted boats of indeterminate purpose fought for mooring space. The air was fresh, tangy with salt, pine and pungent with the recently landed catch. The ruffling breeze quieted the heat, taming it from the fierce, ovenlike blast which ruled the island's interior, to a beguiling warmth that heated without smothering, making the skin tingle and tighten but not burn.

Cordelia perched on the jetty, watching the fishermen repairing their nets, dangling her bare feet into the water. England and all its conventions and inhibitions were almost impossible to imagine. 'I've missed this so much,' she said, turning her face up to the sun. 'The heat, I mean, and the sky. It is so very blue compared to England. The light is so very dazzling, yet it has such clarity.'

Beside her, Iain, who had just returned from finalising the arrangements for their onward journey, shaded his eyes from the glare. 'It certainly makes Scotland seem *gie driech*,' he said. 'Though for shades of grey, there's none can compete with home.'

'I know. Though I have to say, for shades of green, there is nothing like the Highlands.'

'I'd forgotten you'd been there.'

'I have written the guidebook to prove it too. You must take a look at it sometime. I'd like to know whether you think I've captured the spirit of the place.'

'The Governor has invited us to dine with him.'

He had deliberately turned the subject. Cordelia slanted a look at him from under the wide brim of her sun hat. His eyes were impossibly blue, almost the colour of the sky above them. He returned her gaze blandly enough, but the message was clear. Unwilling to spoil the moment, she chose to accept it and, taking his hand, scrabbled to her feet. 'Must we? I can't tell you how sick and tired I am of being chaperoned. I am not sure which the captain feared most, that I would seduce his entire crew, or that our being caught in—*in flagrante delicto* would rouse his crew to mutiny. Either way, he significantly overestimated my charms.'

Iain smiled. 'On the contrary, I think it is you who underestimate them. It's not just that you're a wee beauty, which you must know perfectly well from looking in the mirror, but there's something about you that makes a man's thoughts turn to—what did you call it—*in flagrante delicto*. I know mine do.'

'Iain!' Fire stole over her cheeks which had nothing to do with the Mediterranean sun, though the truth was, she was much more relieved than embarrassed, having spent the better part of their voyage telling herself that Iain was most likely relieved by their forced separation, and that if he was, then so too was she.

'Cordelia. There were times at sea when I

thought one look would send me up in flames,' he said softly. 'That smile of yours, it positively smoulders, did I ever tell you that?'

'No.'

They were standing on the quayside. Iain was dressed formally, in trousers and jacket of pale brown linen, with a white shirt and even a stock tied around his neck. His face was tanned, his eyes seemed to turn bluer every day. She wanted to kiss him. Even though it was every bit as impossible here on the jetty as it had been on the ship, she wanted to kiss him.

'One good thing about all that time I spent wandering the decks on the *Pique*,' he said, 'I got the chance to think. We're very alike, you and I.'

His expression was serious. 'What do you mean?' Cordelia asked warily.

'We're both independent. We don't like to have our minds made up for us. It's one of the things I admire about you most, your determination to go your own road. If you'd been less yourself ten years ago, you would have taken the easy route and gone back to your family with your tail between your legs, or you'd have married D'Amery.'

'If I'd been less myself, as you call it, I'd have married one of the men from my father's list.'

'I hadn't thought of that,' Iain said, looking appalled.

'I'd be a stout matron with a full nursery and an empty bed just like Bella. Though Bella is no longer stout.'

'And her bed is no longer empty,' Iain added.

Cordelia screwed up her face. 'I know I am nearly thirty years of age, but there is something simply not right about discussing such delicate matters when the subject is one's stepmother who is, let us not forget, making a cuckold of my father.'

'Not quite his just desserts for the way he's treated the women of his family, but it's a start,' Iain said grimly. 'But right now, I'm not much interested in Armstrong. I'm trying to tell you that I owe you an apology.' He mopped his brow with a large, very clean and very white square of cotton. 'You were in the right of it to refuse D'Amery both times, and you were in the right of it when you told me it was none of my business what you'd done with the man— I mean when you said that you had...'

'Enjoyed carnal knowledge,' Cordelia said, pleased to hear that she sounded matter of fact, hoping her hat would hide the colour stealing over her cheeks.

'Aye, that.' Iain mopped his brow again, though there was no trace of sweat. 'But I need to be completely honest with you, Cordelia. While I'm glad, more than happy, that you enjoy it, I'd rather not think about you enjoying it with anyone other than me. You can call me a hypocrite, but...'

'If I did, I'd have to apply the description to myself. I know you have been with other women. I know there will be other women after me, but I don't want to think about them.' Cordelia caught at his hand as he made another unnecessary swipe at his brow. 'So I'm forgiven?'

Iain shook his head vehemently. 'There's nothing to forgive you for. It's me who is begging pardon of you. I did judge you, and far too quickly. I'm sorry.'

The relief she felt took her aback, for she had been trying very hard not to think of how she would feel if Iain had judged her as she suspected most others would. 'Thank you.'

'Are we sorted now, do you think?'

She thought about it. She thought about telling him about the other men. It was not only a cowardly desire not to spoil the moment that held her back, nor yet the fact that she was in the habit of keeping her own confidences. They simply didn't matter to her, and Iain had made it very clear he didn't want to know. So she quelled the tiny niggling doubt, reminding her shrinking conscience that she and Iain were not really betrothed, that their future together extended only so far as Arabia, and nodded her head. 'I think we are,' she said.

Iain smiled. One of those smiles that darkened his eyes and gave her that feeling she had eventually decided to call slumberous. He had taken hold of her hand again. She took a step closer to him, and there it was between them, that tingling tension, that acute awareness, that yearning.

She tilted her face as he dipped his. Their lips met. Warm skin, salty with sweat. Kisses were so different under this sky, under this sun. Freer from constraint. It was a climate made for kissing. His tongue touched her lower lip. She opened her mouth to him. Scorching heat, contrasting with the delicacy of the kiss, made her shiver. She felt him shudder too. He reached for her, his hands spanning the flair of her hips where her corset ended, but almost immediately let her go.

'I have no ambition to become a show for our former shipmates.' He nodded in the direction of the *Pique,* easily distinguishable in the harbour, despite the crowd of other ships.

Cordelia swallowed her disappointment. 'Must we really dine with the Governor? I know it's rude and ungrateful of me, but I don't want to make polite conversation about England and politics.'

'I don't think we can avoid it,' Iain said. 'Once I gave him your father's letter of introduction, he insisted we spend the night at his house, and since we don't sail for Athens until the morning tide, I said yes. Besides, I can't lose sight of why I'm here. The man might prove useful.'

Cordelia sighed, leaning on Iain's arm as she pulled on the rope sandals she had purchased from one of the host of vendors who had clustered round the ship in Gibraltar. 'You are so practical.'

'And insightful, I hope,' he said,

'I suppose you are going to claim to have read my mind again?'

'Rather, I'm hoping we are of the same mind. Look over there.'

Iain pointed at the steeply shelving sandy beach. 'Fishing boats,' Cordelia said, puzzled.

'And they are not needed again until the morning. How do you fancy a wee trip?'

'Can you sail one of these?'

Iain laughed. 'Well, obviously I'll have to install an engine, but—for goodness' sake Cordelia, have a wee bit of faith. Do you want to go? It will be just the two of us, mind.'

Her heart did a silly leap, and seemed to catch in her throat. *Just the two of us.*

'If you have changed your mind,' Iain said, 'I need to know. For myself, just so we're clear, I don't think I can bear to wait another day of being with you and not touching you. But if it's just me…'

'It's not just you,' Cordelia said hurriedly. Not something she would ever have admitted to any man before, for she enjoyed the dance—or she had, until she met Iain. No games. Her heart was already fluttering with anticipation.

The merest flicker there was, in response from him. A tightening of his expression, a widening of his eyes, a flare of heat which she would have missed had she not been looking for it. He took her hand without another word and led her down the jetty to the beach, handed some silver coins over to a young boy, who stowed a wicker basket in the bottom of the boat. Cordelia clambered in. Iain and the boy hefted the boat down into the shallow waves, and then Iain too jumped aboard. A final push from the boy, and they were off, bumping over the wavelets and out into the bay.

Iain divested himself of jacket, waistcoat, stock, shoes and stockings, stowing them neatly in the prow of the boat where the nets would customarily be held, before tending to the single sail. Cordelia, perched aft on a narrow wooden board, was, for about the hundredth time since they had sailed from Plymouth, deeply thankful that she had abandoned the layers of petticoats and undergarments necessary to fashion, and pulled her skirts tightly around her knees, for the breeze was already picking up.

It ruffled Iain's shirt, making the soft cambric cling to his frame, giving her the tantalising glimpses of his outline she'd been trying not to notice on board the *Pique.* Now, Cordelia allowed her gaze to rest on him as he focused his attention on sailing them out of the bay along the north coast of the island, on the breadth of his shoulders, the corded sinews of his forearms, the narrowness of his waist and the tautness of his buttocks too, as he bent over the side of the boat to retrieve a trailing rope.

They hugged the shallower waters of the coastline, waters so clear that the sandy bottom could be seen, and the glittering shoals of fish too, darting in formation backwards, then forwards, disappearing under the boat and emerging out the other side. Away from the harbour town of Zante, the island rose steeply out of the sea, high white cliffs topped with their velvetlike carpet of brown and green, eroded by the Mediterranean into vaulted caves and intriguing narrow fissures. The wind teased her hair, the salt stung her eyes and the sight of Iain heated her blood. Cordelia had never felt so elated nor so relaxed, a curious mixture. There was not another boat in sight. Not a soul could be seen on the island's clifftops. They were as alone as if they were at the ends of the earth. Or in paradise.

She laughed to herself, and tilted her head back, closing her eyes, allowing her skin to drink in the sun and the salt and the spray, pulling the pins from her hair and leaning so far back that the ends of it trailed in the water.

Iain wiped the spray from his eyes and tightened his hold on the sail ropes. She was light in the water and highly manoeuvrable, this wee fishing boat, though he doubted she'd survive a day in the rough coasts at home. He cast a quick glance behind him to tell Cordelia so, and his words died in his throat. She was leaning back, her hair, glinting gold from the weeks in the sun, streaming out behind her, long strands of it trailing in the sea. Like a mermaid. Or a Selkie. Or a siren.

Her skin was lightly tanned, and it suited her, and she didn't seem to mind losing her lady-like paleness. There was something incredibly sensual about the line of her body, the arch of her back, the line of her throat, the swell of her breasts. His mouth was dry. He was embarrassingly hard.

Dragging his gaze away, he forced himself to concentrate on navigating. The bay the boy had told him about was almost completely encircled by the cliffs with only a narrow opening where the cross-currents made the boat skitter and bump, making Cordelia squeal, laugh, clutch at the sides of the craft. Inside the shelter of the cove, the water was almost still, the pale gold of the sands glittering in the blistering heat. Iain dropped the sail and jumped out, waist-deep in the water, to pull them the final few yards to the shore.

Without waiting for dry land, Cordelia joined him in the shallows. Her hair hung damp on the thin fabric of her dress, making it cling at the shoulders, the neck, drawing attention to the sweet undulations of her breasts. She was still laughing from the exhilaration of their landing, running on to the sand, shaking out her soaking skirts, showing him tantalising glimpses of ankles and calves. He pulled the boat higher on to the sand, though there seemed to be little tide to worry about, and hauled the basket containing their meal from its hiding place. There was a cave, no more than a low opening, but suffice to shade them from the sun, and to stop their food from spoiling. He pushed the basket into the dark, and his discarded clothes. He spread out the rough blanket the boy's mother had given him, at the mouth of the cave.

Cordelia was standing on the sand, gazing out at the water of the bay. Only the smallest slice of sea was visible through the embracing arm of the cliff. They were completely private. Iain was suddenly nervous. The sand was hot against his bare feet as he went to join her. She turned to him, and he saw his own apprehensions reflected on her face. He was about to tell her that they could forget about it, simply enjoy the cove and their lunch, not because he wanted to, but because the fear of failure had cooled his blood. Then she smiled at him, that smouldering smile of hers, and he stopped thinking and took her in his arms, and kissed her.

She tasted of salt. Of sunshine. Of heat. Exotic. Different, yet entirely the same. There was the same sense of knowing, of fitting, of rightness in their kiss, as there had been that first time, in the hotel in Glasgow. As if they were made for this. Only it was heightened, much more heightened, by the waiting, and released from constraint by the distance and the sunshine. Though he was ravenous for her, their kisses had the languorous, almost leisurely pace of the Mediterranean, tasting, relishing, sensual.

He ran his fingers through the thick, damp tresses of her hair. He felt her hands flutter over his back, up the knots of his spine, flatten over the wings of his shoulder-blades. He lifted his head, and she looked at him, wide-eyed, passion-flushed. Her blatant desire for him sent his own desire rocketing. With a low growl he barely recognised, he picked her up and carried into the shade.

'Like a caveman,' she said, but teasingly, rubbing herself against him as he set her down.

'I hope I can manage to be a bit more civilised,' he said.

Cordelia smiled, catlike and provocative. 'I rather hope you can't.'

Her dress was of pale blue. The bodice buttoned up the front. She began to unfasten it, button by button, all the time watching him. The sleeves were long and tight. She had to wriggle to free herself of them, for the sea made them cling to her skin. As who would not, Iain thought, watching, fascinated, his heart pounding. The skirt of her gown fell to the ground. He had no idea how she'd unfastened it. Her hair, already drying in the heat, was the colour of newly varnished wood streaked with ripe wheat.

Her throat and her hands were tanned, but the swell of her breasts above her corset was creamy, untouched by the sun. He ached to touch her, but he was mesmerised by the way she touched herself, by the way she undressed for him, all the time looking at him, watching him, testing him. His chest heaved with the effort of breathing. His erection strained inside his trousers. He watched.

Her corsets also fastened up the front. She pulled at the laces. Her own breathing was fast, shallow. He was fascinated by the quiver of her breasts. Freed of her stays, she stood before him only in her shift and her drawers. He reached for her now, but only to turn her towards the light, to reveal the body beneath her undergarments. The swell of her breasts. The hard nub of her nipples. The indentation of her waist. The feminine roundness of her belly, the flare of her hips. He traced her shape with his fingers. She shuddered, her eyes closing momentarily. There was a stillness in the air, as if time were suspended. Then their eyes met once more, and the thing which had bound them from the start yanked hard, and they moved together of one accord.

Kissing. No longer languorous, but passionate. Tongues touching, entwined and then thrusting, in a carnal echo of what they sought. Iain tugged frantically at his clothes, fumbling and pulling at the fastenings, all the time kissing her, for he could never imagine having enough of her kisses.

He was naked before she, but not long before. Her shift tore, and fell on to the blanket, was kicked backwards into the damp sand of the cave with her drawers, and the kissing paused as they looked, blatantly looked at each other. Her eyes travelled over the length of his body, and he felt his engorged shaft stiffen further in response. Her nipples were dusky pink, puckered. He took one in his mouth, and sucked, drawing a soft moan from her, making her arch her back. He laid her down then, on the blanket, and began to kiss her. Mouth. Throat. Cupping her breasts to trace their shape with his tongue, before licking, then suckling, first one nipple then the other.

She reached for him, arched under him, rubbed the soft curls of her sex against him. He was in an agony of wanting to thrust into her, but he was too in an agony of wanting this to be different, better. *'Wheesht,'* he said, when she said his name urgently, 'patience.'

'I don't feel patient,' Cordelia said, digging her fingers into his buttocks.

'Tell me,' he said raggedly, 'tell me then how you feel.'

Iain was lying over her, his body covering but not quite enveloping hers. His skin was hot. She could feel the tip of his shaft against her thighs. *Tell me,* he said, and it was part tease and part challenge, the way he looked at her. She had never felt so aroused. She shifted, just enough to allow the hard length of him between her thighs. 'Urgent,' she said, smiling back at him. 'I feel urgent.'

She felt the rumble of his laughter in his chest, vibrating against her breasts. 'I doubt you could feel anywhere near as urgent as I do. Have you any idea what that does to me?'

She arched her back, thrusting up under him. 'Yes.'

Iain swore. Then he kissed her, hard, on the mouth. She kissed him back equally hard. Already, she could feel her climax building, coiling. She clenched tight. 'Iain.'

His eyes were dark, his pupils large, his cheeks flushed. She felt him readying himself to thrust, and opened her legs to receive him. Then he laughed, though it was a strange, harsh sound, and shook his head. 'Did I not promise to prove to you that I had some finesse?'

'Iain, I don't care about finesse. I— Iain!'

He was still between her legs, but no longer touching her. He was still kissing her, but not her mouth. He was kissing her throat again, her breasts again, his tongue, his fingers, teasing her nipples, making her ache, that sweet dull ache that plucked, strained, twisted into a slow, pulsing thrum between her legs.

He kissed her belly. Then he pushed her legs further apart, and entered her, not with his shaft, but with his tongue. She bucked under him and called out in surprise. Then his mouth covered her in the most intimate way, licking into her, over her, and her cry became something more guttural.

His mouth did wonderful things. A new world of kissing. She was vaguely aware of herself moaning, pleading unashamedly for him not to stop, not to stop, when he slowed, waited, started again. She was so tense she thought she might break apart, wanting, not wanting it to end as it built, coiling, coiling, so intense it was on the edge of pleasure, like fingernails on a slate, until she could hold on no more, and he seemed to sense it, and held her, one hand on each of her thighs, licking into her just there, exactly where she needed him, and she came suddenly and so violently that she bucked beneath him, again, and then again and then again, in sharp bursts, which reverberated and ebbed, like consecutive waves, catching each other as they broke and retreated.

She had no idea if she had cried out. She lay panting, spreadeagled, for long seconds or minutes, completely caught up in the shock, the wonder of this most extraordinary experience. She thought she was spent, but when she opened her eyes and saw him kneeling between her, his erection jutting thick and hard, her body began to clamour instantly for another sort of completion.

She smiled at him, that look she knew unravelled him. It was a powerful thing, that smile. He leaned over her and kissed her. She twined her arms around his neck and wrapped her legs around him and, taking him quite unawares, rolled him over on to his back.

He was pressing between her legs once more. This time it was he who arched urgently under her, his expression tight, his desire for completion unbearable. Cordelia kissed his mouth. She moved her hips provocatively. He groaned. 'How urgent do you feel, Iain?'

He sensed her intentions before she moved, and grabbed at her bottom, but she wriggled free of him. She kissed his neck. His chest. His nipples. She kissed her way down his rib cage, kneeling between his legs, in a deliberate echo of how he had kissed her. She leaned over him, grazing her nipples over his chest, sending *frissons* of pleasure rippling through her blood to feed the fire between her thighs. Below her, Iain shuddered. His face was rigid with the effort of control. She felt powerful and, despite her climax, intensely aroused.

She licked into his navel. A thin line of soft hair arrowed down from there. She hesitated. She had never once imagined doing such a thing, never mind attempting it. She sat back, taking him in her hand, curling her fingers around his girth. Such satinlike skin, and beneath he was solid. Not like rock or steel, something very different. She stroked him. He jerked. Her touch was reflected in his eyes. She could see him contracting, tightening. She could feel her insides doing the same. And tingling. A warning. Yet she stroked him again.

'Cordelia.'

Urgent, his voice was. Truly urgent. Yet once again she could not resist. She leant over him, touching the tip of his shaft to the tip of her tongue.

Iain swore. 'Cordelia. I don't think…'

The muscles in his neck were standing out. She couldn't. She didn't want to. What she wanted was what he wanted. Now. She let him go, slid over him, took him inside her.

He went higher than she expected. He was harder. She was tighter. She was already shivering, clenching, shaking, with her impending climax. His hands were on her waist, bracing her.

She lifted herself, and he helped her, almost to the tip, and then down.

He said her name. No one had ever said her name like that. 'Come with me,' she said, the same command he'd given her. He nodded. Gripping. So thick inside her. She lifted herself, and came down on him harder, thrusting her hips forward, drawing a gasp from him. Again, tilting, so that he was higher inside her, and she came instantly, astonishingly, wildly, crying out her delight, the pulsing of her climax triggering his, his warning cry heeded just in time, as he rolled her from him, shuddering to completion beside her, and she lay, eyes wide, watching what she had done to him, feeling utterly replete.

Cordelia stretched voluptuously. Her whole body was singing with satisfaction. Beside her, Iain rolled on to his side and propped his head on his hand. 'Well?' she asked, buoyed up with that heady combination of pleasure and the utter lack of inhibition that seemed to have crept so insidiously over her since leaving England.

Iain ran a finger over the length of her arm,

from shoulder to wrist, his knuckles just grazing her breast, making her nipple pucker in response. 'Well,' he said, 'it certainly was worth waiting for, if that's what you're asking.'

She tried to stop it, but the smile of contentment seemed to push its way over her entire body. 'I feel as if I am glowing,' Cordelia said.

'Sunburn,' Iain said. He ran his finger back up her arm, wrist to shoulder, this time slowing over her breast.

She stared fascinated by her own response to him. The lightest of touches, and it set off a delicious *frisson* inside her. 'We are in the shade.' Her voice had taken on that breathy quality, yet she had only just…

She reached over, copying his action. Shoulder to wrist, her knuckles grazing his chest. Then back up again, more slowly. His shaft stirred. 'You are not inclined to wait another year before we repeat the exercise,' she said.

He caught her hand at the wrist. 'I'm inclined to wait a wee bit longer. Apart from anything else, I'm hungry.'

'And I'm sandy,' Cordelia said, becoming aware

of that fact for the first time. In fact, she seemed to be lying more in sand than on the blanket.

'You're not the only one.' Iain rolled over and got to his feet, hauling her with him. 'Come on then, first things first.'

She gazed out longingly at the sparkling blue of the sea. 'You can't be serious.'

He grinned. 'What, have you suddenly developed inhibitions, Lady Cordelia?'

She had. It was all very well to lie here naked in the aftermath of making love, but to stride out, wearing only one's skin, into the bright sunlight… She caught Iain's eye, and saw that he had once again read her mind far too accurately. There was only one thing for it. Though her inclination was to cross her arms over her breasts and run, she forced herself to walk, arms firmly at her sides, slowly down the beach, praying that no other curious sightseer or fisherman would choose this moment to pay a visit to the cove. The thought that she would have been utterly oblivious to any number of sightseers and fishermen a few moments earlier, made her blush from her toes to the tips of her ears, and sent her into the water at a rush.

It was not cold, but it felt it. Her feet sank into the soft golden sand. The water lapped at her ankles, her knees, made her gasp as it reached the top of her thighs and then her waist. She turned to see Iain not far behind her. A rather delightful sight that made her forget all about the possibility of being discovered.

'I've only ever swum in the Clyde,' he said. 'Even in the height of summer, it's cold enough to freeze the— It's freezing.'

'I've never been in the sea before,' Cordelia said.

'So this is a first.'

He caught her by the waist, pulling her up against him. Cool water lapped on warm skin. 'The second first of the day,' Cordelia said.

'Second? What was the— Oh, you mean that.' Iain laughed, pulling her closer. 'Did you like it?'

'I believe I've already pointed out that you're the last man on earth to need his ego boosted, Iain Hunter.'

'All the same, I like to be sure. I wouldn't like to do it again, if you didn't like it.'

He hitched her legs up around his waist, and slid his hands under her bottom, supporting her in the water. She wriggled, enjoying the lapping of the sea against them, between them, enjoying the way their skin clung. Then he began to walk out. 'What are you doing?'

'Admit you liked it.'

The water was up to her chest now.

'I will not be blackmailed.' She was laughing, but she was also clinging tight, for she could feel her body trying to float away. 'Iain, I can't swim.' There was a note of panic in her voice.

He stopped. 'I can. Don't you trust me?'

In the clearness of the water, she could see the reflection of their joined bodies shimmering. She could feel the bump of his heart against her skin. Above them, the sun beat down. His expression was serious. She looked down at him, and something twisted inside her. This was the kind of day she would remember in all its perfection when she was old. She didn't want it to end.

'Cordelia?'

She blinked. 'Of course I trust you,' she said, 'but if you don't mind, I think I'd rather stand on my own two feet.'

'As ever.' He waded a few paces into the shallows and let her slither down. 'I'm going for a swim.'

Had she offended him? It was difficult to tell, but she did not want to take the risk of spoiling the day. 'Iain,' she said, catching his hand as he turned away. 'I admit it. I liked it rather a lot.'

He laughed, as she had intended he would, and waded out, executing a shallow dive. She watched him, dipping under the waves so that the water covered her to her neck. He swam splashily across the bay twice, then turned to float, arms spread, gazing up at the sky. Though she had no desire to swim, she envied him this, for it looked so relaxing. It could surely not be that difficult. She tried to emulate him, but her body refused to straighten, and her bottom pulled her down. She stood up, spluttering and cursing. Iain was still floating, blissfully unaware. She tried again. This time the problem seemed to be that her neck wouldn't straighten. The effect was the same, only she sank deeper. On the third try, she went completely under, and emerged, hair dripping, eyes stinging, spluttering the very, very salty water she had inhaled, to find Iain standing only a few yards away, laughing.

'I could have drowned!'

'I'd have saved you. You look like a mermaid.'

'Drowned rat, more like. And you were far too intent on enjoying yourself out there to save me.'

He pushed her hair from her eyes. 'I wasn't enjoying myself out there. I was recovering my strength, so that we could both enjoy ourselves. Together.'

He pulled her to him and kissed her, and she discovered that her body too, was fully recovered. She took his hand, and made to wade into the shore, but Iain shook his head. 'It's a day for firsts,' he said, stopping in the shallows, and pulling her down on to the sand.

He kissed her with as much hunger as he had kissed her before, and she found in herself the same hunger. His hands stroked her body, rousing her into passion, as the waves licked at her feet, her calves, her knees, and the grit of the sand in her back contrasted with the soft sureness of his touch. This time it was seamless, the transition from kissing to touching to joining. They moved with the fluidity of sea creatures, arching and bowing, clinging, skin to skin, muscle to muscle, the rhythm of the tide, ebbing and flowing, their passion not violent but something deeper.

When she started to come, he kissed her, drawing her climax out from deep within her, holding back until she was done, rolling away from her into the sea as his own shook him. Turning his back on her, as if he did not want her to see what he felt.

A day for firsts, he'd said, which meant that the other two had not been, not for him. Cordelia shivered. Once before, and only once she had felt this emptiness, a sense of loss. She got to her feet, covering her breasts with her hands, and made for the cave and her clothes. It was the cold, that was all. She was not a mermaid, and she had been in the sea too long.

Watching from the shallows as Cordelia walked across the sand, her shoulders hunched, her arms protectively around herself, Iain wanted to run after her, to console her, but for what? He wanted her more than ever, but he was pretty certain anything more between them would be a mistake.

It frightened him, what he'd felt making love to her. The first time today—that had been—well, it had been powerful. Every bit as good as he'd remembered, but on reflection not at all what he remembered. It was the second time that left him feeling wrung out, and that's what he'd felt the next day in Glasgow more than a year ago now. Turned inside out. As if some sort of storm had passed through him. Confused. And strangely desolate.

By the time he joined her, Cordelia was dressed, sitting tucked tightly into herself on the rug. Iain pulled on his own clothes hurriedly. The picnic he had so carefully selected was delicious, smoked kid, little parcels of rice and lamb wrapped in vine leaves, a salty cheese, olives and flat bread, but neither of them did justice to it.

They talked in a desultory manner of their onward journey. She tried to rouse him with a reference to their former captain's short-sighted attitude to the advantages of sail. He managed a brief eulogy on the power of steam, steel, paddle and screw, but his heart wasn't in it.

A brooding silence fell. Cordelia began to arrange the quartered, but so far untouched, segments of an orange on her plate. 'It was a perfect day,' she said eventually. 'I think it would be a shame to spoil it with something less perfect. Which is what it would be if we—you know—again.'

He ought to be relieved. And flattered too. Instead, contrarily, he was annoyed that she had pre-empted him. *'If we—you know,'* Iain said sarcastically, 'it's not like you to be so prudish. Though now I come to think of it, I hadn't thought you'd be so inhibited either. Maybe you're a wee bit more conventional than you like to imagine.'

She coloured, looking offended. 'I thought I'd overcome my inhibitions rather well. Obviously, I lack your experience. Only one first for you today, compared to my three.'

And now he'd hurt her. He felt like a right bastard, and at the same time he felt a ridiculously male sense of pride that he'd been the first to do *that*. And now who was being prudish! 'I'm sorry,' Iain said gruffly.

'I was not being prudish,' Cordelia replied. 'If you must have it, I simply don't know how to describe what we did. And, no, I pray you, do not use the Latin term, for that is not what I meant. I meant the second time, in the sea, I meant...'

'I know what you meant.' Iain reached over to remove the plate and the orange from her restless fingers. 'Perhaps we shouldn't try to put it into words,' he said. 'Perhaps there aren't any.'

'Do you think it was a mistake?'

Dear God, but what he was thinking was that he wanted to pull her into his arms and start again, but that really would be a mistake. *Too much.* Cordelia's words, that first night. He should have listened. He was damn sure he'd pay attention now. He'd caught himself just in time. 'I think you're right,' Iain said heavily. 'It was perfect. Let's just leave it at that.'

'For good, do you mean?' Cordelia asked. She sounded a little desperate. 'Despite the fact that familiarity has not bred indifference?'

Iain forced himself to nod. 'A misjudged ambition, on reflection, don't you think? Apart from anything else,' he said, attempting levity, 'we are alone on so very few occasions that it would likely take us years, and we don't have years.'

'We haven't really discussed how long we do have.' She blinked. If he did not know her better, he'd suspect she was trying not to cry, but her next words gave that impression the lie. 'You are quite right.' She got to her feet and began to pack up the remains of their meal. 'It would be a mistake for us to repeat this—this exercise. We have far more important things to be thinking of than planning our next—our next conflagration. I have a guidebook to write and more importantly, I have my sister to see. And you—you have your boats to build.'

'Ships.'

'What?'

'Ships. They are not boats, they are ships.'

'Ships.' She crossed her arms, then uncrossed them. 'So we are agreed.'

'I'm afraid we are.' Iain sighed. 'Your honesty puts me to shame. It was perfect, and it was too much. I would have said it had you not. You stole my thunder by doing so, that's all. I don't want to be—preoccupied—any more than you. I have my business to attend to, as you so rightly pointed out, and I don't want to be distracted.'

'Well then. That's—that's good.'

'Cordelia.' He got to his feet, removing the empty plates from her hand and placing them in the hamper. 'Now that's out of the way, do you think we can put it behind us?'

'I don't know. I have never— Do you mean we shall be friends?'

Iain shrugged. 'Must we have a name for it?'

'A friendly alliance. That is what Sir Edmond, the British Governor in Athens, calls his relationship with King Otto.' Cordelia held out her hand. 'We should shake on it, as gentlemen do.'

He took her hand, covering it with both of his. 'Neither of us is a gentleman, thank God.'

He meant to let her go, but instead found himself closing the distance between them. She tilted her head, and he bent towards her. His mouth hovered over hers. Time seemed to stop. Then start far too quickly. He jerked away. She yanked her hand free.

Chapter Nine

From the moment they returned that night to the Governor's official residence later that day, Lord Armstrong's far-reaching influence could be felt. The talk at the dinner table was all of London, the King's health and the implications for the Government. Cordelia, dressed more formally than she had been since they set sail from Plymouth, smiled politely and spoke when she was addressed. She retired with the Governor's wife and the other ladies to drink tea, while Iain was forced to watch as the Governor and his male guests drank port, cracked warm jokes and discussed the private lives of people he had never heard of and would certainly never wish to meet.

From Zante they sailed to Athens and on to Cairo on the cargo ship *Ariadne,* where conditions where even more claustrophobic than aboard the *Pique,* in the presence of a surly and sullen ship's company who obviously resented having their foreign passengers foisted upon them. Iain seemed preoccupied with his plans. Cordelia tried to preoccupy herself with her guidebook. There were times when that *thing,* as she called it, caught her by surprise. When they found themselves staring into each other's eyes, or when Iain's forearm brushed hers as they leant on the deck's railing, or when their hands crept unchecked towards one another. Then, they would jump back, pretend it had not happened.

In Cairo, they learned that King William had died on the twentieth day of June. During their brief visit to the Consul-General's residence, they toasted the new queen, Victoria, and raised a reluctant glass to Lord Armstrong too. The heat in the city was stifling. The noise and the dust and the smells were quite alien. The nearer they came to the end of this much longed-for journey, the more nervous Cordelia became, the more she dreaded their arrival not as a beginning but an ending.

* * *

'Whatever happened to Peregrine?' she enquired of the Consul-General's young and extremely raw-looking assistant. The man looked blank. 'I met him only the once, but he played rather a pivotal role in the marriages of both my sisters,' she explained, turning to Iain, who was seated beside her in the shade of the veranda. 'A very portly young man, I remember, and he used to turn the most astonishing colour of puce whenever one addressed him. Mr Finchley-Burke, that was his name.'

'Ah, yes, Finchley-Burke.' The assistant looked uncomfortable. 'Most unfortunate.'

'Oh, surely he did not—is he dead?'

'As good as,' the young man said drily. 'Really, Lady Cordelia, it is not a tale that I would sully your ears with.'

'Goodness, I can't believe it can be that bad. Mr Finchley-Burke was most frightfully proper.'

'And now he's gone native and is frightfully rich and very definitely *persona non grata* here.'

Iain laughed. 'That, my lad, was exactly the wrong thing to say. Both Lady Cordelia and my-

self are very fond of outcasts, I'll have you know.
What heinous crime did the poor man commit?'

'I believe I told you, he has gone native,' the
young man said stiffly.

Quite unaccustomed to being teased, Cordelia
surmised, or perhaps, if he too were an Old Har-
rovian as every member of staff at the Consulate
appeared to be, he was far too accustomed. She
smiled encouragingly at him. 'I liked Mr Finchley-Burke, and he was very kind to my sisters, in
his own way. Please do tell me what happened.'

'He married a Bedouin princess—at least,
she claimed she was a princess,' the young man
said, unbending in the light of Cordelia's smile.
'By all accounts, a most ample woman, just like
Finchley-Burke himself, though not a tooth in
her head, I'm told, and not a word of English either. How they communicate I don't know, for the
Consul General says that Finchley-Burke mas-
tered not a single word of Arabic in the ten years
he was here. I am told that they are very happy.'

'Perhaps the language barrier is the reason they
are so happy,' Iain said.

'I trust they will continue to be so,' the assistant

said primly, 'for his family have disowned him. He is the son of an earl too. Such a waste. You will excuse me now, Lady Cordelia, Mr Hunter. I have important business to attend to.'

'And good riddance to you,' Iain muttered under his breath. 'Pompous wee arse.'

Cordelia chuckled. 'I suppose I ought to pretend not to understand your meaning, but your words have a poetry quite their own, and you are quite right, he is. My brother James is very like him. Do you suppose they breed it into them at school?'

'Very likely they empty their head of brains, stick a poker up their...'

'Arse,' Cordelia said softly. The word sounded much more shocking than she expected. Iain looked quite appalled. She stifled a smile, and gave him an innocent look. 'What would you prefer? Nether regions? Backside? Bottom? Buttocks? Or perhaps you would rather I said *derrière?*'

'I'd prefer you didn't mention it at all,' he said.

'Because it is vulgar? I would remind you that you said it first.'

Iain tugged at his stock. 'Because you have a particularly delightful one. I have a very vivid memory of it, swaying in front of me on the beach, and I'm not allowed to think about it.'

Colour flamed her cheeks. She picked up the fan which lay on the rustic table in front of her, and waved it frantically.

'I'm sorry, but you shouldn't have—I'm trying, but there's only so much a man can do to distract himself. There are only so many times I can strip back a steeple engine in my head.'

'Is that what you do?'

Iain shrugged, looking sheepish. 'Sometimes I count rivets. I try to work out the number you'd need depending on the size of the hull.'

'And do you—arrive at a number, I mean?'

'Oh, I always get *a* number. Whether it's the right one or not—well, that's another question.'

'I calculate odds,' Cordelia confessed. 'If coal goes up by a shilling, what will be the impact on iron? When will it become cheaper to import American printed cotton than to merely import the raw material? Is the cost of investing in one of the new gas companies outweighed by the risk of them blowing themselves up?'

'And I thought I was daft. Does it work?' Iain asked.

'Like you, I always arrive at a number.'

'And like me, you've failed to answer the question.'

They had done it again. Somehow, while their minds were engrossed in conversation, their bodies had moved of their own accord. Iain's arm rested against hers on the table. His knee was brushing her thigh. She knew she ought to remedy the situation, but she lacked the will. What she wanted was for him to kiss her. Just one kiss. What harm could it do? 'Do you think that we were precipitate when we agreed we should not— That that particular element of our relationship had been concluded?' she asked.

'I do at the moment.' Iain moved his hand closer, so that his thumb could stroke the inside of her wrist.

Cordelia's eyes drifted closed in pleasure. But if she kept them closed she would not see what was happening, and she had discovered that she liked to see. Iain's face. Iain's hands. Iain. She leant over, and touched her fingers to his temple, then let them feather through his hair. It was longer now. He had not had it cut since they left England. 'Do you think that once more would be a mistake?' she asked, following her fingers with her lips, whispering the words into his ear.

'Cordelia, I can't think when you're this close to me.'

'I should move.'

'No, you're missing my point. Don't move. I don't want to think.'

His arms slid around her waist, pulling her towards him. She half slid from the chair, but his knees caught her. And then his mouth captured hers, and their lips clung, her breath quickened, her body began to thrum and his mouth began to move against hers, and she thought, yes, yes, yes, and gave a sigh of relief, and a voice that belonged to neither of them gave her such a shock that she would have fallen, had Iain not caught her.

'I say. I am most terribly sorry.' The Consul-General's assistant was blushing furiously.

Iain helped her to her feet. 'What is it?' he snapped. 'Could you not have knocked?' The assistant looked around at the open veranda in confusion. 'Or made a noise, stamped your feet, coughed?' Iain said. 'Maybe you could even have gone away and left us to it, since it was perfectly obvious that we thought ourselves alone?'

'I have word from Prince al-Muhanna. I was under the impression that you were somewhat anxious to hear from him.' The assistant held out a sealed letter.

'Right.' Iain took it. 'Sorry about that.'

'As indeed am I. You will, I am sure, excuse me.'

'And you will not, I am sure, be forgiven,' Cordelia said, watching the stiff-backed young man retreating.

'An annoying but timely interruption.' Iain broke the royal seal and began to read the letter.

Cordelia watched him, trying to regain control of her breathing. *Annoying!* If that is all it was, then she was glad she had not surrendered. Because she'd had no intentions of surrendering. It was just a kiss. 'Annoying,' she said, 'yes, but you are right, very timely.'

Iain looked up, his eyes narrowing as he scanned her face. He cannot read my mind, Cordelia told herself, and even if he could, all he would see would be exactly what he is thinking himself. A timely interruption. It would have been a mistake. 'Well?' Her voice sounded snappy, but that could not be helped. 'The letter, what does it say?'

Iain handed the heavily embossed paper over. 'Read it for yourself. We're expected in A'Qadiz. The royal barge awaits our convenience.'

It was not a barge which awaited them at the end of the journey south from Cairo, but rather a larger and extremely ornate version of the traditional dhows that ploughed up and down the Red Sea. The long thin hull came to a point like a gondola. There were two large triangular sails, one at the front, a smaller one in the middle. A second deck was built aft, with cover provided by a fringed gold canopy. They were welcomed aboard by Prince Ramiz al-Muhanna's captain, immaculate in the traditional white tunic which bore their kingdom's discreet embroidered crest depicting a falcon and a new moon. Each member of the crew, ten in all, was lined up to meet them, similarly clothed, their heads covered by a red-and-white checked head-dress, bowing low as Cordelia and Iain made their way aboard. On this ship, as with all the others, they would be well chaperoned.

The journey took several days. The Red Sea was as busy as a river, with dhows of all shapes and sizes, one-, two- and three-masted, contesting for the best part of the channel with feluccas and caiques. Oranges, lemons, dates, bananas, grapes, limes and a host of fruit and vegetables Cordelia, for all her travels could not name, were transported up towards Cairo from the lush, fertile banks.

The deep waters were amazingly clear. Shoals of multi-hued fish moved in apparent synchronicity from one side of the dhow to the other, forming and reforming, morphing from arrow to triangle to a sphere and then a rhomboid. Coral reefs of every shade, from the palest of pinks to vermilion red, could be seen shimmering below the surface, shaped like starbursts with willow fronds, magical places where the tiniest of fish darted about their business.

Cordelia spent a great deal of time leaning precariously over the narrow rail of the main deck, fascinated by the endlessly changing seascape. Iain, who had in his possession one of Robert Moresby's precious maps of the Red Sea, was equally fascinated, tracing their journey carefully, marvelling at least five times a day, at the accuracy of Mr Moresby's work.

'I hear that Captain Haines of the HMS *Palinurus* is even now surveying the southern coast of Arabia,' he told Cordelia. 'It is a vital exercise if we are to put steamships on the route to India,' he explained.

'So your interest in building a shipyard in A'Qadiz, it's not only to provide ships for Celia's husband?'

'If Prince Ramiz is the visionary his reputation would have us believe, he'll already be thinking beyond the Red Sea. I believe the British have their eyes on the port of Aden. If you look at the map, you will see that A'Qadiz is halfway from Cairo, halfway to Aden, and so perfectly placed for refuelling and repairs. And here you see is India.'

'You are set to conquer the world with your steamships then,' Cordelia said, studying the map, marvelling at the breadth of Iain's ambition. 'Prince Ramiz is not the only one with vision. If you are right, my new guidebook will be in great demand.'

'Then I hope I am right.'

Iain rolled up his map. They climbed the shallow steps which led to the upper deck. Here was their main living quarters. A thick carpet covered the varnished decking. Two low divans strewn with mountains of cushions of velvet, satin and silk, sat at right angles to each other, with a very low marble table between them. Dusk was falling, and they were nearing the shore, for the dhow did not sail through the night. The scent of jasmine perfumed the air, and soon it would mingle with the delicious smells of cooking coming from the main deck.

Dinner was delicate, fragrant, a series of tiny morsels designed to entice the palate. Pastries filled with goat and minced lamb. Olives stuffed with almonds. Vine leaves stuffed with rice and herbs. Tomatoes and the lush purple fruit called aubergine, grilled and dressed with olive oil. Yoghurt flavoured with rose-water. They ate with their fingers, rinsing between each dish in the glass bowls scented with orange blossom.

Afterwards, Cordelia gathered a heap of cushions on to the floor, leaning against one of the divans, while Iain stretched out upon it, as relaxed as she was with this strange but infinitely comfortable arrangement, which allowed a view of the shore on one side, the sea on the other. 'The night falls so quickly here,' she said, 'like a curtain coming down. And the stars are so big, they seem so much nearer.'

'It is very beautiful,' Iain replied. 'I had always thought it a sailor's tale that you could reach out and touch them, but it's almost possible, lying here, to believe that you could.'

Cordelia twisted round to look at him. 'Iain Hunter, I believe you are turning into a romantic.'

Her shoulder was brushing against his knee. He smiled lazily at her from his prone position. 'Moonlight, stars, a royal barge, a waiting desert and a beautiful woman. It would turn any man into a romantic.'

'Any man who was not a rough Glasgow ship-builder.'

Any man, Iain thought, restraining the impulse to touch her, even *a Glasgow shipbuilder.*

Cordelia's face was in shadow, for the lamps were not lit, but he sensed her looking at him. She was unbearably close, unbearably out of reach. The silence between them was intense, filled with an acute longing. 'We arrive in A'Qadiz tomorrow morning,' he said bracingly, though in truth it made his heart sink. 'You'll be with your sister soon.'

'Yes.' She shifted out of his reach, curling her legs up to her chest, and wrapping her arms around them.

'What's wrong?'

'Nothing.'

Which meant there was definitely something,

and it wasn't the thing which must not be talked about, which left only one thing. 'Tell me about Celia,' Iain said.

'What do you want to know?'

Prickly, definitely on the defensive, which, knowing Cordelia, meant she was much more worried than she wanted to let on. 'What age were you when she left?' he asked.

'Thirteen.'

Her terseness confirmed his thoughts. She sat huddled, so patently struggling with whatever fears and insecurities this eldest sister aroused, yet equally patently determined not to let him see them. He wanted to help her, and the only thing he could think to do was to tell her of his own sister. To talk about something he had never talked about, in the growing dark, on what might well be their last night alone. *Could he?* Iain pulled his kerchief from his waistcoat pocket, shook it out and began to fold it methodically into ever smaller squares. 'I was twelve when Jeannie— when I lost Jeannie,' he said. 'She was only just turned seven.'

Cordelia edged closer to him.

'She was a bonny wee thing,' he continued. 'She had one of those smiles that could wind you round her wee finger. A terrible liking for barley sugar, she had, her hands were always sticky with it. Hair the same colour too, just like—like our mother's, and eyes the blue of the sky on a rare summer day.'

'Like yours,' Cordelia said.

'The only likeness we shared. Also from our mother.'

'So you take after your father?'

'I have no idea.' The words were out before he could stop them, betraying the anger and hurt he'd thought long buried. 'He's been dead a long time,' he said, which could well be true, for all he knew.

Cordelia reached for his hand, forcing open his clenched fist, removing the crushed square of cotton, twining her fingers his. He looked down at them, and forced himself to recall that other little hand, so trusting.

'Did you lose your sister at the same time as your parents?' Cordelia asked softly. 'You told me that you were an orphan, I remember.'

Had he? Iain tried to recall. So accustomed was he to thinking of his mother as dead, he could well have led Cordelia to believe it was true. He didn't want to talk about his mother. He tried to remember why he'd decided to talk at all. He moved, instinctively making to escape, but Cordelia's grip on his hand tightened.

'Tell me more about Jeannie.'

He did not know if he could, but he wanted to. He really did want to. 'Funny to think that you are a wee sister,' Iain said. 'I can't imagine you trailing about after anyone, not even as a bairn.'

'Oh, but I did. I was forever wanting to be let in on Celia and Cassie's confidences. I thought Celia the most elegant person it was possible to be, and Cassie the most beautiful, while I was just a—a ragamuffin in comparison.'

Iain laughed. 'I find that very hard to believe. I'll wager you were every bit as able to wind them all around your wee finger, just as Jeannie was.' He leaned back against the divan, closing his eyes. 'I remember,' he said, and allowed himself to do so, for the first time. Maybe it was the darkness. Maybe it was the fact that they were so very far from home, here on a wooden barge on the Red Sea. Another climate. Another continent. Or maybe it was just that Cordelia was the right person to tell. Whatever it was, his memories were golden for once, untinged by the dreadful loss, dancing into his mind and tripping from his tongue as lightly as Jeannie had danced and laughed, full of the joys, a wee sprite of a thing who could make even their mother's drunken husband, the man they called father, smile.

Iain opened his eyes and sat up. 'It was a Tuesday morn, the day of the accident. Our father was supposed to be working, but by then he was fonder of the hard stuff than hard labour. Jeannie must have seen him going into the tavern. She ran out in front of a dray.' He heard Cordelia's sharp intake of breath, but forced himself to finish. 'Two huge Clydesdales there were pulling it, and she was such a wee tiny thing, she didn't have a chance.'

He didn't cry. He hadn't cried since that day, but he hadn't talked about it either. His throat closed over. He felt it working, swallowing repeatedly, and couldn't seem to control it. He couldn't bear to look at Cordelia, though he could feel the force of her concentration, the strength of her grip clinging to him as if she would save him. Not that he needed saving.

He forced himself to unpick his fingers from hers, and shifted so that his back was to her. He breathed, deep gulping breaths of the warm, salty air, as he tried to get the image from his mind, the white feathers of the great gentle horses, the jingle of their heavy bits, the grinding of the dray's wheels on the cobbled stones of the dockside road, the shouts, the screams, the crack of bone.

Soft hands slid around his waist. A body pressed against his back. Cordelia held him tightly, her cheek against his shoulders, and only then did Iain realise he was shaking. 'I don't know what she was doing there,' he said, the question Cordelia hadn't asked but he knew she was thinking it, for who wouldn't? And it wasn't true, that he didn't know, though he had never asked for confirmation. By the time word reached him, his mother was hysterical, beyond questioning and reason, the man he called father was dead drunk, and Jeannie…

'They said she didn't suffer,' he said.

'You must hope so.'

It was that. The way she didn't simply agree, the way she didn't pretend she could know otherwise, the way she didn't offer him false comfort. It was that, that wrenched the choking sob from him. It was the way she held him, her face to his back, her arms tight, holding him together yet allowing him his privacy that allowed the second sob out, and the third. He felt no shame, only an enormous relief. His shoulders heaved, then gentled. He felt strangely disconnected from himself, intensely aware of Cordelia yet at the same time, quite alone. He breathed, in and out, in and out, and let it wash over him, the grief, until it calmed, and though it was a cliché it was true, he felt emptied.

'I was twenty miles downriver at the docks in the Port,' Iain finally continued, turning, but still in the circle of her arms. 'He—my father—he'd lost his job there, and had taken another at a yard not far from the Broomilaw, where you and I first met.'

'So that is why you don't drink.' Cordelia

touched his cheek, then burrowed her face into his chest. 'You must think I am an ungrateful wretch, the way I have complained about my own family. I feel absolutely dreadful.'

'In many ways, he was a better father than yours. He tried to do his best for me, and he loved Jeannie, even though...' Iain caught himself. There had been more than enough revelations for today. He felt better, but he had no doubt lifting up that particular stone would make him feel a lot worse. 'He was a drunkard, but he had cause,' he said, and before Cordelia could comment, disengaged himself from her embrace. 'I didn't tell you all this to make you feel bad,' he said gruffly. 'I told you because I wanted you to know.'

Cordelia froze. *I wanted you to know.* It was a dangerous thing, this knowing, for it led to wanting more, and it led to more being demanded in return, and that wasn't part of their agreement. She didn't want to be known. 'You wanted to reassure me,' she said, because that made sense. 'Because you could see I was worried about meeting my sister. To reassure me that at least I have a sister.' She could have kicked herself. Not only did she sound ungrateful, she sounded callous. 'I mean, you were trying to show that you understood what it is like to lose a sister,' she continued ineptly, 'not that I've lost a sister. Not the way you have, but…' She trailed off, realising she was digging a bigger and bigger hole for herself. She'd mentioned her nerves merely in order to deflect him from seeing how upset and confused she was, but now she wished she had not, for she had inadvertently broached the subject she had been so keen to avoid. 'It's late,' she said.

She should have known Iain would not be so easily deflected. 'What is it that's really bothering you?' he asked.

This was the downside of confidences, Cordelia thought, this expectation that they would be returned. And the strange thing was, she wanted to, and that frightened her almost as much as the doing. 'It's nothing.'

It came out sounding exactly like the lie it was. Iain made an exasperated sound. 'Our betrothal, as you never fail to remind me, might not be real, but I do understand what makes you tick. You don't like it, but there it is. Now, you can either embrace it and let me help you with what is obviously troubling you, or you can do what you usually do, which is bottle it all up and hope it will go away. It's up to you. Cordelia.'

She was angry, not with him but with herself. She hated being in the wrong, and she hated that he was so horribly right. She felt chastised, and she knew she deserved it, for she had behaved as pettishly as a child. 'I'm sorry,' she said, sounding far from it, 'it is simply that I am accustomed to sorting out problems myself.'

A statement so obvious, and so mutually applicable, that she was not surprised when Iain did not deign to reply to it. With difficulty, she forced herself to examine the issue. 'It's not that I think Celia won't like me, or that I won't like her, but she is very—opaque. A diplomat, if you like. It is the one way in which she resembles our father. I am sure she will welcome me, but I am afraid that she— Oh, if you must have it, I am devilish scared that she will disapprove of me.

She might not even like me!' She folded her arms across her chest and glared at Iain in the gloom. 'There, are you happy now?'

'What do you think she'll disapprove of?'

'Well—you know—my being unmarried and—and unrepentant of my experience.'

'So you're planning on telling her all then, as you told me? Though I'm assuming you've never told your other sisters, since you did not turn to them for help when you left that ba—that man.'

'I did not need help,' Cordelia said. A lie. She could almost feel his mind probing hers, seeking out the truth. Looking down, she realised her arms were still defensively crossed, and quickly unfolded them, tucking her hands under her thighs. 'I suppose now you will tell me that there is such a thing as being too independent,' she said, unable to prevent herself falling back on her usual tactic of attack as the best form of defence, 'but I am willing to bet that you never asked anyone for help either.'

'I have not the wide selection of siblings you have to turn to. And, no, I did not say that because I wanted you to pity me, merely as a statement of fact.'

'What about that man, Jamie?'

'What *about* Jamie?'

'You have entrusted him with the custody of your precious shipyard. That must surely mean he is a friend as well as a business partner?'

An uncomfortable silence followed. Cordelia would have given a lot to see his face, but lighting a lamp would mean he would then be able to see her, so she refrained. 'I haven't needed to ask for help,' Iain finally said.

'Any more than I have,' Cordelia retorted. This time, the silence was weighted against her. She could positively feel Iain's scepticism boring into her. 'When I left Gi—the man who shall not be discussed, Caro was in the middle of her own scandal. She had left her husband. Not her current husband. And Cressie was still in the first flush of love with her husband, the Italian painter she eloped with. Actually, Cressie and Giovanni seem still to be besotted with each other. As are Sebastian and Caro. Sebastian is Caro's second husband.'

'Your sisters seem to be almost as unorthodox as you,' Iain said.

'Yes.' Cordelia chewed on her lip. 'I didn't even try to get in touch with any of them, if you must know. Of course you know. Have guessed. Not at first. I was too—not ashamed. Yes, ashamed, but mostly I felt I'd failed, and I wanted to have succeeded in something, or not failed in something before I contacted them, and you might think that is just silly pride and foolishness, and so it was, but I would most likely do the same again,' she finished in a rush. 'Caro and Cressie are so happy, Iain. All of us have been damaged by our upbringing one way or another, but I am the only one who has not managed to put it behind me. You've witnessed how—how furious my father can make me, how he can hurt me.'

'And I've witnessed you starting to come to terms with it.'

'Come to terms, but I have not *triumphed* as they have. I know that is a strange word to choose, but it is how I am made to feel. You heard Aunt Sophia. And even Bella, when I told her that I was a wealthy woman in my own right, she was completely unimpressed, and seemed to think it was much more important that I made my peace with you. A man, you see. That is the pinnacle of success for a woman, having a man by her side.'

'And all of your sisters have that while you don't.' Iain touched her shoulder briefly. 'Yet you have succeeded on your own terms, Cordelia. Or don't you actually believe what you preach?'

'I don't preach. Merely, I have to speak louder to be heard above the—do I preach?'

'Not half as much as I rant on about steam engines.'

'I suppose that what it comes down to is that I am on tenterhooks all the time, waiting to defend myself,' Cordelia said sadly. 'That is what is so difficult to bear. Being reunited with Cressie and Caro was one of the happiest days of my life. A huge consolation and an enormous disappointment, for I cannot ever make myself be wholly open with them.'

'You know best of course, but do you think you were ever really that close, Cordelia?'

'Yes, we were! Well, we were younger then and

there was not— Oh, I don't know. Do you mean that I expect too much of this reunion?'

'I think you're expecting Celia to plug a big hole that she can't possibly fill. I think maybe you've always been much more alone than you realise. I'm thinking—' Iain broke off. 'You know what? Maybe it's best that I stop telling you what I think. I'm just a shipbuilder, not a philosopher. Why don't we just wait and see what happens tomorrow?'

'Tomorrow. I can't quite believe it.' Cordelia felt quite ill at the thought. 'Iain, will you— Can I ask that you refrain from telling Prince Ramiz the truth about us until I have spoken to Celia? If you can do so without compromising your business deal, that is?'

There was a pause before he answered. 'That's an awful lot to ask, Cordelia.'

Her heart sank. 'You're right. I should not have—'

'The thing is,' he interrupted her, 'I'm anxious to make the most of all these concubines I'm sure the prince will have waiting for me, and I don't want you to feel your nose is out of joint.'

'Iain! You are outrageous.' Cordelia chuckled. 'I cannot imagine my sister tolerating even one concubine, never mind a harem full.'

Iain sighed theatrically. 'In that case, I'll just have to make do with you.'

'I am terribly sorry, I know a plain English-woman cannot compare with an Arabian houri straight out of the pages of *One Thousand and One Nights.*'

'I very much doubt any woman could compare to you,' Iain said.

The laughter had gone from his voice. Cordelia caught her breath, quite taken aback by this admission. Iain too seemed startled. She sat frozen to the spot, her heart pounding, knowing that she should make some light riposte, unable to think of a single word. When he pulled her into his arms, she told herself that she would resist, but could not.

His kiss was soft, almost tender. He held her face between his hands as if afraid she might break, and tasted her as if she might dissolve. He kissed her slowly, carefully, keeping enough distance between their bodies so that they touched but did not press.

Water lapped at the dhow. A camel bleated. Somewhere on the sea side of the boat, there was a splash. The kiss went on and on and on. And then it stopped, long before it was enough, long after it was too much.

When Iain helped her to her feet, the boat was quiet, the crew sleeping, save for the night watchman, who looked at them impassively as they descended to their bedchambers. The small porthole was already open, covered with netting to keep out the mosquitos. Cordelia undressed and lay naked between the cool sheets, touching her lips, closing her eyes and weeping, a silent steady flow of tears she could not explain that left her emptier than she had ever felt before.

Chapter Ten

They arrived at the port of A'Qadiz in the late morning. The harbour was crowded with people, camels, mules and cargo of every kind. Bales of cloth, terracotta urns, crates, boxes, sacks and parcels were stacked in precarious heaps on the quayside. Chickens cheeped, dogs yapped, donkeys brayed, and above it all the musical ululating of the Arabic language could be heard.

Cordelia watched it all, her eyes wide, so entranced that she completely forgot to take any notes. She must have seen this before, when she had visited Celia just after she was married, but she could not recall. 'It's absolutely fascinating,' she said to Iain, who was as usual standing by her side. 'Entrancing. No wonder Celia fell in love here.'

'Has the romance of the desert caught you in its grasp then?'

'We are not even in the desert.' Her fingers went automatically to her lips. There was something different about Iain today, though perhaps it was something different about herself. She didn't know what to make of last night, and would much rather not make anything of it at all because no matter how hard she tried, she could not persuade herself it was nothing, which meant it was something, and it felt like an important something, and she already had too many important somethings to think about.

'I'll see Celia soon,' she said. 'I confess, the nearer I am to her, the more nervous I am.'

'You've no need to be.'

'Iain, did you ever want something so much you thought it was the only thing worth having, and then when it was quite within your grasp, you were afraid it might not be what you wanted after all, and so you thought maybe it would be for the best if you forgot all about it?'

Iain looked at her most strangely. 'Are we still talking about Celia?'

'Who else?' she replied, puzzled.

'Who else, indeed.'

He sounded hurt. No, that wasn't right. Resigned? But that couldn't be right either. Maybe he simply thought she was talking nonsense. 'You think I'm being silly?' she said.

Iain shook his head. 'Sometimes all you are, Cordelia, is human. You're making too much of this. Your expectations are set so high you're bound to be disappointed. You know that, for why else would you be scared?'

'I could be afraid that you were right, when you said Celia could not possibly be all that I want her to be.'

'I said she couldn't possibly be all you want her to be *to you.*'

'Yes, you did, and that's what I'm afraid of. So you were right, as you always are. You must be pleased. You will be sorry when you no longer have me to make you feel so superior.'

'What do you mean?'

'When our betrothal is over.'

'Cordelia, I...'

'What? You wish it was over sooner rather than later?'

Iain shook his head. She was struck once more by how sad he seemed, but when she looked at him again, she thought she must have been mistaken.

'I wish you didn't think I liked to prove you wrong,' he said. 'Let's not talk about when our betrothal is over. It's not over yet.'

He put his arm around her and pulled her close, and she allowed herself to lean against him because it was a harmless thing, and it didn't mean she felt protected or needed protection. There would come a time, maybe in as little as a few weeks, when Iain would not be by her side. A time when her life would go on, and his life would go on, but they would take quite separate paths. A time she didn't want to think about right now.

They were met on the quay by a tall, elegant figure whose white silk robes proclaimed his higher status. He introduced himself in softly accented English as Akil, Sheikh al-Muhanna's trusted man of business. 'The prince very much regrets that he has been detained,' Akil explained, 'and begs that you will make use of his hospitality at the Second Palace until he arrives.'

'What about my sister?' Cordelia asked.

'The Lady Celia is well, be assured, and she sends you her warmest greetings. It has been arranged that I will escort you to her myself, Lady Cor—Cordelia.' Akil struggled with the name, and made an apologetic little bow. 'It is three days across the desert to the First Palace in the city of Balyrma. We will travel like the wind as soon as Prince Ramiz arrives in the morning.'

'But—but what about Iain—Mr Hunter—is he not to come to Balyrma too?'

'Prince Ramiz is to honour Mr Hunter with his time and most wise counsel here by the sea, where the ships are to be built. After that…'

Akil spread his hands in a gesture Cordelia remembered from her first visit to Arabia. Who knows, the gesture implied, we are in God's hands, or the hands of fate. What it meant was that she had very little time left with Iain. That Iain wouldn't be with her when she met Celia and Cassie. That Iain might even sail back to England without her. Or on to India. He seemed very interested in India. She would be interested in India herself if it were not for Celia.

'Are the arrangements not to my lady's satisfaction?'

Akil was looking worried. Iain was looking—distant. Cordelia shook her head and smiled brightly. 'No. They are fine.'

'Then if you would be so good as to follow me.'

Out of the docks, where Akil's presence made the crowds part, they followed him to a narrow street lined with warehouses emanating the same potent mixture of smells she remembered from the Isle of Dogs.

'It seems all docks are the same in some ways,' Iain said, tucking her hand into his arm.

Cordelia had on a wide hat. The few women she had seen were veiled, though some only lightly, with the thinnest of gauze, while others were swathed from head to foot in black with slits only for their eyes. She was glad that her gown covered both her arms and her neck. It was not merely Akil's presence, she noticed, which made the people stop and stare, and though a few children came close enough to touch her skirts and to smile, wide-eyed, up at her, it was Iain, in his plain buff clothes, who drew most of the attention. And it was Iain who, with his usual casual authority, was now conversing with Akil, making the man smile and gesture, eyeing him, when Iain's attention was elsewhere, with dawning respect.

She began to feel alone. As if she were fading, already disappearing from Iain's sphere. He had said nothing when it became obvious they were to be separated. Most likely he didn't care. No, that was wrong, for it was to assume that he cared more about her than the business he had paid such a high price to come here to execute. It wasn't that he didn't care, it was that he had more important things on his mind.

They walked, Akil explaining that his prince and Lady Celia preferred to do so themselves whenever possible, for it kept them as one with their people. All around them were signs of growth, from the civic buildings and port authorities to the newly cobbled streets, where cooling fountains doubling as water pumps stood on every corner. The Second Palace was not as grand as the one Cordelia remembered in Balyrma, but it was just as beautiful, the flowing lines of the walls embellished with turrets and minarets, the high arch over the entrance decorated with a falcon and a new moon made of tiny mosaic tiles.

'Your sister really does live like a princess,' Iain said, looking around at the tiled courtyard they entered, with its central fountain and vista through a columned gallery of at least three other such courtyards.

'Lady Celia is much respected and admired here,' Akil said. 'There have been many changes since our prince took her as his only wife.'

'Only?'

'The tradition of taking more than one woman is dying out, though some of our Bedouin tribes still practise it. I myself am a man of the nineteenth century, and like our prince have only one woman to warm my bed.' Akil permitted himself a small smile. 'Like our prince, I too am most happy with my choice. The blessing of a true companion in life is indeed one of the greatest.

Without my Yasmina, I would be a lesser man. You see how I am not ashamed to say so? That is one of the teachings which the Lady Celia has given. I must congratulate you, Mr Hunter, on your choice of wife. A sister of Lady Celia can be nothing other than a great asset to a man.'

Akil beamed, entirely unaware that this surprising speech had had quite the opposite of its intended effect on Lady Celia's sister. Cordelia smiled back woodenly, feeling like a complete fraud and a complete failure.

'If you will excuse me, I will investigate the arrangements which have been made for you.'

'What's wrong?' Iain asked, as they stood alone in the courtyard.

What's right? Cordelia would have liked to reply, but it was a little dramatic. 'Celia is revered here. You heard Akil. Not only does she have the heart of one of the most powerful men in Arabia, she seems to have his people eating out of her hand. While I have been priding myself on my stupid guidebooks, she has been changing lives.'

'With the help of one of the most powerful men in Arabia.'

'Who no doubt worships the ground she walks on and would travel to the ends of the earth just to procure her a—a thistle, if she wanted it.'

Iain laughed. 'I could have brought one with me. We have them in abundance in Scotland.'

'I know.' Cordelia managed a weak smile.

'If Celia is anything like you, then one of the things she'll have wanted more than anything is to see her sister. Prince Ramiz has not arranged that for her.'

'No, you have, and I am being an ungrateful wretch.'

'You're nervous, and you're tired, and you're being irrational, but you've no cause to say you're ungrateful, for your being here has as much to do with you as me. We did this together, Cordelia.'

She nodded.

'And you're not a wretch. You're my ain wee darling.'

'Not for much longer. I am to go to Balyrma alone.'

'Aye.' Iain stretched his hand out, spreading

his fingers under the cooling water which rushed from the horn of the marble unicorn which cavorted in the middle of the fountain. 'It's probably for the best.'

Because she had served her purpose. Because he found her too distracting. Because Celia was not his problem but hers. Because she was not really, and never had been, his *ain wee darling.* She would never be anyone's ain wee darling. She didn't want to be anyone's ain wee darling!

Iain turned back towards her. 'Because the sooner you deal with it the better,' he said. 'Don't get me wrong, I would dearly like to be with you, but I know you don't need my support, and I don't want to compromise things.'

'Compromise?'

'Cordelia, you need to be honest with her. You need to try very hard to be your own true self. If I come with you, with things as they are between us at the moment, it wouldn't be right.'

'You mean I'd have to lie about us?'

'I'm tired of lying, aren't you?'

He was looking at her so strangely again, and she couldn't understand it. As if he was trying to tell her something without saying it. Something important. But she couldn't read his mind the way he could hers.

The return of Akil accompanied by a small, round beaming man whose bright-red tunic stretched tight over his belly, saved her from having to answer. 'Mr Hunter, if it pleases you, I have some preliminary business to discuss,' Akil said, stepping aside.

Iain made a noise that might have been irritation, quickly disguised. He cast a frustrated look at Cordelia then turned to Akil. 'I am all yours,' he said.

As she followed the berrylike man alone to the first of the inner courtyards, Cordelia wondered, sickeningly, if this was the last she would see of Iain.

Akil had left him alone at the proposed site for the new dockyards. Despite the fact that building a yard from scratch was one of his life's ambitions, Iain was finding it difficult to concentrate. Work had always been a panacea for him before. Work had seen him through Jeannie's death, and that of the man he called father. Work was what defined him. He had worked his way up from apprentice to shipwright to shipowner to dock-yard owner. If things went well for him here in Arabia, he would be the joint proprietor of the first dockyard to build steamships on the Red Sea. The markets it would open were beyond his wildest dreams. He was rich and would be much richer. He owed nothing to anybody and wanted for nothing either. So why wasn't he happy?

He hadn't slept last night, but he had grown ac-customed to insomnia on this long and protracted journey. He was used to being kept awake by his body's aching for Cordelia. He was accustomed to doing just as he'd told her he did to counter-act it, mentally stripping back engines, count-ing rivets. Last night had been different. Today was—worse.

He gazed unseeing at the few tentative plans he had drawn in his notebook, then slumped down on an upturned terracotta urn, and resorted to gazing blankly out at the Red Sea. Something that might be a frog was croaking, a mournful sound like a door creaking open, and shut, open and shut. Last night he'd wanted to go on kissing Cordelia forever. He'd wanted to fold her up inside him and keep her safe. He'd wanted to make her his. Only his. Always his.

The frog stopped croaking at about the same time Iain thought his heart had stopped beating. He'd seen what love did to his father. The man he called father. The man who had been married to his mother, poor sod. There had been times, when Iain was wee, before Jeannie arrived, when they'd been happy, his mother and her man. He knew they'd been happy, because his mother smiled a lot, and his father—that man—whoever the hell he was or was not—would smile too, a big, beaming, proud smile. In those times, Iain was like an outcast in his own home, for they wanted only their own company. It never lasted long. His mother had no patience for love of any kind. His father—what the hell, he might as well call him father, for that was the role the man had taken on, even if he was not his flesh and blood—his father had too much patience.

Love meant subservience for one, dominance for the other. Love meant there was a winner and a loser. Love was not an equal thing. Not in Iain's experience. Not that he had any experience. Not until now.

No. He was not in love. He was in lust. Though last night hadn't felt like lust any more than that time on the beach at Zante. What he was feeling was homesick, most likely, and Cordelia was home. Which was a daft idea because apart from anything else, he hadn't missed Glasgow at all.

So it must have been the combination of the stars and the desert and the sea and the beautiful woman last night after all. The romance of it. Would he have felt the same if it had been another beautiful woman? He'd known a few. He tried to imagine them, but none could replace Cordelia. No one compared to Cordelia. He shouldn't have said that last night. He shouldn't even have been thinking it, for he had no intention of spending the rest of his life comparing.

Which reminded him he'd be spending the rest of his life without her. A fact he immediately shied well away from. It was proximity, that's what the problem was. It was being constantly in her company that had deluded him into thinking he could not do without her company. It was the way she was so like him and so unlike, he thought, half-conscious that he was becoming a bit desperate. It was because he felt protective of her, because she made him feel like a knight errant.

No, another daft idea, and while he was on the subject of daft, what did he think he was going to do, even if he was in love with her, which he wasn't? She had made it very clear that all she was interested in was meeting her sister. She had made it even more clear that she valued her independence above all. She'd turned down D'Amery, and no matter that Iain thought D'Amery was a fool, he was a pretty good proposition for a husband. The right kind of man for Cordelia, in fact, while Iain was most definitely the wrong kind of man. Though Cordelia was here with Iain, and she'd refused D'Amery. Twice.

What if he was in love? What if all the things he'd taken as truths were only the product of two totally screwed-up people like his mother and father who should never have been together in the first place? Cordelia was nothing like his mother. He was certainly nothing like his father.

Iain groaned. You could twist logic any way you liked. There was no such thing as truth, only gut feel, and his gut told him that what had gone on between his mother and his so-called father was not something he wanted to get into. But his gut also told him that he didn't want to spend the rest of his life without Cordelia. Was he just lonely then? He thought about this, and then re-membered what he'd said last night. It had come out without him even thinking about it too. In-stinct. If he couldn't have Cordelia, no one else would ever do.

'Aye, which leaves me right back where I started. I'm a bloody eejit.'

'Sir?'

He turned to find Akil had returned. The man must be thinking he really was an idiot, talking to himself. 'I was just saying to myself that it's a perfect site,' Iain said inanely.

Akil bowed his head. 'Chosen by Prince Ramiz after much consultation. The bay here is much deeper than further along the shore at the existing docks. If you have seen enough, I will take you back to the Second Palace, and then I must bid you goodbye. I leave with the Lady Cordelia before dawn. That way we make the most of the day before the sun becomes too hot.'

Which statement left Iain feeling so sick to the stomach he could only nod. There was no use in trying to decide whether this strange, tender, protective feeling that squeezed his guts and made his heart skitter really was love, because even if it was, there was no point in saying anything until Cordelia had seen her blasted sister, by which time the feeling might well have passed, and if it hadn't—well then, he would deal with it then. In the meantime, he had much more important things to worry about than whether or not he was in love. Which he wasn't. Such as Sheikh al-Muhanna's arrival. And ships. Ships were the thing. But as he followed Akil back to the palace, Iain discovered that not even steamships mattered more than Cordelia. Which was definitely a first.

It was a beautiful palace, and Cordelia seemed to be its only occupant, save for the small army of servants who were so discreet as to be non-existent. She surrendered to the temptation of the hammam baths, lying naked on a long marble slab in the steamy heat while a dark-skinned woman rubbed scented oil into her skin and pummelled and kneaded her tired muscles until she felt as if her bones had been removed. She lay, wrapped in a towel, quite limp, as the steam from the water poured over hot stones wafted around her, then allowed herself to be led to the deep-green pool, gasping as the icy water enveloped her.

More oils made her skin feel softer than she had ever known it. Her hair was braided, and she was dressed in a long silk tunic in her favourite shade of blue, the hem and cuffs intricately beaded with turquoise, her only other garments a pair of organdy pantaloons pleated into the waist and held under the tunic with a belt made of gold threads, with matching slippers.

Cleansed, invigorated and looking satisfyingly like one of the illustrations from *One Thousand and One Nights,* Cordelia felt sufficiently restored to take herself to task. How many times in the past ten years had she wished herself here? And now here she was, and instead of thinking about Celia, she was obsessively dissecting a betrothal that wasn't even real. What's more, she was in danger of compromising the one thing she'd fought so hard to earn over this past decade, and that was her precious independence. She didn't need Iain to be at her side when she met Celia. She didn't need Iain by her side at all.

This, while true, was not at all palatable, for the thought of not having Iain in her life made her feel quite sick. She had obviously become far too accustomed to him, that was all. She had spent too much time in his company.

Though two years with Gideon had not made her feel like this.

Two years with Iain, and she would almost certainly feel the same indifference she felt for Gideon, Cordelia told herself stoically, ignoring the fact that she'd never felt for Gideon what she felt for Iain. Iain, who had kissed her last night as if—as if he did not want to stop kissing her. Iain, who had said he suspected no one could compare to Cordelia.

'Which meant absolutely nothing more than that I am different from every other female,' she said to herself firmly. Which was most likely true, but not necessarily a good thing. Men did not want their wives to have a past. They did not want their wives to challenge them and upbraid them and they certainly didn't want them to be independent. Not that a wife could ever be independent. Not that she was thinking that she wanted to be Iain's wife, even if he did want her, which he didn't, and…

'Devil take it, what is the point in thinking about any of this when I leave first thing tomorrow morning?'

She had been pacing the innermost courtyard of the palace, working her way round the colonnades which bordered it. At the corner of each was a fountain. Iain stood at the one diagonally opposite her. He was wearing a long dark blue tunic. It suited him, the silk caressing his lean frame, clinging to the long length of his legs. His feet were, like hers, clad in leather slippers.

The colour of the tunic made his eyes seem even bluer, though that surely was not possible.

'You look—you look as if you belong here,' Cordelia said, unable to take her eyes off him.

'I like it here. I've just spent the last half-hour being beaten up by a ferocious man wearing only a towel.' Iain grinned. 'I feel as though my bones have been broken and put back together. I could get used to this. Are you still worried about Celia?'

'I don't want to talk about Celia.'

Iain crossed the courtyard. 'I'm not much interested in her either right now, I confess. I'm not the only one who looks as if he belongs here. You look like you should be in a harem.'

'They don't have harems here in A'Qadiz. Not the sort of places you imagine anyway. My sister would not tolerate it.'

'I thought we'd agreed we weren't going to talk about your sister?' Iain ran his hand down her arm, shoulder to wrist. 'Call me old-fashioned, but when I see you like this, I can understand why the men of this country used to lock their women out of sight. Have you anything on at all under this thing?'

She lifted the hem of her tunic, revealing the flimsy pantaloons, and heard his sharp intake of breath. 'Dear God, Cordelia, I don't know how I'm supposed to keep my mind on what I need to say when you look like that.'

She knew then that she had been fooling herself. He had come to say goodbye, and she didn't think she could bear it, because it was suddenly, horribly and fatally apparent that the turmoil she was going through was love. It was the only thing that made sense. She had fallen in love with him.

'What's wrong? You look as if you've been shot.'

Stabbed through the heart, more like. 'Indigestion,' she said, though she had barely touched the food which had been served to her.

Iain was frowning. 'Look, I know you've a lot on your mind. I was going to wait until you saw Celia—you see, there's no getting away from her, it seems—but I can't. You might be gone days. Weeks. I don't know how long you will be gone, and I know the timing is not right, but when would the timing ever be right for such a thing and...'

He was nervous. 'You don't want to lie to Celia's husband. You're right. I shouldn't have asked you. It doesn't matter now anyway, you can tell him as soon as you meet him, since Celia will not be with him and...'

'This is not about Celia or Celia's husband,' Iain interrupted. 'I'm sick to the back teeth of talking of the pair of them, if you must know. Cordelia, ever since last night...'

'I know. You need not fear, I did not take it seriously,' she said quickly. Her voice was pitched too high. She sounded odd. No wonder Iain was looking at her strangely.

'Cordelia, would you just hold your tongue and let me speak? This is hard enough to say without you interrupting me. In fact, I wasn't going to say anything...'

'Until I saw Celia.' Goodbye is what he was trying to say, and she didn't think she could bear it. 'Don't say it, Iain, because—because...' If he didn't say it, then she could carry on pretending. But he had had enough of the lies. He had said so just today, she remembered, so the worst thing, the very worst thing she could do would be to tell him how she felt, and if she opened her mouth again, she was afraid that the words would come tumbling out. So there was only one thing to do.

'I'll be leaving first thing in the morning,' Cordelia said. 'And even though I am not really the type of woman to be taken in by the romance of the desert and the stars, to say nothing of a royal palace and a very, very attractive man, I cannot help thinking it would be a terrible shame to let such a rare combination go to waste. Look at us, Iain. We look as if we belong here. A desert prince and his concubine. Let us pretend, just for one night, one last night, that is what we are.'

'I won't think of you as a concubine.'

'A princess then.' He was still looking at her strangely. He still seemed as if he would persist in saying what she did not want to hear. So Cordelia twined her arms around him, and pressed her body against his. 'Just for tonight Iain, let's not talk. Let's just enjoy what we have,' she whispered, and kissed him.

He surrendered to her with a low groan, kissing

her back, wrapping his arms around her and pulling her tight against him. He was hard. There was something extremely sensual about the slither of silk against his erection. She deliberately rubbed herself against him.

He swore, tearing his mouth away from hers. 'Cordelia, if you carry on like that, I'll never remember what I came to say, let alone actually say it.'

'Then don't.'

She pulled him back towards her, and kissed him again. His hands slipped on the silk of her tunic. Delightful, but it was getting in the way. She grabbed his wrist and tugged him towards the nearest of the rooms which lay cool behind the terrace. The bathing chamber. She was about to try another, softer room, when the low marble counter, similar to the one on which she had been massaged, caught her attention.

'Take it off,' she said, tugging at his tunic, pulling her own over her head. The soft hiss of his breath expelling told her he liked what he saw, as she stood before him naked from the waist up, draped in perfectly translucent organza from the waist down. But tonight was not about what Iain could make her feel, it was about what she could do to him. This might be their last time. It might be the only time she could make love to him and love him. She was going to make sure he remembered it.

Lifting his tunic at the hem, she helped him ease it over his head. He was completely naked underneath, had already lost his slippers. She feasted her eyes on his body, on the lean, long lines of him, feeling herself heat, tighten, at the sight of his obvious arousal. She kissed him extravagantly, curling herself around him, pressing herself into him, her mouth clinging, her hands roaming, trying to memorise every inch of him, dragging her lips away only to lead him to the marble bench.

'What are you doing?'

She smiled at him, the smile she knew he could not resist, the smile he called smouldering. 'When in Rome,' she said, indicating that he should lie down. 'Or rather, when in a harem.'

She picked up the bottle of oil from the shelf by the mirror and tipped some on to her hands before climbing up beside him, kneeling between his legs, to smooth the oil over him in one sweeping movement, from chest to belly, then back up. His skin glistened in the soft lamp light. His muscles clenched and rippled under the sliding palms of her hands. She picked up the bottle and smoothed on more oil, until he was sleek with it, and then she lay down on top of him, her breasts sliding over his chest, their skin clinging, sliding.

When he said her name, his voice was hoarse. She kissed him lingeringly, then lifted herself just a fraction, allowing her nipples to graze his chest, his belly, and his shaft.

He swore. That word he had used back in Glasgow that first day. She teased him again, kissing him first, then working her way back down from chest, to belly, to the straining length of his erection.

'Take those things off, Cordelia. I need to be inside you.'

She shook her head, circling her fingers around him. Her hands, slick with oil, slid up with ease. Iain closed his eyes. His hands curled into tight fists. She slid her hand down to the base of his shaft, leaning over him, so that he was nestled between her breasts. 'Open your eyes, Iain. I want you to watch.'

'You will kill me.'

'No.' She kissed him again, forcing him to kiss her back slowly. 'I won't kill you,' she whispered, 'but I will make sure you never forget this.'

'Cordelia, I don't know what you're planning to do, but I can assure there's no need. This is already more than memorable, but if you don't take those things off and let me— It will be memorable for all the wrong reasons.'

She laughed then. 'Iain Hunter, I think you underestimate us both,' she said, and began her assault.

This time, she did not hesitate. She remembered how he had kissed her in this most intimate of ways, and it seemed the most natural thing in the world to kiss him in the same way, her tongue flicking over his tip, her lips nuzzling down the length of him and back. She glanced down at him. His eyes were wide open, utterly focused. She wrapped her hand around his member and stroked him, then dipped her head back down to kiss the tip once more.

His chest rose and fell rapidly, but he lay rigid, holding himself clenched tight, his eyes riveted on her. She opened her lips, and took him inside her, letting her mouth do the work of her hands, letting her tongue slide over his most sensitive part as his had slid over hers. She forgot herself as she kissed him, stroked him, tenderly, lovingly and then finally, when she sensed he was about to lose control, passionately.

As his climax tore through him, he pulled her up against him, kissing her wildly, his arms like manacles, binding her body to him as he came, his heart hammering against hers, his mouth hot, hard on hers, and between them, the shuddering, pulsing of his orgasm.

Not even that first time had she felt such an elemental joy, the elation of being one being, of abandoning everything she was and surrendering it all to this new creation. She lay as sated as he, spread over him, their breaths mingling, utterly at peace.

'Cordelia.' With a horrible sense of doom, she

lifted her head. She should have known that Iain would not be so easily put off.

'We need to talk,' he said.

The moment he had seen her in the courtyard he knew. He was in love. He really was in love. Still, he had not intended to tell her, determined to allow her to get this meeting with her cursed sister out of the way, unsure of whether he had even a chance of her returning his feelings, until she had done this.

But now! Surely she would not have done this most intimate act unless she loved him? And surely nothing mattered more than that he told her he loved her? Not even the blessed Lady Celia.

Studying Cordelia as she sat on a heap of cushions, resting her back against one of the corner fountains, Iain felt an unwelcome shadow of doubt creep into his thoughts. If he did not know better, he'd have said she looked quite dejected. But he did know better. Bloody Celia. *Was* he being selfish?

He grimaced inwardly. It was hardly selfish to

tear open the wound that had never quite healed, just so Cordelia could inspect it. He felt quite ill at the thought of it, but it was the only way he could think of to show her how he felt, and the only way he could think of to persuade himself he had nothing to fear. 'Ach!'

Cordelia looked up with the ghost of a smile. 'Iain, whatever it is you are torturing yourself with, there is no need. I know what you're going to say.'

He had been pacing the courtyard as if it were the deck of a ship. Now he came to sit beside her, not on the cushions but on the edge of the fountain. 'You guessed?'

'It wasn't so difficult. After last night…'

'Aye. It was then I realised, though not until today that I was sure.'

'Then Akil made the decision for you.'

'Akil?' Iain frowned. 'I remember now. *The blessing of a true companion in life is indeed one of the greatest.* It was well put, but I think I'd already made up my mind. The only question was the timing of it. I was going to wait until you'd seen your sister, but after tonight, I can't.' He held up his hand when she would have spoken. 'No, don't say anything, for it's hard enough. I've never told anyone before, you see, what I'm going to tell you. About my mother.'

'Your mother!'

'Aye, you may well look surprised, but she's the reason, you see, why it took me so long to— to…' Iain stopped. His head was in a tangle. He didn't want to just blurt it out. He had to explain first. 'I'd best start at the beginning'.

'My mother was a very beautiful woman,' Iain said. 'I mentioned she was from the Highlands, I think. Well, what I didn't tell you was that she didn't leave of her own accord. She got herself into trouble, as they say. She was pregnant.'

Cordelia stared at him. This was not at all what she had been expecting. 'But didn't they—in the Highlands—I am no expert, but they seemed to me very tight-knit communities. Was not the man who was responsible made to marry her?'

'Aye. No doubt he would have, but my mother was having none of it.'

He looked distinctly uncomfortable. With a

horrible feeling of déjà vu, she began to understand why. 'She didn't love him,' she said.

'No. She didn't.'

'I can see now why my story resonated so deeply with you,' Cordelia said with a sinking feeling. She frowned down at her fingers, which had found the golden belt holding up her pantaloons to play with, and had already managed to unravel one strand. 'But she did marry him though, in the end, because you said your father...'

'The man she married wasn't my father. I called him that, but I knew, for she told me on several occasions, that he was not.'

'Yet he took care of you.'

'As best he could, when he was sober. He wasn't a bad man, just a very disappointed one. He loved my mother, you see, to his dying day.'

'But it was the loss of his daughter that killed him,' Cordelia said.

Iain shook his head. 'Jeannie was no more his flesh and blood than I was. My mother called herself a passionate woman. Our neighbours called her a floosie.'

'Oh, hell, Iain, I am so very sorry.' She made to get up, she wanted to sit beside him, to offer him some sort of comfort, but he warded her off.

'I need to get this out of the way. I need you to understand.'

Indeed, she thought she did now, in a dreadful, final way, but she bit her tongue, refusing to let her selfish, heartbroken tears fall, for what good would they do Iain? 'Go on.'

'There's not much more to tell. As you can imagine, it's coloured my views on love and marriage so that they've always been more or less black.'

'Considering your formative experience, I think you have done remarkably well.'

Iain shrugged. 'I thought I'd succeeded in life despite the odds, but I'm coming to think that my upbringing was the making of me. No, don't get me wrong, I'm not going to tell you I wouldn't have had it any other way, but one thing I've learned since getting to know you, that being born with a silver spoon makes not a whit of difference.'

'You cannot possibly compare us, Iain. I have had every advantage…'

'Save for a mother's love. Or a father's. Think how different you'd be if your mother hadn't died, or if Celia had stayed longer to play the mother. Think what your life would have been like if your father had given a toss about you.'

'Pray, don't mince your words.'

'I would, if I thought you cared, but I think you've finally grown out of that.'

Cordelia's smile was bittersweet. 'You are the only person on this earth who knows me so well.'

'I used to think that was a weakness to be avoided at all costs, but that's another thing you've taught me,' Iain said. 'No, for once just take the compliment, Cordelia. I've accused you a good few times of not trusting anyone, but I've never, until you forced me to, considered that the fault in me might be just as big a problem.'

'Thank you,' she stammered, for tears were clogging her throat.

'And I wanted to be absolutely honest with you. I—when you told me about D'Amery, I— It was wrong, but I…'

'It made you think of your mother.'

Iain nodded. 'The circumstances are not at all the same. *You* are not like her, but…'

'But what if I am?'

'But you're not.'

She felt sick to her stomach, but he had been so painfully honest, she could not bear to allow him to continue in ignorance. 'I have never had a child. I have never married, but Gideon is not the only man I have taken into my bed, Iain. There have been others.'

'Others?' He looked at her blankly.

'Other lovers,' Cordelia said.

'"How many? No, don't answer that.' He cursed. 'I wish you hadn't told me. Why are you telling me now?'

Because she loved him. Which was no reason. 'Because I don't want you to feel guilty about telling me to go.'

'Go?'

She could sit still no longer. 'It's what you've been working up to, and I can't bear it. I know you are tired of the lies, Iain, but I find I am not.

Though in a way I am. Oh, God, I'm not making any sense.'

She took a hasty turn to the next fountain and back again, remembering as she did how she had counted out her steps in his lodgings, when she had told him the truth about Gideon. So long ago. As if she was a different person. But she was not, and she could no longer deny her history.

'Five,' Cordelia said, 'not counting Gideon. I have had five other lovers. I told myself they were none of your business. Then, when you reacted so—after what happened between us the night of my father's party, I decided I didn't want any other man getting between us. I wanted you, you see. And I— Yes, I will say it. I thought that you would judge me more harshly for six men than one. They meant nothing to me. Until you told me about your mother, I thought that was a fact in my favour. I see now that you cannot but hold it against me.'

'Yet you told me all the same,' Iain said. 'Why?'

He did not sound angry, but she was far too overwrought to judge the matter. 'I told you, I don't want you to feel guilty.'

'Guilty! God almighty Cordelia, do you know, I came here tonight pretty sure of what I felt and what I wanted to say to you. And then you— we—you did that. I thought it was because you felt— I thought— And now you tell me this. And it's not just this either, for this damned thing with your sister is still hanging over you, and it's my belief until you get it out the way, then I haven't a hope in hell of getting through to you. I should have waited.'

And if he had waited, if he had not made the parallels between herself and his mother crystal clear with this shocking revelation, Cordelia shuddered to think how the conversation would have gone. She would have told him that she loved him, and then they would both of them have been hurt. At least she had spared him the shame of having to reject her. 'I am glad you did not,' she said. 'At least now you know the full truth you need not feel guilty.'

'I don't feel guilty. I feel bloody confused.' Iain ran his fingers through his hair. 'Just what was that all about, any road?' he asked. 'All those things you said about making me remember you.

Do you think there's any chance in hell I'd ever forget you! I sometimes wish I could, do you know that? My life would be a damned sight easier without you in it.'

Which brought them right back to what she'd been trying to avoid hearing him say. And which confirmed without doubt that her confession had done exactly what she'd expected it too. 'Then it's as well that I will be gone from it sooner rather than later,' Cordelia said.

'I didn't mean that. Cordelia, what you did, I thought…'

'No!' She could not bear it if he realised what she felt. She simply could not bear it. The urge to run, to flee from him right now, was so strong that she had to curl her toes up inside her leather slippers to prevent herself. 'What I did,' she said, 'was prove to you that I am not so inhibited as you accused me of being.'

Her words came out sounding satisfactorily careless. Dismissing her feelings, making so light of what had meant so much, made her curl up in-side, but she held his gaze and stood her ground, and she refused to think about what that wounded look of his meant. He was not hurt. Or if anything was hurt, it was simply his male pride.

'I see.' Iain's expression tightened, and then became unreadable. 'Another first for you to chalk up. I should be honoured. I assume it was also farewell?'

'You were the one who said you were tired of lying, Iain. I thought— I did not think— I was being selfish. You are right. As ever,' Cordelia said with a lopsided smile. He looked as if he would protest, though she could not understand why. Tears threatened to clog her throat. She fought desperately to contain them, forcing a yawn and another queer little smile. 'I am very tired and I have an early start, and you will no doubt want to be fresh for my brother-in-law's arrival, so I will bid you goodnight.'

She could not bring herself to say goodbye. It was not really goodbye in any case, because their paths would be bound to cross at some point in the near future at least.

Iain hesitated, then turned away without another word. At the far entrance, he turned back. 'The reason I told you about my mother,' he said, 'was because I wanted you to understand. All my life, I've thought that it was her fault for failing to love my father as he said he loved her. I was wrong. My father made himself miserable. If he'd really loved her he'd have walked away and let her be herself. There is no surer path to destruction than one-sided love.'

Chapter Eleven

Royal Palace of Balyrma—two weeks later

'A letter has just arrived from Cassie. She is very sorry, but must postpone her trip here for another few weeks. It seems little Katie has the measles.' Celia crossed the courtyard, smiling. Tall, graceful and unmistakably English despite her Arabian clothing, with her glorious crown of Titian hair falling loose over her shoulders, she looked at least ten years younger than her forty-three years. 'You know, I am beginning to think it might be easier for you to visit Cassie than for her to come here. That way you can meet all of her brood at once—if you have the stomach for it.'

Cordelia smiled, shifting on the cushions to

make way for her sister beneath Celia's favourite lemon tree. 'Seven children, as well as her stepdaughter. I still can't quite believe it.'

'Well, they are all much older than Katie. She was quite a surprise to everyone when she arrived last year.' Celia floated down on to the cushions with a grace that filled Cordelia with envy. 'She is named after our mother, as you will have guessed.'

'Yes.' Cordelia smiled distractedly. A visit to Cassie ought to be a prospect that filled her with joy. Instead, all she could think of was the extra miles it would put between herself and Iain. She wondered what he was doing now. She wondered if he ever thought of her. She castigated herself for the thousandth time for wondering.

Beside her, Celia was pouring fragrant mint tea from an ornate silver pot into tiny glasses. Conscious of her sister's too-perceptive eye on her, Cordelia dragged her thoughts away from Iain and forced another smile. 'I've been meaning to ask you,' she said, 'about our mother. Bella made the most intriguing remark about her.'

Celia took a sip of tea. 'I married George to get

away from Bella, you know. I thought she would put my nose out of joint. You were too young to remember, but I was very proud to have acted as Papa's hostess at his diplomatic soirées.' She made a face. 'I can't believe how naive I was back then.'

Celia began to arrange the unused tea glasses on the silver tray, first lining them up and then placing them in a circle. Her attention caught by this very familiar habit which betrayed the so-assured Celia's discomfort, Cordelia abandoned her own tea. 'What do you mean?' she asked.

'For a start, our father did not marry Bella to play the hostess, but to provide him with sons. I have no doubt that if I had not married George, I'd be playing Papa's hostess still—though perhaps he has less need to hold soirées now that he is part of the Opposition?'

'You know our father. It is not so much party loyalty that matters as having a finger in every pie,' Cordelia said wryly. 'At the party he held to announce our betrothal, there were Whigs there as well as Tories.'

'The man who bends with the wind will never

break,' Celia said. 'One of my husband's sayings, though I doubt he would take it as carte blanche to play the turncoat, as I don't doubt our dear parent would do if he considered it politically expedient.'

'You don't like Father much, do you?' Cordelia said in some surprise.

Celia shrugged. 'I wonder if he has even the faintest idea that every single one of his womenfolk holds him in such low esteem. I always knew Bella did not love him of course. I confess, though I should be shocked, I am rather pleased to hear that she has taken a lover.'

'She sees it as her just reward.'

'And who can blame her?' Celia abandoned her exercise in regimenting the tea glasses. 'Have you ever wondered why, when he was so desperate for sons, it took Papa eleven years to marry again?'

'Actually, yes. In fact, it was exactly that topic which triggered that intriguing remark of Bella's I was going to ask you about.' Cordelia frowned, trying to recall the conversation. 'I said our father must have loved Mama very much because it took him so long to get over her death, and

Bella said, quite adamantly, "he never loved Catherine." Then she would say no more, and told me I must ask you.' Cordelia looked expectantly at her sister. 'Ask you what though?'

'If I tell you, you must not take it the wrong way.' Celia took her hand. 'It was not that Mama didn't love you. She loved all of us, I am sure of it, for I remember, I was almost fourteen when she...'

'Died. I know.'

'You don't. She didn't die, not for another ten years. She left.'

'Left?' Cordelia repeated blankly.

'She eloped, to be precise. With her lover. And, no, before you ask, her lover was not your father. Those eyes of yours, I am sorry to say, are undoubtedly Papa's.'

'Good God. How do you know this? Why did our father not— No, no need to answer that one. Scandal. His biggest fear.' Cordelia shook her head, as if doing so would clear the jumble of questions whirling around in it. 'Have you always known?'

'I guessed early on. Aunt Sophia confirmed

it. I did not tell any of you because— Cordelia, forgive me, but I knew Papa would never allow Mama back into our lives, and you were just a baby, it seemed much kinder to allow you to think her dead. Was I wrong?'

'I don't know. No, I don't think so. Was she happy?'

'I believe so. I certainly think she must have been very, very unhappy to leave all of us. She wrote to Aunt Sophia regularly for news of us, you know. It was always my intention to meet with her once I was married. It is one of my biggest regrets that I never did, for she died the year before my wedding.'

'Do our sisters know?'

'No.'

'Why did you tell me?'

'I do not do it lightly, but—you do an excellent job of covering it up, Cordelia, but I can see that your mind and perhaps your heart are not here.' Celia frowned down at her hands. 'One of the things we all have in common is a deep-rooted sense of duty. So deep-rooted, that we have each of us, including Mama, tried to conform, and each of us have been mightily unhappy in doing so. I hate Papa for that. I hate him for making it so hard for us to find happiness.'

'But you have,' Cordelia said, totally taken aback by the vehemence in her sister's voice. 'You have all found happiness, despite his best efforts to make you miserable.'

'All of us except you.'

Cordelia picked up a cushion and began to worry at the tassel. 'I'm not unhappy, not now that I am here. You have no idea how long I have wished for this, Celia.'

Her sister removed the cushion and once more took Cordelia's hand. 'I know how much it cost you to tell me about Gideon. I need you to believe me when I say that I'm proud of you, my dear. To refuse to buckle under the pressure I am sure you must have felt is—well, it is more than I managed, for I married George, and he was on Papa's dratted list.'

'Do you think you would have been terribly unhappy if George had not been killed?'

'I don't think I'd have known any better. How can one know if one is unhappy, without true happiness to compare it to?' Celia smiled mistily. 'It was not until I met Ramiz that I discovered what love was, and it was not until I discovered love that I found the courage to put myself first. I knew it would cost me, you see,' she continued, pressing Cordelia's hand tightly. 'The biggest price I have paid has been not seeing you and Cressie and Caro growing up, but if I had put you first and not myself, I would have made a very miserable sister, and you have always been in my heart...'

She stopped, her voice suspended by tears. 'I know,' Cordelia said fervently. 'It has been the same for me.'

'Yes, I do know that,' Celia said with another misty smile, 'and I hope that now we are reconciled— But that is not what I've been trying to say. This is difficult for me, I am not in the habit of confiding, any more than you are—any of us, I suppose. Another of Papa's legacies. However, I think I know enough of you, from what you have told me— Cordelia, I'm not saying that you need a man to make you happy, but I am saying that if this man, this Iain Hunter, makes you happy then you are a fool to run away from him. For that is what you have done.'

'I didn't run. I came here to see you. It was what I had always intended.'

'You ran away when you were twenty-one. You ran again, from Gideon D'Amery two years later. You ran away from Cressie and Caro when they could have helped you. You ran from Mr Hunter when first you met him in Glasgow. You've been running most of your life, Cordelia. Isn't it time you stopped?'

Celia's voice was gentle but firm. Desperate as she was to deny what her sister said, Cordelia could not. 'He doesn't love me,' she said miserably.

'If he does not, then you cannot be happy with him.'

'"*There is no surer path to destruction than one-sided love.*" That's what Iain said.'

'Are you sure he was talking about himself?'

'Yes, I—I don't know. It was all so— I was so upset, and I just wanted to get away without breaking down and…' Cordelia flushed. 'Don't say I told you so. I wanted to run away.'

'Dearest, I am not interested in being in the

right. I simply want you to be happy. Do you love him?'

Cordelia nodded miserably. 'But, Celia, the parallels with his mother—I cannot explain, but even if he did have feelings for me, after what I told him...'

'If he truly loves you, it won't matter, because if he truly loves you, he truly knows you, warts and all,' Celia said, smiling. 'Which would be worse, Cordelia, sacrificing your silly pride to take a chance on happiness, or letting that chance pass you by because you don't want to lose face?'

'You make it sound so easy.'

'Trust me, I know that it is not, but I also know that the price is worth paying.' Celia got to her feet. 'Now, shall I ask Akil to be ready to escort you to the port tomorrow?'

'What about Cassie?'

Celia raised her delicate brows. 'Prevaricating, Cordelia?'

'You promise you will pick up the pieces if he rejects me?'

'If you need me to, but we are strong women, we Armstrong sisters. I don't think you'll need me.'

* * *

Cordelia was packing for the caravan which would leave the next morning when the door flew open.

'Ramiz!' Celia ran to her husband.

'Celia, my love. My apologies for the lack of warning, but the Scottish man was like a caged lion with far too much on his mind to concentrate on building our ships. He threatened to cross the desert alone. From what I know of him, I suspect that he would have too, but I decided not to take the risk of having to look for his bones, and so I escorted him here myself.'

Prince Ramiz let go of his wife reluctantly to make his bow. 'Lady Cordelia, a belated welcome to our home. I look forward to getting to know you, but as you can see, I am in need of a bath and a change of clothes. My quickest journey yet from the port to Balyrma, I believe, but Mr Hunter would not stop for such trivialities as food and sleep.'

'Prince Ramiz.' Cordelia managed a low curtsy, though her knees were shaking and her heart was hammering. 'Please, has something happened to Iain?'

'Alas, he has been struck with that most fatal of diseases.'

Her heart stopped beating. She felt the colour drain from her face. 'He's ill?'

'Ramiz!' Celia exclaimed. 'He is teasing, Cordelia. He means—'

'He means to let the man speak for himself,' Ramiz said. 'Mr Hunter awaits you in my library, Cordelia.'

'Actually, I couldn't wait.' Iain appeared in the doorway. Like Prince Ramiz, he was dusty, dressed in the full Arabian attire, complete with the lightweight cloak known as a *bisht* worn to protect the tunic from the sand, and head-dress. His face was now darkly tanned, making his eyes seem bluer than ever.

'It seems you have been spared a journey, Cordelia,' Celia said archly. 'My husband, as he said, is in need of a bath. Being a prince and a man, he cannot bathe himself, and so I must go with him. I am sure you will excuse us.'

Celia, closely followed by Ramiz, left the

chamber, closing the door softly behind them. 'I do believe my sister has just propositioned her husband,' Cordelia said, because she had to say something, and she couldn't possibly say the thing she wanted to say. Not yet.

Iain cast off his head-dress and ran his hand through his hair. He'd had it cut, Cordelia noticed, and it was much more gold than auburn now. 'I was not expecting you,' she said inanely.

He looked around him, at the clothes strewn across the divans. 'You were leaving?'

She nodded.

'Cordelia, I don't want you to go.'

'I wasn't…'

'No.' Iain placed a hand over her mouth. 'This time, I will finish what I want to say.'

'But I was only…' He looked quite desperate. He looked quite devastatingly attractive. She swallowed, her mouth suddenly dry, and laced her hands together tightly to stop them from trembling. 'I'm listening.'

'Aye. Right.' He unfastened his cloak and cast it on to the floor beside the head-dress. 'I should have known, when not even the thought of building ships could distract me, that you were trouble,' he said. 'I've been trying, the whole time since you've been here, I've been trying to concentrate on what I came here to do, but it's just not worked. I can't think of anything but you.'

Her heart was hammering again, but not in the same way. She no longer felt sick. She felt— giddy. Terrified she might be wrong. Strangely sure she was not. 'Iain.'

'Let me finish.' He began to wander around the room, picking up items of clothing, staring at them sightlessly, putting them down. 'We got each other in a right fankle that night in the other palace. I wasn't telling you about my mother to draw comparisons. God forbid. I was telling you because I wanted you to see— To explain— Dammit!'

Iain threw down a slipper, and strode over to her, grabbing her by her shoulders. 'I love you, woman. I'm in love with you. I don't give a damn about those other men. I wish I was first, but it doesn't matter. What matters is that I'm the last. Now for God's sake put me out of my misery and tell me how you feel because—'

'I love you.' Cordelia threw her arms around him. 'I love you so much, Iain Hunter, and if you'd just let me speak I'd have told you that five minutes ago. I wasn't packing to run away from you but to run to you. I am done with running away, and I never want to be more than this much apart from you for the rest of my life.'

'Cordelia, do you mean it?'

She laughed. She closed the tiny gap there was between them. And then she kissed him.

He kissed her back, with a hunger that matched her own. His hands slid down her shoulders, wrapping her tightly to him. He tasted of sand and sweat. 'You rode across the desert for me,' she said, panting. 'Just like a prince from *One Thousand and One Nights.*'

'Cordelia, I'd have gone to the moon to get you, if that's what it took.'

He kissed her again. Her hands roamed over his back, his shoulders, his arms. She could not quite believe he was here. 'I thought you meant me,' she said. 'When you said that about one-sided love. I thought you had guessed how I felt.'

'And I thought you had guessed how I felt. What a pair of numpties we are.'

'I have no idea what that means, but…'

'Idiots. Does this thing have buttons?'

'Here.' She turned around for him, so that he could unfasten her tunic. He kissed her nape. She curved her bottom into his thighs, relishing the hard ridge of his erection. He gasped, then slid his hands around under her tunic to cup her breasts, and it was her turn to gasp. 'Iain, I never loved any of them, those men.'

'I know.'

'Did you— Have you ever…?'

'No. Never. I thought that was obvious.'

She wriggled against him. His fingers stroked her nipples. 'It was,' she said. 'Only I just wanted to hear it.'

He laughed, a soft growl in her ear. 'You're the first, last and only love, my ain wee darling.'

She turned around in his arms. 'And you are my first, last and only love, my ain, most decidedly and deliciously large darling,' she said, pulling him towards the divan.

* * *

He wanted to relish it, to take it slowly, to make every moment last, the first time he made love to the woman he loved and who loved him back, but it was quite beyond him. Cordelia lay under him, hot, flushed and every bit as aroused as he, and all he wanted was to be inside her. She kissed him as if she were starving, and he was every bit as starving as she. Her hands touched, stroked, cupped, tugged, and her body arched into his, and her legs curled around his, and they would have all their lives to relish and to make every moment last, and so he surrendered. When he entered her, it was as if he was always meant to be there. She clung to him, thrusting up under him, and he could feel himself thickening, pulsing, already painfully close.

He held her still, kissing her, gazing deep into her eyes. 'I love you so much,' he said.

'Then show me,' she replied. With one of those wicked looks of hers, that nearly sent him over the edge. 'Show me now, Iain,' she said, digging her heels into his buttocks. 'Now!'

So he did. He laughed, he kissed her and he

thrust. And she laughed too, wildly, and he thought he'd never felt such unadulterated joy in his life as he thrust again, and felt her tighten, and thrust just once more, and felt her pulsing around him, and he stayed there, inside her, kissing her, eyes wide open, heart wide open, and he'd never felt so exposed and so completely possessed and so utterly happy in his life.

'Iain?' Cordelia lay draped across his chest, her arm around his waist. Their legs were tangled together. Her heart had almost returned to normal.

'Mmm?'

'Are you sleeping?'

'Recovering,' he said with a grin.

'We cannot—not again. Not yet. Celia will be wondering where we are.'

'Celia, my wee love, is most likely doing exactly what we are doing right now. I doubt very much that she cares where we are.'

'Iain! That's my sister you are talking about. And she's been married to Ramiz for nearly twenty years.'

'I hope we're still like that in twenty years.'

Cordelia propped her head on her elbow, the better to see his face. 'Do you think we will be?'

'Do you want an honest answer?'

'I never want anything else from you.'

He frowned. 'We're bound to argue. We're both far too independent-minded not to.'

'You've thought about this.'

'Cordelia, I've thought of little else.' Iain sat up, pulling her with him. 'This love thing, it's only a ball and chain if it's unequal. That's what I was so ineptly trying to say when I told you about my mother.'

'I know. I just— Goodness, Iain, you will never believe what Celia told me. My mother did not die in childbirth, she ran off with her lover.'

He shook his head in disbelief. 'Another of the skeletons your Aunt Sophia was talking about. You're quite a family for them. Speaking of which—listen, there's one thing I didn't tell you. I gave you the impression— The fact is, my mother isn't actually dead. She's alive and as far as I know, for she certainly gets through the substantial allowance I give her, she's still kicking, though I haven't seen her in years. My own skeleton she is, and I was thinking...'

'Good heavens, yes!'

'I haven't asked you yet.'

'Yes, I would like to meet her.' She kissed his cheek. 'Yes, I think it's a good idea that you make your peace.' She kissed his other cheek. 'Yes, I'll support you if you decide when you've seen her that once was enough.' She kissed the tip of his nose. 'Yes,' she said and kissed him on the mouth. 'I can't believe this. Darling Iain, isn't it wonderful being in love? Do you think I might even learn to love my father?'

'I don't think you've ever stopped loving him. As to liking—honestly, my darling, no.'

Cordelia giggled. 'Celia cannot abide him, and she is practically a saint. I can't tell you how much better that made me feel. Though nothing can compare with how you make me feel.'

'And nothing will ever compare to you. When I said that, do you remember that night on the dhow? That's what made me realise I was falling in love with you.'

'Iain, are you sure? I don't mean are you sure

you love me, but—I don't know, I have been on my own for so long, I am not at all sure I can adapt to being part of someone else.'

Iain smoothed her hair away from her face. 'I don't expect you to be anything other than yourself, which is why I think we're bound to argue. I don't expect you do my bidding, or to think that what you want is less important than what I want.'

'But there will be times when one of us must compromise, won't there?'

'And times when it falls to the other. You will be accountable to me, just as I will be to you, but that's a small price to pay, is it not, for having someone always on your side?' Iain said. 'I want you to love me as much as I love you, Cordelia. I want you to be on my side, as I'll always be on yours. I want to be first with you, as you'll always be with me. I want you to always be yourself. That's all, and I don't know what I've said to make you cry.'

She blinked rapidly. 'I'm not.'

He wiped her eyes with his fingers. 'Of course you're not.'

'It's probably sand from your hair. You have half the desert on you.'

'It's a magical place, the desert at night. I should like to be in it with you. How do you fancy spending our honeymoon there?'

'Our honeymoon?'

Iain laughed again, pulling her tight against him. 'Oh, aye, I forgot that comes first. Will you marry me, Lady Cordelia Armstrong?'

'Just as soon as it can be arranged, Mr Iain Hunter. That is—if we are married here, will it be recognised in England—or Scotland?'

'I've no idea, and I don't really care, if it means getting married once, twice or three times. In fact, I quite like the idea of three honeymoons.'

Cordelia wriggled against him provocatively. 'I do believe you are recovered enough to practise for our first honeymoon right now.'

Iain rolled her on to her back, trapping her between his legs. 'I do believe I am,' he said, and kissed her.

* * * * *

Historical Note

I'm indebted to Alistair Deayton and Iain Quinn's book, *200 Years of Clyde Paddle Steamers,* for the details of any ships and yards I've named. With one exception—the *Eilidh,* which I named for one of my nieces—all of the paddle steamers named are real, and if you want a description of Napier's steeple engine you'll find it detailed in that book. The Broomilaw in Glasgow, where Iain and Cordelia meet, is now the site of, among other things, the Science Centre, the Armadillo and several of the new-built Commonwealth Games auditoriums, but the paddle steamer *Waverley* still berths there.

I've tried to be true to the time scales in terms of the development of paddle steamers and their various engines—and I could probably bore for

Scotland on the subject. For those of you interested in the detail, I first came across Robert Napier when visiting my grandparents' graves in the tiny churchyard of Kilmun. Coincidentally, it's where the Dukes of Argyll were traditionally buried, and Robert Napier was their blacksmith—though actually he's the brother of the engineer Napier in my story—with the same name—who owned the Millwall Iron Works.

As to paddle steamers in the Red Sea—well, this I *did* make up, although at the time of Iain's visit to Arabia the British were indeed eyeing up the port of Aden with a view to establishing a fast steam-powered link to India. My thanks to my cousin Mhairi for telling me about Robert Moresby and the team of surveyors who made the first detailed maps of the Red Sea, which Iain has managed to get his hands on. On a point of detail, at the time Iain and Cordelia arrive in the Red Sea Captain Haines of the HMS *Palinurus* really was continuing with the survey.

The route of Iain and Cordelia's journey to Arabia follows, more or less, the route taken by Lady Hester Stanhope. At the time, the now notorious holiday island of Zante was under British protectorate. I've never been to Zante, but I lived on Cyprus for four years, and I've tried to evoke the spirit of that island in my descriptions of Zante's scenery. HMS *Pique,* the frigate on which Iain and Cordelia travel, was a real Royal Navy ship, though her journey through the Mediterranean to Syria was in 1840—a few years later than theirs.

And finally, a note on dialogue. I have absolutely no idea how a Glaswegian would have spoken in 1837—no more, really, than I can know how Cordelia would have sounded. I did want to make a distinction between Iain and Cordelia's language though, so I've taken the liberty of using some modern-day Glaswegian—*eejit* and *numpty* spring to mind. Not historically correct, I know, but I do hope it's more effective than any attempt at an accent.